HIGH FORCE

A DCI RYAN MYSTERY

LJ ROSS

ISBN: 978-1-912310-05-0

First published in 2016 by LJ Ross

This edition published in July 2020 by Dark Skies Publishing

Author photo by Gareth Iwan Jones

Cover layout by Stuart Bache

Cover artwork and map by Andrew Davidson

Typeset by Riverside Publishing Solutions Limited

Printed and bound by CPI Goup (UK) Limited

"Let your plans be dark and impenetrable as night, and when you move, fall like a thunderbolt."

~ Sun Tzu

PROLOGUE

Tuesday 29ᵗʰ March

As soon as she awakened, MacKenzie knew that he meant to kill her.

There was no confused, fumbling recollection of what had happened. On the contrary, she remembered everything with horrifying clarity.

Dark eyes. White smile.

A flash of his fist, and then nothing.

The car lurched sideways and she was thrown violently against the hard interior of the boot. It was impossible to brace herself against the impact because her wrists and ankles were bound tightly with wire cord. The darkness was heavy and impenetrable, suffocating her.

She drew great, shuddering gulps of air into her lungs and felt the warmth of her own breath surround her in the cramped space. Perhaps she could pretend it was all a terrible nightmare and she would open her eyes to find

Frank sleeping peacefully beside her. But the scent of diesel invaded her nostrils and the dream evaporated, leaving only blunt reality. Her mind was shockingly awake and would not be fooled.

The car wound its way up and over a steep hill. MacKenzie's stomach heaved and she recognised the symptoms of shock: she was shivering uncontrollably whilst also sweating profusely. Her head felt fuzzy and it was as if she were floating above her own body, watching another woman she barely recognised. She sucked air through her teeth, chest tight with anxiety. Her bowels wanted to loosen but she bore down and tried to think clearly.

How long had she been here?

It was impossible to know for sure whether it was night or day; not a shred of light glimmered to relieve the oppressive blackness of the small space and she had no idea how long she had lain unconscious. But she knew the terrain had changed. They were no longer travelling on smooth tarmac and the car jerked unsteadily across uneven ground as it trundled towards its unknown destination.

She lay there without any idea of the passage of time nor the distance she had travelled and thought of Frank Phillips.

I love you, Frank.

The car sped through the desolate countryside, away from the men and women who began a frantic search for Detective Inspector Denise MacKenzie. Slow clouds passed across the moon but occasional beams of white light broke through and illuminated the solitary vehicle as it crawled up and down the peaks and troughs of the dales. When the clouds shifted again, night fell like a shroud and was relieved only by the light of the car's headlights as it motored further away from civilisation. Now and then, they passed through a hamlet or village but there were no people on the streets and no lights in the windows at that hour. The driver and his passenger continued onward, alone amid a vast expanse of land and water, of ruined farmhouses and the remains of hefted sheep who had wandered too far from home. The *whirr* of the car's engine pierced the silent sky as it rose over the brow of another hill, where it was suspended for a moment before disappearing down into the protective, secretive fold of the valley.

CHAPTER 1

Monday 4ᵗʰ April

One week later

The sleek grey car slowed to a crawl, its tyres sloshing through deep puddles at the edge of the road as Detective Chief Inspector Maxwell Finley-Ryan peered through the windscreen at a row of unremarkable houses.

"This can't be the place."

He glanced down at the scribbled note he'd made on the back of a dog-eared envelope and then up at the street ahead.

"Nothing but a dead end," he muttered.

The street was tucked away in an area of Newcastle upon Tyne known as Benwell. It was a poor part of town, west of the upmarket city centre and not far from the river. Years ago, a colliery and munitions factory had fuelled a booming industry and rows of uniform terraced houses had been built for the workers. Now, they stood derelict or run down, some of the red bricks around the doors and windows bearing the evidence of arson. Ryan's ordinary duties as a murder detective took him into the city frequently but it was easy to forget the old heart of the metropolis.

He turned on the windscreen wipers as rain started to fall again. It was barely eight o'clock in the morning and the sun was struggling to break through the blanket of thick grey cloud overhead, lending an even more depressing air to proceedings. He was about to turn the car around when he spotted the place he had been looking for.

Buddle's Boxing Gym was little more than a seventies prefab consisting of a square, boxy building with a flat roof, sagging with rainwater. It rested on the foundations of two demolished houses and nobody had bothered to do away with the remaining concrete which surrounded it like a dystopian moat. It lacked the kind of warm, welcome feel he might have found inside one of the higher-end city gyms but, since Ryan never bothered to go to any of those, he wasn't in any position to judge. He sat for a long moment, then took a deep breath and slammed out of the car to stride purposefully through the rain.

"Howay, man! Is that the best you've got?"

Detective Sergeant Frank Phillips wiped the sweat from his brow with a threadbare grey towel and threw it back into the corner of the ring.

"We've had a good spar, Frank, let's call it a day—"

"Aye, if you can't take the pace," Phillips jeered.

Irritation won over tiredness and the other man tapped his gloves together, signalling that he would go another round after all. A boy of eleven or twelve took his cue and banged an old brass bell with the edge of a spoon and the two men began to dance around the ring.

Ryan pushed through the swing doors into the main gymnasium, ignoring the frankly enquiring and suspicious looks from the locals, who huddled in groups to watch the fight that was underway. Testosterone was palpable on the air and he almost reeled at the smell—a heady combination of male sweat and cigarette smoke. Several pairs of eyes continued to watch him, clocking the striking, raven-haired man who looked vaguely like someone they had seen on the television. He gave them a friendly nod. They didn't return the gesture but turned back to the fight, so Ryan moved further into the room and settled himself against the back wall to watch along with the rest of them.

"How's he doing?"

The man beside him could have been anywhere between the ages of fifty and eighty. His head was completely bald and it shone like a halo around his weather-beaten face.

"Which one?"

"The shorter one," Ryan said, nodding towards the stockier of the two fighters.

"Frank," the man provided. "He's like a man possessed, t'day. Pummelling the bloody life out of anybody who'll come close. Billy's doing his best but he'll not last much longer."

Ryan said nothing and continued to watch the two men who stood centre stage in the old-fashioned boxing ring, illuminated by a row of bare light bulbs hanging from cheap ceiling squares. Both were stripped to the waist and perspiration gleamed against their skin, flickering as they moved in and out of shadows thrown by the patchy light.

"Who's the ref?"

"Nobody in particular, since Frank floored him an hour ago. He's gone home to his missus, for a bit of tender loving care."

Ryan frowned at that, black brows drawing together.

"What if things get out of hand?"

The man cast him a wary glance.

"You're not from the Boxing Association?"

Ryan gave a slight shake of his head. Turning away again, the man took out a leather pouch of tobacco and began to roll himself a thin cigarette.

"We've had men boxing in here since before you were born. We know how to handle our own. It's you who should watch yourself, else you might spoil your smart clothes."

The ghost of a smile passed across Ryan's face. Buddle's was what he might have described as a 'no frills' establishment but he admired its lack of pretension. It wasn't the dirt that worried him, it was the apparent absence of safety measures. He folded his arms across his chest and continued his silent observation, wondering why they bothered to wear gloves at all if the object was to inflict as much damage as possible.

Frank Phillips was oblivious to the crowd. All he felt was anger, deep and raw, coursing through his body like a torrent. It needed to get out and this was the best way he knew how.

Whack, he took a blow to the midriff and felt the air rush out of his body but a second later he was back again, coming at the man who had ceased to be 'Billy from the gym' and now represented everything he hated in the world.

Smack, left hook.

Smack, right hook.

Billy stumbled backward against the safety barrier, arms flailing, and Phillips hopped impatiently from one foot to the other before going at it again.

Ryan watched his sergeant inflict a series of fast jabs, face contorted into something almost unrecognisable from the cheerful, mild-mannered man he had come to know.

Another thirty seconds and Billy fell to the ground, defeated.

There was a smattering of half-hearted applause and people began to chatter and disperse. Billy crawled out of the ring on legs that were less than stable, sporting a face that was already beginning to swell.

"Howay then, who's next?" Phillips shouted, to nobody in particular.

There was a series of rumbles in the negative.

"This place has gone downhill since my day," he called out. "If a bunch of lads are too precious to take on an old man like me. What's the matter wi' ya?"

His friends looked among themselves and wondered what to do. They'd all heard about what had happened to Frank's girlfriend and they sympathised, but there were limits to how much baiting they would take and the mood was becoming tense.

At the back of the room, Ryan came to a decision and pushed away from the wall.

"If the offer's still open, I could do with the workout."

Phillips squinted at the sea of faces from his elevated position inside the ring and watched a tall figure materialise. When he saw who it was, he shook his head slowly from side to side.

"I'm in no mood for games."

"If you're feeling tired, I'm sure one of these other gentlemen will go a round or two with me," Ryan said, bobbing his head towards the crowd that had gathered once again to see how this fresh drama would play out.

He began to shrug out of his navy wool overcoat and thanked one of the teenagers who took it from him. Next, he unbuttoned his shirt.

"Don't test me, boy. I won't fight you."

Phillips' face was hard as granite but Ryan could see deep shadows beneath his eyes, the evidence of sleepless nights. Another few minutes and the fight would drain from him entirely, Ryan thought.

Keeping a dubious eye on the other man's thick-set physique and murderous expression, he unclasped his watch and entrusted it to a spotty-faced teenager, who palmed it and scuttled away.

Shouldn't he be in school?

Shrugging philosophically, Ryan dropped his shirt onto a nearby bench and then boosted himself up and under the heavy elasticated barrier of the ring.

"Didn't you hear me?" Phillips growled. "I told you I won't fight you."

"If you're feeling the strain, just say so," Ryan returned.

He accepted a pair of gloves and began to pull them on. There was no offer of taping or headgear.

"How did you know I'd be here?"

"Does it matter?"

"It matters to me."

Ryan lifted one bare, muscled shoulder.

"I asked around."

"You had no business coming to find me," Phillips ground out. "If I'd wanted you to know where I was, I'd have told you."

"In case you've forgotten, I'm still your superior officer," Ryan said flatly, although the words stuck in his throat. "You can't expect to go AWOL for two days and have nobody come looking for you. You have responsibilities; to the department, to yourself…and to Denise."

"Don't you *dare* bring her into this!"

With that, Phillips lunged forward and planted a gloved fist squarely into Ryan's face. The force of it snapped his head backward and sent him careening into the barrier behind. There was a collective gasp from the crowd.

In the silence that followed, Ryan shook himself off and accepted a towel to dab at the trickle of blood which ran from his nose. A quick wriggle told him it wasn't broken, at least. He didn't like to think what Anna would have to say about that.

Phillips swallowed and began to apologise.

"Sorry, lad, I—"

But Ryan waved it away.

"I think that was the bell for Round One, wouldn't you say?"

With that, he landed a hard blow to Phillips' stomach.

"If you *think* that I'm going to go *easy* on you—"

Phillips fought back and Ryan had a fleeting moment to regret his earlier decision before raising his gloves to block a series of blows. He parried, circling the ring to tire them both out, but Phillips had energy to spare.

"You don't need to do me any favours, boy," he said, feigning a left before planting his right glove into Ryan's chest.

Ryan doubled over, winded.

"You're stubborn as an old mule," he panted.

Phillips cupped a hand to his ear.

"What's that? You've had enough of a beating for today?"

Ryan looked up, slowly.

"Hard of hearing, as well," he concluded, before surprising Frank with a sharp jab to his midriff, followed swiftly by a solid *crack* to his jaw.

Phillips landed hard on his arse and looked up in shock.

"Where the hell did you learn to box?"

"Boarding school," Ryan puffed. "And the *Rocky* franchise."

Phillips' lips trembled.

"Have you had enough?" Ryan asked, eyeing the red marks he'd inflicted with a small stab of conscience.

Phillips looked around at the faces in the crowd, let out a long sigh and then pushed himself back to his feet.

"Aye, I've had enough."

Ryan unstrapped a glove and held out a hand. Phillips did the same and, swearing roundly, pulled him in for a hard hug.

"I needed that," he said roughly.

"Any time, any place," Ryan said dryly.

They pulled apart and faced each other again.

"I don't know what to do," Phillips said simply. "I can't stand to think of Denise, of whether she's still alive, somewhere out there—"

Ryan could imagine, only too well. Her abductor was an infamous serial killer called Keir Edwards, a former medical doctor better known in the press as 'the Hacker'. Less than a week ago, Ryan and his team had been dealing with the fallout from another murder case. While their backs were turned, Edwards had escaped from his maximum-security prison in Durham and kidnapped Detective Inspector Denise MacKenzie from her own home. Every man and woman in Northumbria CID knew the violence Edwards was capable of inflicting but none more so than Ryan himself, who had brought the man to justice and lost his sister in the process.

The memory of it still haunted him.

Now, he looked into the bleak eyes of his sergeant. Neither of them knew what had happened to Denise and history was not on her side. Ryan understood the feeling of failure that had driven Phillips back here to the people who knew him from the old days. He remembered the driving need to fight back, to expel the hate and the anger that grew stronger every day that he was without the woman he loved.

But now it was time for Detective Sergeant Phillips to get back to work.

"Don't think about the 'what ifs,'" Ryan said. "Think about how to find her."

"*How*?" Phillips burst out. "Nearly a week has passed and we've got nothing. No leads, no sightings…what if he's killed her already?"

Ryan mustered a confidence he didn't entirely feel.

"We have to believe that MacKenzie isn't his main objective. Edwards will make contact and tell us his demands. He must know that we're watching the airports and the ferry ports; he has limited means and his face has been splashed all over the regional and national news. There's a nationwide manhunt underway. He can't hope to escape without trying to use Denise as leverage."

"What if he doesn't want to escape?" Frank said.

Ryan's mouth flattened. There was always the possibility that Edwards had an entirely different motive in mind, one that didn't require him to keep live hostages.

"If he wants a crack at me because I'm the man who put him away, he'll have his wish just as soon as we find him." He raised a hand to give Phillips' shoulder a reassuring squeeze. "But I need you on board, Frank. I need you with us, helping us."

Phillips blinked a couple of times and looked away.

"I let her down. I should have been with her."

"You haven't let anybody down," Ryan said forcefully. "There was no way you could have known. Now, for God's sake, put your shirt on and come back to work. I don't know how much longer I can stand here looking at your belly."

Phillips' chin jutted out in a manner reminiscent of his former self.

"There's a layer of pure muscle beneath this belly."

"I'll take your word for it."

CHAPTER 2

The atmosphere was hushed when Ryan and Phillips walked into the Northumbria Criminal Investigation Department on the leafy, western border between Newcastle and the county of Northumberland. They stood inside its scuffed double doors and breathed deeply of the homely smell; a potent mix of pine cleaning detergent and casserole that wafted its way upstairs from the direction of the canteen.

Ryan was relieved to see a healthy number of staff in attendance, although the room was nowhere near the hive of activity it had been when news had first broken of Edwards' escape and MacKenzie's disappearance. Durham CID were leading the investigation into how Edwards managed to engineer an escape from HMP Frankland, while Northumbria CID focused their efforts on tracing the whereabouts of their colleague and her abductor. Tyne and Wear Constabulary and several other neighbouring constabularies had offered their time and resources. Despite it, they were now entering the seventh day of a joint investigation that showed no sign of light at the end of the tunnel.

Detective Inspector Denise MacKenzie was a popular woman and a good murder detective with a solid history of public service. Her kidnap had elicited an outcry from local and national media, who rallied around to ensure that ordinary people could not fail to recognise her abductor's face as they went about their daily lives. But inevitably, as time passed, the news bulletins began to refer to her in the past tense, betraying an assumption that the worst had already happened. They discussed her life and profession as they would a fallen soldier, sacrificed in the line of duty. Newscasters began to speak of institutional failings and budget cuts to explain how a notorious killer had escaped his pen and opinion was divided on whether the police were doing enough to find her. Was there a lack of resources or were they merely incompetent? Chat shows re-opened the hackneyed debate on capital punishment, stoking a fire that already burned in the hearts of the men and women of the North East. It was inconceivable to think of a man such as Edwards roaming free again, able to hunt new victims and devastate other families. The idea of putting down such a dangerous animal was tempting and Ryan couldn't deny that the prospect held a certain allure.

But that would make him no better than a killer.

Underneath all the scaremongering was a generous dose of good, old-fashioned fear. It was the kind that kept people awake at night and led them to imagine that their neighbour was a homicidal maniac. They rang the Incident Room to report a killer living next door; one who looks *exactly* like that escaped convict everybody's been talking about and, oh, would they mind sending a couple of policemen around to arrest him?

Time-wasters, every one.

Ryan looked around the tired faces of his team. Despite what the papers said, he knew they had worked tirelessly for six days. Their loyalty was commendable but he had not been able to prevent their gradual reallocation to other casework. After all, serious crime had not stopped in the wake of CID's own tragedy.

"Alright, listen up!"

Conversation was suspended as detectives and support staff noted the arrival of the two newcomers.

Poor old Frank, Phillips imagined them saying.

His button-brown eyes darted from one display board to the next, images of Denise blurring with those of Keir Edwards in blown-up technicolour. One of the constables hastily moved to stand in front of one board but it was too late: he had already seen the lurid photographs of Edwards' previous victims. He remembered each of their faces, anyway. He had seen their mangled bodies lying on an impersonal metal gurney at the mortuary and he had mourned every one of them.

Now, the same man was at large again and this time he had Denise.

Denise.

Phillips took a long, shaky breath and dragged his eyes away from the board to look at an enormous map of the North East. It was dotted with pins to denote areas of interest while a bank of photocopiers and printers hummed along another wall. A single telephone began to ring plaintively across the room, in painful contrast to the incessant ringing of several telephones only a few days ago.

The trail was going cold and people were beginning to lose interest.

Just then, a hand came to rest solidly on his shoulder. He whipped around and saw a young man wearing an earnest expression on his clean-shaven face.

"Good to have you back," he said, and practically threw himself into Phillips' arms.

"There, lad." Phillips gave him a manly pat on the back as his face was crushed against the shiny fabric of Detective Constable Jack Lowerson's suit jacket. The overpowering scent of some flashy aftershave filled his nostrils, damn near choking him.

Ryan grinned and took the opportunity to address the room at large, making sure his voice carried into all four corners.

"As some of you may know, DS Phillips has been out of the office on a short period of special leave," Ryan lied smoothly. "He has now returned and is eager to get on with the business of policing, which is what we all do best. Let's keep the idle chatter to a minimum and welcome him back."

There followed a short, spontaneous round of applause and Phillips felt a lump rise in his throat.

"Aye, thanks for all the cards and messages," he managed. "I know—I know Denise would appreciate it."

Ryan waited a beat and then clapped his hands together.

"Alright, get back to work!"

The summons came exactly twenty minutes later.

Ryan and Phillips retraced their steps along a wide, utilitarian corridor and up an equally minimalist stairwell towards the Chief Constable's office. In other circumstances, they might have made a pit-stop at the ancient vending machine for a cup of bad coffee, but not today.

Ryan's footsteps slowed as they approached the door with its tarnished brass plaque.

"You ready?"

Phillips patted the collar of his shirt in an automatic gesture and was dismayed to find his necktie hanging in a loose knot. He took a moment to adjust it, smoothing down the fabric.

"Ready."

Ryan decided to keep his opinion of Phillips' apparel to himself. He had chosen a tie of bright emerald, embroidered with a series of tiny dancing leprechauns. At any other time, it would have been ridiculous, but he imagined Phillips had acquired it on one of his visits to Ireland with Denise, and so he held his tongue.

He rapped a knuckle against the Chief Constable's door.

"Come!"

When they entered, Chief Constable Sandra Morrison had a telephone handset wedged between shoulder and ear as she flipped through a large file of paperwork with one hand and scribbled notes on a dog-eared notepad with the other. Her sandy-blonde hair had been tamed into a tortoiseshell hair clip at the back of her head, but it was starting to come loose amid the stress of the morning.

She paused to raise her index finger, indicating that she would be another minute.

Taking advantage of the brief lull, Ryan made a beeline for the coffee machine in the corner of the room. He happened to know it served a far better standard of caffeine than the machine downstairs.

"I think another press conference would be premature… yes, of course, I understand your position—"

Morrison dropped her pen and began to knead an ache developing at the back of her neck. Ryan and Phillips edged towards the visitors' chairs arranged in front of her desk and settled themselves.

"I can assure you that we are pursuing every possible avenue, sir. He's as good as vanished into thin air."

Phillips took a small, scalding sip of coffee and felt his stomach quiver.

"Yes, sir. I'll have an update ready for you by the end of the day."

The air thrummed with leftover tension from Morrison's conversation for a full ten seconds after she ended the call. In the residual silence, they could hear the everyday sound of traffic from the main road below, reminding them that ordinary life continued beyond the walls of CID.

Morrison allowed herself a moment to collect her thoughts and used that time to study both detectives. There, on the one hand, was Phillips. A reliable man, one she had worked with for nearly thirty years and whom she would venture to call a friend. Like a bloodhound, he followed the scent of a case until its conclusion through a combination of common sense and raw intelligence. He was often brash and straight-talking to say the least, but he was also scrupulously honest which was a quality she admired and encouraged among her staff. Studying his face, she saw clear signs of strain. His skin bore an unhealthy grey pallor and bruises were beginning to bloom on his face and jawline. Framed against the bright light filtering through her office window, she was saddened to note that he looked at least ten years older than he had a week ago.

Then, there was Ryan. The media's darling, most of the time. Despite being several years younger, he was senior to Phillips in rank and, at one time, she had wondered how they would get along. She needn't have concerned herself because the two men were more like family these days. But where Phillips was what she might call a 'people person', Ryan was a strategist: a born leader capable of viewing an investigation with the precision and detachment of a field marshal, with no compunctions whatsoever about giving offence if it reaped results. He had the capacity for great things and his track record proved it, but he followed instinct as much as he did rules and regulations. That meant she could never entirely trust him to follow orders, but his heart was in the right place. She knew that his family owned an old pile of bricks somewhere down in Devon and yet he had chosen to leave those soft, rolling hills for wilder, untamed northern shores. He had chosen hard work over an easy life and, looking at him now, she thought that he had made a wise decision. Being a healthy, red-blooded woman, she might as well admit that he wasn't hard to look at, either.

Even with a swollen nose and the beginnings of a black eye.

"Well," she said briskly, gesturing to their coffee cups. "I see you've already made yourselves quite comfortable."

Phillips set down his cup with a bit of a clatter, while Ryan took his time finishing the last couple of mouthfuls.

"Thank you, ma'am."

Morrison rested her elbows against the scarred beech desktop and linked her fingers.

"In case you're interested, that was the Commissioner on the phone," she said. "As if the enormity of our task isn't enough, his media liaison had a tip-off about our Senior Investigating Officer brawling with another senior detective this very morning." She flicked a glance towards Phillips' bruised face. "One with a remarkably similar description to you, Frank."

Phillips squirmed in his seat.

"I can explain that," Ryan interjected. "Given the turn of events and the fact Edwards is considered armed and dangerous, I felt it would be wise to brush up on my self-defence skills, in the event they're needed. Phillips kindly offered to share some basic boxing skills with me this morning at a fully-licensed boxing gym."

Ryan had a strong inkling that Buddle's hadn't been on the official radar for years, but he wasn't about to mention that.

Morrison fixed Phillips with a direct stare.

"Is that what happened?"

Phillips cleared his throat.

"Aye—yes, ma'am. Just like the man said. I kept the moves basic, since he's such a novice." He smiled winningly.

Morrison looked between the pair of them and knew when she was beaten.

"Look," she said wearily. "I don't know what happened, or why, but let that be an end to it. Phillips, I hear you've been out of the office for the last two days on a period of leave. I don't recall you mentioning this to me, Ryan, but given the circumstances I think it was best all round."

Morrison licked her lips and wondered how best to approach the next question.

"The fact is, nearly a week has passed. Nobody will be more aware of that fact than you, Frank," she said carefully, "but questions are now being asked. We're accountable for our management of the situation—"

"What are you saying?" Ryan sliced through the waffle.

Morrison sighed.

"I'm saying that the Commissioner has doubts about whether the officers investigating MacKenzie's disappearance can remain objective, given the clear conflict of interest. This isn't just a matter of being unbiased; it's about making sure that we are *seen* to be unbiased in the public eye."

"If you're insinuating that Phillips—"

"I'm referring to both of you," Morrison interrupted the beginnings of an angry tirade. "Ryan, your relationship with Keir Edwards is already a matter of public record. The man killed your sister and nearly killed you. Nobody could blame you for wanting to be part of the task force that will eventually see him returned to a maximum-security prison. But, if anything were to go wrong…well, you can imagine the backlash."

Ryan said nothing but his eyes darkened to a turbulent grey, the same shade as the North Sea.

"As for you," she said, shifting slightly to face Phillips. "Your relationship with Denise MacKenzie is an open secret around these parts. To all intents and purposes, you're her next of kin. That being the case, how on earth do you think yourself capable of following the avenues of this investigation with the level of detachment that we need?"

Phillips' face fell into aggrieved lines and she was sorry for it but forced herself to continue.

"Believe me, Frank, I feel for you. Everyone in this department is feeling the impact and we all want to help.

I know that you want to be an active participant because I would feel the same way myself. That's why I gave you this past week to end things quickly. But as your commanding officer, I can't allow it to continue."

Ryan broke the uncomfortable silence that followed.

"Let me see if I understand you correctly. The Commissioner is beginning to feel the heat from the Powers That Be. They're fielding accusations from the press about police incompetence and they're looking to shake things up, so they can appear to be on top of things. Correct?"

Morrison inclined her head.

"That's hardly breaking new ground, is it? I haven't worked on a single major investigation where the papers haven't taken a pop at our methods at one stage or another. Have you, Phillips?"

"Can't say that I have," came the reply. "It's a thankless job."

"Exactly. We don't do this work for the plaudits and we're not interested in playing at politics so that we can be popular with the tabloid press," Ryan said, scathingly. "We're interested in justice, whatever the hell that means."

He leaned forward and Morrison felt the full force of his anger transmitting itself across the expanse of her desk.

"So, with all due respect, *ma'am*, don't sit there in your ivory tower and talk to us about detachment or conflicts of interest. Because whether it's my sister, his girlfriend"—he jerked a thumb in Phillips' direction—"or a total stranger, once we've agreed to take care of them, they matter to us. Every one of them *matters*."

"You're too close—" Morrison tried again.

"Every time we get a call from Control, we have to be objective. We put on the mask of indifference and set aside that creeping feeling that tells us, just maybe, this one won't be coming home. We visit the mothers, the fathers, the sisters, the brothers—and we shatter their lives. We try to ignore the terrible instinct warning us that there will be more lives ruined before all is said and done. So, if you want MacKenzie found, if you want Edwards back behind bars, then you won't do any better than Phillips or me. Because not only do we do this job every day, we know MacKenzie and we know *him*. We know how they both tick and we're invested. We can bring this home for you, we just need more time."

Ryan fell silent and sank back into the foamy chair.

"I see." Morrison linked her hands again and turned to his colleague. "Do you have anything to add?"

Phillips was no public speaker, but he set his jaw and sat up a bit straighter in his chair.

"I won't beg," he said forthrightly. "I won't grovel for a place on the team. I've earned the right to be there. Edwards has vanished into thin air, you said? I say that's bollocks. He's not a ghost, he's flesh and blood and he's out there, somewhere, with the woman I love. I'll tell you this, Sandra"—he didn't bother with formalities since they had cheerfully sailed over the line of insubordination long ago—"I was born here and I've spent my life getting to know this land. I'll turn over every rock, I'll look behind every tree and search every building and outhouse from John O'Groats to Land's End if I have to. But I'm going to find Denise MacKenzie with or without the support of the bigwigs at Northumbria CID. D'you know what else?" He jerked his head over his shoulder. "There's a room full of people down on the second floor who'll help me do it. Every last one of them has a personal connection with Denise as a colleague and as a friend, so good luck finding anyone *unbiased* in this building."

Morrison drained the last of her coffee.

"Good. That's all I needed to know."

She gave them a small nod. Taking their cue for dismissal, both men exchanged a look and rose hastily to their feet. They had almost made it to the door when she called out.

"Ryan?"

He turned back and raised an eyebrow.

"Don't let me down."

A muscle ticked in his jaw but professionalism won out, as it always did.

The door clicked shut behind them and Morrison sat staring at it for a long time afterward, wondering if she had just made the biggest mistake of her career.

CHAPTER 3

Water sluiced over MacKenzie's bare skin in a miserable, icy-cold trickle. She stood facing the wall, focusing her vision and her mind on the dated bathroom tiles.

Cream with a pattern of faded brown flowers and she'd counted forty-seven of them in total.

The bathroom suite was bottle-green and equally old. The cheap plastic tub was cracked and mould grew in the corners. Every other surface was covered in a layer of dust and insect decay.

"Turn around."

She fought back tears of humiliation.

Stay calm. Survival is key.

She wasn't ashamed of her body and her mind was far, far away, somewhere he could not touch. Slowly, she turned from the wall and fixed her eyes on a point above his head. She had learned that it was possible to remain in control if she could avoid looking directly into his eyes. Somebody had once said that the eyes were the windows to the soul, but what did they say of a man without a soul? When she looked into Keir Edwards' eyes, she saw nothing but dark emptiness, a fathomless chasm where his soul should have been.

The man himself lounged against the wall and took a leisurely survey of his prisoner.

"You know, Ruth, you're really not bad. Not bad at all," he said, with the tone of one making a great concession. "Not my type, regrettably."

Relief must have shone in her eyes because he added, "I could always make an exception. It would certainly pass the time, wouldn't it?"

He smiled, enjoying the fear and confusion racing across her face.

The arms she had thrown around herself to protect her naked body tightened, fingernails digging small arcs into her own skin.

"Would you like that, Ruth? I seem to remember you sending me several very flattering letters while I was incarcerated. Perhaps you'd like a demonstration, now that you have the real thing?"

He spread his arms and caught his own reflection in the spotted mirror above the pedestal. Like a true narcissist, he took a moment to admire himself, flexing his considerable muscle and watching it ripple beneath the woollen jumper he wore.

She wanted to scream, to shout, to lash out. But she'd tried all three and had earned herself a smattering of injuries in return. Her left ankle was sprained and she suspected that at least one of her ribs was fractured. Dark purple bruises covered her torso and kidneys.

"My name is Denise," she whispered, then instantly clamped her lips shut again.

"She speaks!" Edwards exclaimed, clapping his hands together in delight. There was no fun to be had while she retreated behind her silent armour.

He stepped closer and was gratified to see her shudder and cringe away from him. He ran an idle finger along her leg, feeling the goose pimples against her frozen skin.

"In prison, you told me your name was Ruth. Don't tell me that was a *lie*?"

His voice was mild, as if remonstrating with a small child.

"Tut tut," he continued, tracing a fingertip around her belly button. "I don't like liars."

MacKenzie clenched her jaw so tightly it cracked. She understood that he was punishing her. A year ago, she had worked undercover, assuming the persona of 'Ruth' to elicit information from him about another case. She had worn a wig and played the part of a sad, lonely woman obsessed with a charismatic serial killer. She had flattered and cajoled him, gone through the motions of being infatuated by him. In short, she had played him for a fool.

Somehow, he had found out her real identity and it must have made him even angrier to find that she was part of Ryan's team, the man responsible for putting him behind bars. She wondered how long Edwards had planned his revenge, this campaign of psychological torture, or whether he improvised as he went along. It didn't really matter.

She continued to stare at the wall and eventually, he sighed.

"I have to go out soon, Ruth. I hope you'll manage without me?"

MacKenzie's heart quickened, beating like a bird in her chest.

He was leaving her alone?

"Here you go." Solicitous all of a sudden, he handed her a moth-eaten towel. She snatched it from him and quickly wrapped it around her skin.

Then, he held out a hand to help her step out of the bathtub. She imagined herself slapping it away, clawing at his face, his eyes, crushing his skull against the porcelain sink.

But her body was so broken and stiff with pain, she could barely move.

She stared at his hand and thought about the violence it was capable of inflicting, then took it and struggled over the edge of the tub. She winced as the movement jogged her ribs and sent shards of pain arrowing through her chest.

"Thank you," she mumbled.

It did no good to provoke him, she thought. So long as she was courteous and polite, agreeable and conformist, she stayed alive.

At least for now.

Immediately after getting the green light from their Chief Constable, Ryan called a briefing. It was held in the largest conference room at CID, designated as a 'Major Incident Room' to investigate what had affectionately been named 'OPERATION IRELAND'. Within the space of half an hour, it was brimming with staff ranging from admin support to trainee detectives and data analysts, all of whom had set aside their other work and foregone their lunch in a display of solidarity. Ryan had taken a moment to rearrange the board—which was the entire length of one wall—to redirect their attention to the facts in their possession. He knew there were computer programs that could do it all for him, but he was of the old school and believed that there was no substitute for the visual impact of seeing MacKenzie's image front and centre, reminding them why they were all there.

As the clock struck twelve, Ryan strode to the front of the room and shoved his hands in his pockets, sweeping a glance around the sea of faces. He watched Tom Faulkner, the senior CSI, hurry through the doors with a gaggle of CSIs in tow while Phillips took his seat in the front row next to Lowerson, who clucked around him like a mother hen. He opened his mouth to quieten the chattering din but, for once, the room fell silent of its own accord.

"It's been a week," Ryan said without preamble. "And, before we go any further, I want to thank all of you. Nobody could have asked for a more loyal or hardworking team. The sad fact is, despite our efforts, we still haven't found our friend."

He didn't give them time to mourn before moving swiftly on.

"Current thinking is that we've missed something, somewhere. So, we're going to do the only logical thing and go back over our tracks. That includes re-opening every one of Edwards' old case files."

It was a tall order to retrace every report, every sighting and every piece of forensic evidence generated over the last seven days in addition to every year Edwards was an active killer, but it was the only way forward.

"I don't need to tell you that we've ground to a halt." He met Phillips' stare and didn't flinch. "Until Edwards shows himself, we're treading water. But experience tells me there has to be a trail, one that we're not seeing. I propose we start again and, this time, we find it."

There were murmurs of agreement, nods of heads.

"As you know, Durham Police have been leading the investigation into Edwards' escape." He moved across to a large board with a list of action points and pinned photographs. "To recap, at approximately eleven-thirty on the evening of last Monday 28th March, a Sikorsky S-92 helicopter belonging to the Search and Rescue base at Humberside Airport landed in the central courtyard at HMP Frankland, in Durham. It was able to land thanks to a lack of wire netting to protect the overhead space, something Edwards exploited—"

"Not to mention the press," somebody piped up. "The Prison Service has come in for a hammering since it happened."

Ryan lifted a shoulder.

"They were unlucky. That prison houses hundreds of dangerous men under one roof for years at a time. Only one of them had the means and the sheer bloody audacity to organise a helicopter pick-up."

"He always was an arrogant bastard," Phillips spat.

"The helicopter was piloted by this man," Ryan continued, pointing to a headshot photograph of an average-looking, middle-aged man in dress uniform. "This is Andy Hayworth, Chief Pilot at the SAR base in Humberside. He has over fifteen years' experience behind him in private employment and the Royal Air Force."

Ryan paused to check he had their undivided attention, then continued.

"Hayworth has an exemplary track record and a string of commendations, so the first thing our colleagues in Durham have done is ascertain what led a man of his standing to forget his principles and help the Hacker to escape."

He picked up a marker pen and drew a line from Hayworth's photograph to one of a woman holding a blond-haired toddler with a gummy smile.

"His wife and child are the reason why," Ryan explained, circling their photograph with a swirl of red pen. "We tracked the helicopter to open farmland approximately four miles northeast of MacKenzie's home, not far from here in Ponteland. The helicopter was intact, but its pilot was found unconscious with severe bruising to his face and head, alongside the beginnings of hypothermia after being stripped of his clothing and left out in the elements.

Hayworth was taken by ambulance to the Royal Victoria Infirmary, where he was treated for exposure under police guard. When he regained consciousness, he was able to tell us that he had returned home from work on the same day to find his wife and child missing. A note had been left giving detailed instructions about what he should do to avoid either of them being killed. The time constraints and gravity of the situation led him, under severe duress, to carry out the instructions in that note. Hayworth proceeded to commandeer the helicopter without proper authority from his air base and flew northward without radio support."

Ryan shook his head, remembering the conditions that night.

"Let me remind you that last Monday night we saw four inches of rainfall, winds of up to thirty miles per hour, and he was flying low across the North Sea."

Phillips cleared his throat and looked down at the stack of paperwork resting on his knee. He wanted to feel pity. Looking at the faces of the pilot's wife and child, he almost did. Then he thought of Denise, who was now at the mercy of a madman thanks to the actions of Andy Hayworth, and his heart hardened.

"He got his wife and son back, didn't he?"

Ryan pulled an expressive face.

"They're both alive, but severely traumatised after their experience. They were found dumped at the side of the A1 at Scotch Corner, terrified. Traffic police picked them up on the Tuesday morning."

Phillips' eyes strayed to the picture of the little boy and his mother.

"Aye, that's tough," he conceded. "Nobody would want that for the little feller. But surely the mother can tell us who's behind it all?"

Ryan rubbed a hand across the back of his neck and prepared to deliver more unwelcome news. "She gave a preliminary statement with a physical description of the assailant who gained entry into her home, posing as a steam-cleaning salesman. He proceeded to kidnap them both in a blue van bearing the logo of a company we now know to be false."

"We tried tracing the whereabouts of the van, guv," one of the support staff said. "We have patchy footage of Mrs Hayworth and her son being dropped off near the junction at Scotch Corner and more footage of the van heading southbound along the A1 as far as Wetherby. After that, nothing."

"We have the make and model," Ryan said. "What progress has been made to trace all abandoned vehicles matching its description?"

"No blue vans—"

"Forget the colour," Ryan interrupted. "It's an easy job to spray over the bodywork if you know the right people. This man was a professional and the pick-up was slick. The whole operation was slick, for that matter," he was forced to admit. "Go back and check again."

A scribbled note was made.

"She got a good look at him." Phillips picked up the thread of their earlier conversation. "That means she could do a line up."

"That's the issue," Ryan said, as he hitched a hip onto the edge of his desk. "Since making her initial statement, Mrs Hayworth has clammed up. She claims that she can no longer be sure that her description of the assailant was correct."

"Somebody got to her—" Phillips burst out.

Ryan shook his head.

"We've had the Hayworths in a safe house under surveillance for the past week. They haven't been compromised but it's highly probable she was threatened before she and her son were dropped off. Now she's scared to talk."

"Let me speak to her." Phillips tried to remain calm, though he wanted to punch the closest hard surface. Sensing it, Lowerson moved a fraction further away.

"I can't allow that." Ryan swiped a hand through the air. "Two senior personnel from the Durham Constabulary will be re-interviewing Mr and Mrs Hayworth first thing tomorrow morning."

"But—"

"Frank." Ryan's tone was uncompromising. "Durham Constabulary have been fully cooperative so far. The last thing we need right now is to jeopardise that relationship. Leave it to our colleagues in Durham; they know their business as well as we do. As soon as something breaks, they'll tell us."

Phillips leaned forward to rest his forearms on his knees and stared down at the grubby brown carpet tiles covering the floor, hands clenched tightly together.

"So, we just sit around, twiddling our thumbs?"

Ryan chose to ignore that remark.

"As for our side of things, over the past week we've retrieved and analysed every available piece of CCTV footage within a ten-mile radius of MacKenzie's house thanks to a very prompt turnaround from local businesses and the Council. As it stands, we know that Edwards had the nerve to walk from the helicopter drop-off site across open farmland to the taxi rank at Newcastle Airport, and this was all in plain sight. We have extensive footage of him approaching the main entrance to the airport, wearing Hayworth's clothes, then making his way to the taxi rank where he got in a cab. We have partial footage of the cab making its way from the airport—"

"Past our front door, under our noses," Phillips interjected.

Ryan continued as if he hadn't heard.

"We have no footage around MacKenzie's house, unfortunately, but we do have footage of the taxi entering the top of her road at 12:18 and leaving two minutes later. Phillips and Lowerson have told us that they drove directly there in the early hours of last Tuesday morning, as soon as they became concerned by MacKenzie's lack of response. They arrived at the scene at around half past midnight. Prior to that, we have a record of five missed calls from DS Phillips' mobile to MacKenzie's, the first one being received at 12:24. Factoring in average journey times and the footage we do have, we can make an educated guess that MacKenzie was taken sometime between 12:18 and 12:30."

Phillips' jaw clenched and his eyes burned holes in the carpet.

Minutes, he thought. *They had missed her by only a few minutes.*

"We believe Keir Edwards used MacKenzie's red Fiesta as a means of transport. He didn't take her mobile phone or bank cards, so the telephone companies and banks won't be much use to us this time. However, her car is equipped with police GPS tracking and we were able to trace its whereabouts quickly. It was found abandoned near the Styford Roundabout, off the A69 heading in a westerly direction. Lowerson?"

His head snapped up in surprise.

"You're in charge of CCTV accumulation and analysis. Give us a rundown of what has been done to trace her movements since then."

Lowerson got to his feet and turned to face a roomful of stony-faced police staff.

"Right. Yes." His voice wobbled like a teenager. "We believe that the Styford Roundabout was carefully chosen by Edwards as a changeover point. It's like a compass, with roads turning off in all directions and there is no Automatic Number Plate Recognition nearby. In fact, very limited CCTV footage on any of the roads leading off that roundabout, since you're getting right out into Northumberland, away from the city—"

"There has to be something," Phillips put in.

Lowerson swallowed and moved across to the giant map on the wall. He pointed to the location of MacKenzie's home in Ponteland, less than a mile away from where they were all gathered now.

"Edwards drove the Fiesta through Ponteland along this road"—he traced his index finger along the high street—"and then he must have taken the back roads to avoid cameras. He picked up the A69 motorway here," he said, and tapped his finger above a bright blue pin on the map. "We know that he didn't turn east into the centre of Newcastle, he travelled west until he reached the Styford Roundabout. Once there and under cover of darkness, we believe that he transferred himself and MacKenzie to a new vehicle. That leaves four possible routes for him to take: the A68 southbound through the North Pennines towards Weardale; the B6530 southwest into Corbridge town; he could have continued further west along the A69 with an option of picking up the road north towards Scotland; or he could have doubled back and taken the country road that runs parallel to the route he had just taken, sneaking back towards Newcastle without using the motorway."

"What have you eliminated so far?" Ryan prodded.

"Um, well, we've been studying the footage covering the B6530 into Corbridge during the hours of 12:30 and 02:30

last Tuesday morning and we're pretty certain that Edwards didn't take that route. There was a total of forty-four vehicles captured by the CCTV as you enter Corbridge during those hours and all of them have been accounted for."

Ryan nodded thoughtfully.

"I agree that Edwards is unlikely to have waited any longer before continuing his journey; he knew that we would find MacKenzie's Fiesta fairly quickly, therefore he wouldn't hang around the area. No need to extend the search timescale," he concluded. "What else?"

Lowerson flicked a dubious glance towards Phillips, who watched him like a hawk.

"Unfortunately, sir, that's about it. There is no roadside CCTV coverage along any of the other three roads until you reach a major town and we've already checked the cameras outside Hexham. We also looked at the speed cameras along the A69 and the A68 for completeness. No hits for speeding vehicles during the relevant timeframes, I'm sorry to say—just a stream of ordinary vehicles passing by various civilian CCTV cameras, which we are slowly analysing. It's a long process," he added, with a note of apology.

Ryan scrubbed a palm across his face.

"Alright. What about further along the major roads? We could pick up the vehicle…" He trailed off as his brain caught up with his mouth. "And that would be a pointless task, considering we have no idea what Edwards' replacement vehicle looks like. Might as well stop every single vehicle using the national road network in the early hours."

Lowerson nodded miserably and sat down again.

"Alright, so he didn't leave a nice little trail of breadcrumbs," Ryan shrugged. "We'll do this the conventional way. Faulkner? What can you tell us about forensics?"

Like a meerkat, the senior CSI popped his head up from a line of police staff, adjusted his glasses and moved cautiously to the front of the room.

"Ah, yes, well. We went over MacKenzie's home and car with a fine-toothed comb days ago and I doubt we will find anything new there. There is no evidence that Edwards moved beyond the hallway of MacKenzie's home and judging by a small pattern of blood spatter on the inner left-hand wall…" He looked up from his sheaf of papers, caught Phillips' eye and began to stutter. "Ah, that is, it's fairly certain—"

"Spit it out, Tom," Ryan ordered. "We all need to know the facts."

"Well, we're pretty sure he hit her as soon as she opened the front door, taking her by surprise. That's probably how she was disabled."

Phillips remembered his last conversation with Denise before she was taken. They had both worried for Ryan and his fiancée, Anna, mistakenly thinking that she would be the Hacker's first target.

How wrong they had been.

"Denise was hurrying to get ready and come down to the station, to help out," he said dully, and heads swivelled towards him. "She was distracted, worrying about Anna. That's probably why she didn't check before she opened the door."

Ryan stiffened. He wouldn't—couldn't—feel guilty that his fiancée was safe at home, much as it churned him up to know that his friend was suffering instead.

"MacKenzie is a good woman," he said quietly. "But remember, Frank. No matter how distracted she was, no matter how well trained, Edwards came to her home intending to take her. Whether she opened the door or he kicked it down, that was always his goal. It's unlikely she could have prevented him—he had the element of surprise."

Phillips flinched as the words hit home but something clicked in his brain. When he looked up again, his eyes were clear.

"You're right," he said, decisively. "Tom? You said there was spatter? How about inside the Fiesta?"

Faulkner's throat bobbed up and down.

"Only a few spots of blood in there, crusted onto the felt lining of the boot. We didn't find any significant blood spill," he said, understanding what they all really wanted to know. "We took our time looking at the driver's seat and compared the skin samples with existing DNA records we have on file for Edwards. There was a positive match."

"So, he disabled her, put her in the boot and then got into the driver's seat," Ryan surmised.

"Yes. We went over the area around the abandoned Fiesta beside Styford Roundabout but I'm afraid we weren't quick enough to beat the weather. It was raining heavily last Monday night, just as it is today."

They all followed the direction of his myopic gaze and watched the rain battering against the dirty windowpanes outside, the dim light doing nothing to motivate their spirits. Ryan muttered something unintelligible and moved to flick on the heavy strip-lighting in the centre of the room. Immediately, they were bathed in garish yellow light from the industrial fluorescent bulbs.

"That's better," he said. "Faulkner? You're saying there were no tracks or traces found whatsoever?"

Faulkner pushed his glasses further back on his nose.

"I didn't quite say that. It's true, there were no tyre or foot prints around the site where we found the car. However, we pushed our search further back into the shrubbery on the outskirts of the roundabout and we noticed something. There was a fresh gap in the bushes, large enough to have been made by a vehicle entering or reversing. We also found a partial tyre track, but not enough to draw any meaningful conclusions at this stage. When we find the other vehicle, we should be able to match it."

"Somebody hid the vehicle there, in readiness for him to pick it up. Who?"

"His solicitor."

Lowerson spoke the words without thinking and reddened as attention turned to him once again. Ryan pointed a finger as if to capture the thought.

"Yes, it's possible. She's currently being investigated for fraud."

Edwards' former solicitor was currently out on bail while the fraud team put together their case, following a tip-off from the Solicitors Regulation Authority. Apparently, the woman had accepted bribes from her client in exchange for performing a series of illegal acts. It wasn't too much of a stretch to imagine that she might have provided Edwards with money or transportation.

"I want her questioned again. Lowerson? Liaise with the fraud team on this and set up an interview ASAP."

Ryan leaned back against the desk and crossed his ankles.

"Carry on, Tom."

Faulkner paused to remove his glasses and rub at his eyes. It would be easy to reel off facts and figures but what everybody needed to hear, Phillips most of all, was not what his team of CSIs had found but what they *hadn't* found.

He slipped his glasses back on and tucked his file under his arm.

"We made a full search of the ground around the Fiesta stretching back through the shrubbery and beyond. It was a fingertip search that went on until last Thursday. Although there were alterations to the landscape suggesting that one or more persons had walked through the grassland, at no time did we find any evidence suggesting foul play."

Phillips looked up at that, eyes hopeful.

"There was no...no burial site or anything of that kind," Faulkner added. "And no human blood or tissue."

Silence dawned as the room wondered whether to be optimistic following that remark. Although MacKenzie had not been found dead at the side of a roundabout, there was every reason to suspect that she might be found elsewhere.

Sensing the change of mood, Ryan decided to nip it in the bud.

"*If* and until we are proven wrong, we will be working on the basis that Detective Inspector MacKenzie is still alive. I won't sugar coat the fact that Keir Edwards is dangerous and severely disturbed. He has a history of extreme violence and a personal dislike of our department, for obvious reasons. But his previous MO has been to kill his victims relatively quickly and all of them have been brunettes in their twenties."

An image of his sister flashed into his mind, a beautiful young girl lying dead in his arms. Ryan shoved the memory aside and ordered himself to focus on the present. He could not change the past, much as he wished to.

"MacKenzie isn't his usual physical type, being a woman in her forties with red hair. That gives us reason to hope that her kidnapper has an alternative motivation in mind."

"Why does he usually go for brunettes?" Lowerson queried, curiosity getting the better of him.

Ryan frowned, thinking back.

"We never found out and he never told us." *It was a damn good question.* "Why do anything? Maybe there was a girl at school who rejected him. Maybe he had an Oedipus complex but mummy said 'no'. Maybe he just likes the way brunettes look dead. Who the hell cares?"

Ryan shoved away from his desk and paced around a bit to shake off the irritation. He didn't want to think about why the man killed dark-haired women because it was an immediate reminder that Anna was one of them. Her safety was a constant worry and would be until Edwards was safely back behind bars.

He sucked in a long, calming breath.

"You're right, though, Jack. We need to know how this arsehole thinks and try to understand what goes on inside his twisted mind. I'm going to re-open the old case files and go back over every statement we've ever had from him. Maybe something will turn up."

Ryan turned to look at the board behind him and into the dark eyes of a smiling man that society deemed handsome. A man who, at first glance, looked uncomfortably like him. But that was where the similarity ended. Where he spent his days fighting to protect human life, Edwards was a former doctor who had rejected his Hippocratic Oath to inflict the worst possible abuse on another human being.

"Edwards has a driving need to be recognised," Ryan murmured, rubbing a hand across his chest to stave off a sudden chill. "He needs everybody to know how clever he is."

"He could be out of the country by now," somebody chirped up.

Ryan laughed and gave a small shake of his head.

"And miss out on the opportunity to show off? No, he's still in the region, festering somewhere. He's so close, I can almost smell him."

CHAPTER 4

Nothing moved inside the empty house, not even MacKenzie.

She sat on the extreme edge of a rickety single bed frame listening for any sound that might alert her to his presence, but the house had been quiet for almost half an hour without the usual noises coming from downstairs.

Normally, it was the radio. On a good day, he would tune into the classical station and Puccini or Mozart would fill the air. On other days, he brought the old transistor radio onto the landing outside her room and turned the volume so high that the sound of *The Beatles* became deafening. MacKenzie swore that if she survived—*when* she survived—she never wanted to hear anybody singing about the virtues of getting by with a little help from their friends so long as she lived.

The irony of his choice of music was not lost on her either.

Not content with the injuries he had already inflicted, Edwards went about the business of breaking her spirit, reminding her of how alone she really was. And, oh, he was masterful at the game, pouring poison into her ears as often as he could.

I don't want to hurt you, Ruth.

Where are your friends? I'm your only friend, now.

He never used her real name. It was just another way to dehumanise her, to diminish everything she had ever been.

"I am Detective Inspector Denise Mary MacKenzie. I was born in County Kerry, Ireland—" she whispered.

A tile slipped on the roof and she jumped, acutely aware of every creak and groan in the old house. Her eyes darted around the room but nothing had changed. The walls still bore the remnants of peeling wallpaper redolent of the seventies or eighties, darker shadows of varying rectangular shapes indicating where pictures had once hung. Aside from the single wooden bed with its grubby, stained mattress, the only other furniture in the room was a plastic bucket he had placed in the corner in lieu of a toilet.

He ran the place like a prison. It gave him a peculiar delight to inflict the monotony of his experience behind bars upon one of the detectives who had contributed to him being there in the first place. He never tired of opening the door to find her waiting to be led to the bathroom, or to be handed a measly plate of beans or tuna. Always canned goods, she noticed, and the water he sometimes gave her tasted raw. She had been violently ill during the first three days but now her stomach seemed to have accustomed itself to the change of circumstances.

She didn't know whether to be pleased or not.

When the trembling in her hands stopped, she bent down to retie the makeshift bandage on her sprained ankle. Fluid pooled around the joint and it was painful to touch, but not as painful as bending over with a couple of cracked ribs. Sweating from the effort, she stared down at her bare feet with their dirty soles. Her boots had been one of the first things to go and her skin was covered in splinters from the old wooden floor.

Come on, Denise.

Transferring her weight onto her good foot, she stood up and hobbled across to the single square window to peer through the broken glass. It was far too small to squeeze through and the drop was too high for her to come out of it unscathed, in any case. The air was crisp and cold as it flooded into the room but she didn't care about being too cold, or too hot for that matter.

Either was better than the alternative.

Her eyes scanned the farmland outside, drawing a mental diagram of the terrain. The front door was on this side of the house—which was east-facing, judging by the direction of the sun—and it led directly onto open fields which stretched as far as the eye could see. The mossy turf undulated down into the valley towards a forest or woodland of some kind, although only the tips of the tallest trees were visible. There were a couple of tumbledown outhouses nearby made of the same thick stone as the house but neither of them was large enough to hold more than a few chickens or some firewood.

Crucially, there was no sign of his car. She hadn't seen it since the first day and she wondered where he had hidden it.

Come to think of it, there was no sign of a road either.

She squinted through the window from every angle, leaning out as far as she could, but she couldn't see anything resembling a garage. There were no traffic sounds carrying on the air, only the whisper of the wind as it slipped through the gaps in the walls.

Slowly, she made her way to the bedroom door, pressing her ear against the wooden frame to listen for any sound of life on the other side.

She wiped her clammy palm on the side of her jeans and then grasped the handle.

The door swung open.

MacKenzie stood there, staring through the open doorway into the empty hallway beyond, unable to believe her eyes. It was not possible that he had forgotten to lock the door. Edwards was a methodical psychopath; he never did anything without having a reason.

Knowing that it had to be a trap did nothing to dim the overwhelming sense of hope that fluttered in her chest but there were her injuries to consider and she was weak after six days of malnutrition and lack of sleep.

And yet, the door was open.

It was foolish to try but, then again, she would be a fool not to.

She took the first, careful step out of her room and onto the landing. The floorboards whined in protest and she stopped dead, blood thundering in her ears as she waited.

Still nothing.

MacKenzie took another tentative step, leaving a wide berth around a sizeable hole in the landing floor where the wood had collapsed entirely three days ago. On that occasion, when he unlocked her door, she had taken a swing at him with one of the wooden slats from her bed, then tried to make a run for it. She hadn't made it three feet before he caught her, throwing her body to the floor with enough force to break through the old wood.

That was how her ribs were fractured.

Gritting her teeth, she hobbled further along, clutching the banister for support. She paused to look down through the gaping hole, into what passed for a living room. She could make out the edge of a ratty blue sofa, faded with age and covered with dust and fragments of wood.

Her fingers curled around the rail and she continued along the landing as quietly as she could. She passed three doors: the bathroom door was closed and the other two bedroom doors stood open on creaking hinges. One of them must belong to him and she braced herself for the sight of Edwards jumping out at her, but he didn't appear.

She reached the top of the stairs and hesitated.

"You have to try," she whispered.

The pressure on her ankle was intense, so she crouched down to sit on the top step and began to make her way downstairs on her rear end, like a child.

One, two, three, four…

She counted off the stairs in her head and stopped again when the front door came into view, straight ahead of her. Involuntary tears sprang to her eyes and she brushed them away impatiently with the heel of her hand.

…five, six, seven…

Her legs wobbled as she drew herself up again, gripping the newel post like a lifeline. She risked glances to either side and saw the living room to her left and an ancient kitchen to her right. And there, atop one of the worktops, was a large carving knife.

She looked between it and the front door, torn between expedience and good sense.

Sense won out and she limped into the kitchen, her panting breaths impossibly loud in the quiet space. The metal clattered against the counter as she grasped it by the handle. She spun around, eyes wide and poised for attack.

Moving quickly now, she made for the front door and found that unlocked as well. She threw it open and clutched the knife in her other hand, ready and able to use it if he should be waiting around the corner. The sight of verdant green fields and pale sunshine nearly overwhelmed her as she stood there, on the cusp of freedom.

A sob escaped her lips as she limped out into the light, letting her feet sink into the thick grass. It was still damp from rainfall earlier in the day and, to her starved senses, it was like a balm. Her toes curled into it and she felt a wave of emotion wash over her.

A bird flew overhead, letting out a long cry.

She shrank back against the outer stone wall and wondered which way to go. Straight ahead led to the forest in the dip of the valley, but it might lead her further away from the nearest town. Gnawing the inside of her lip, she decided to trace the perimeter of the house to see what lay on the other side.

Perhaps there would be a road.

Please, let there be a road.

Another tile clattered off the roof and fell to the ground not far from her head. She stumbled and looked up to see the same bird perched on the edge of the guttering, watching her slow progress.

"Shh," MacKenzie warned it, raising a shaking finger to her lips.

She emerged on the western side of the house to find a mirror image of the view she had just left. More farmland, rippling in a patchwork of green and brown far off into the distance, broken only by outcrops of woodland. It was an Arcadian scene that she might have appreciated, in her old life.

But now all she saw was vast emptiness and miles of painful walking ahead.

East or west?

North or south?

Every direction looked the same.

She turned too quickly and trod on a sharp pebble jutting from the grass beneath her feet. She threw a hand across her mouth to stifle a cry but found herself wondering if there had once been a driveway hidden beneath the undergrowth. If so, perhaps this was the right direction to follow.

MacKenzie scrutinised the ground, looking for more patches of rubble. She found traces leading back towards a wooden gate in the hedgerow nearby. It had long since fallen from its rusted hinges, but her heart swelled.

She had found the way out.

Frank Phillips stared down at an image of Keir Edwards, taken sometime after his arrest back in 2014. Edwards stared boldly back at him from the glossy photograph in his file; unrepentant, defiant.

"Put it away," Ryan said mildly, from his desk a few feet away.

Phillips shoved the image away from him and tugged his lip between thumb and forefinger.

"Have you heard from Durham yet?"

Ryan didn't bother to look up.

"I've already told you, they're re-interviewing the pilot and his wife tomorrow. Lowerson has set up an interview with Edwards' former solicitor in the meantime. He'll be interviewing her first thing in the morning, alongside one of the DIs from the fraud team."

"Is he up to the job? He's barely out of short trousers."

Ryan merely raised an eyebrow.

"Alright, he's a decent lad," Phillips relented. "But it would be better to have one of us in there—"

"Morrison is watching every move we make. Lowerson has the impartiality she's looking for, at least on paper. Give him a chance, Frank, he cares about her as much as you and I do."

Phillips swallowed his frustration and looked down at the stack of papers scattered across his desk.

"I've gone back over all the statements we received last week. The taxi driver who picked Edwards up at the airport said he seemed like, 'a really nice bloke.'" Phillips let out a bark of laughter that held no humour whatsoever. "A *nice bloke*. What kind of idiot has a serial killer sitting on his back seat and thinks he's a canny body?"

Ryan set his file to one side and turned to face him.

"Edwards operated in society for years before he was captured. Think about all the doctors and nurses who worked with him at the hospital; all the patients who said how charming he was and who found it hard to believe that *nice* Doctor Edwards could ever hurt anybody. But we know better. The man is an operator and manipulating people is one of his greatest skills. He doesn't go around wearing a t-shirt saying *I'm The Hacker*, to alert people. He moves among them, blending in."

Phillips sighed and looked back down at the statement on his desk.

"The cabbie also describes him as tall and very muscular. That doesn't seem to tally, does it? I mean, he liked to keep fit but he was more of an athletic build, a bit like you," Phillips said, unguardedly.

A shadow crossed Ryan's face and Phillips instantly regretted his casual remark.

"Ah, that is to say, you're both tall and that…"

"Well, apparently, he's bulked out quite a bit which is hardly surprising given the time he's spent in prison. What else did he have to do, except mastermind his escape and work on his physique?"

"Didn't the taxi driver also say he had close-cropped hair and a beard? That's another change from his usual foppish hairdo," Phillips added.

"The prison officers confirmed he had grown a beard," Ryan said. "But they didn't have an up-to-date photograph, just the old one from when we first booked him back in 2014."

Ryan searched the files on his computer and found a facial composite which had been produced using a combination of Edwards' old image and new, overlaid features based on eyewitness accounts of his recent appearance. He brought the photofit up on his computer screen and turned it towards Phillips.

"This new image has been plastered all over the news and there are leaflets and flyers all around town. Let's hope somebody recognises him."

The rain had stopped, leaving clear blue skies in its wake. Ryan was quiet for a moment while he watched the sun begin its slow descent, blazing trails of light through the remaining clouds. He thought of all the people going about their lives, never thinking that they might be the Hacker's next victim.

He envied them their naivety.

"Edwards was behind bars for nearly two years," he continued. "That's two years when he was cooped up and unable to kill anybody. He's been outside for a week now and I don't need to tell you that it will have been a feat of superhuman restraint for him to have lasted this long without sating his aggression."

Ryan turned to look directly at his sergeant.

"I still believe MacKenzie is alive because she serves a special purpose and she's got the training and the will to survive. But there are thousands of other people out there who serve no purpose to a man like Edwards, except as a vessel for his needs. He was never one for delayed gratification."

Phillips knew it was true.

"He's gone to ground but he'll have to surface at some point. When he does, we'll be ready."

"I hope so."

Freedom was intoxicating.

MacKenzie dragged herself across the grass towards the broken gate in the far corner of the field as quickly as she could, tripping over potholes in her haste to get away. She didn't know how long she had until Edwards returned and there was a possibility he would see her, fleeing the house in the same direction. As soon as she reached a road, she would keep to the hedgerows, out of sight. Her ankle protested with every agonizing step and one arm clutched her midriff to quell the stabbing pain in her ribs. Her other arm swung at her side, still clutching the kitchen knife.

Gradually, awareness crept in.

A prickle worked its way along her spine, causing the fine hairs on her arms and the back of her neck to stand on end. Her heart rate quickened to a roar and she could see the gate a few feet ahead of her, tantalisingly close and wide open, beckoning her onward.

But the feeling would not go away, it only grew stronger.

She came to a gradual standstill, drawing shuddering breaths into her body. Through blurred vision, she saw the edge of a dirt-track road leading from the gate and down into the valley. It was almost hidden by years of undergrowth but it was there, directing her towards safety and civilisation.

It might as well have been on the other side of the world because she knew she would never reach it. She knew that he was behind her somewhere, watching.

Laughing.

Impotent tears began to fall as she stood immobilised, frightened to move forward yet afraid to look behind. She waited for long minutes until the tears completely dried against her skin. She would not give him that satisfaction.

Drawing herself up to her full height, she took one last lingering look at the road and then pivoted on her good foot to look back towards the stone house that was her prison. The sun had dropped lower in the sky, grazing the uppermost edge of the moss-topped roof. She raised a hand to shade her eyes against its bright glare but then a tall figure moved, eclipsing the light.

Defeat weighed heavily against her heart. The hand holding the knife began to shake and it fell from her nerveless fingers into the thick grass at her feet.

Edwards had been on the roof all along, with a rifle aimed at her head.

CHAPTER 5

Day moved seamlessly into night as the occupants of CID worked with their heads bowed, and the sun went unnoticed as it dipped into the horizon, throwing out wide arcs of amber and gold in a final display of light as it fell off the edge of the world. When he eventually looked up, Ryan was surprised to see that it was well after eight o'clock and he had been working for twelve hours straight. Half of his staff, particularly those with children waiting for them, had gone home. He arched his back to ease out the kinks and ran a hand through his hair in a habitual gesture, thinking of what else could usefully be achieved that night.

Not much.

He had already delivered his obligatory report to Chief Constable Morrison, detailing the problems they faced tracking down Edwards' phantom vehicle without first having a lead, which might come from their interview with his former solicitor the next morning. Forensic work had ground to a halt after an extensive operation covering every nook and cranny of the stolen helicopter, of Edwards' old prison cell and of MacKenzie's home and car. All the prison staff working on Edwards' section at HMP Frankland were due to be re-interviewed in the coming days, alongside the pilot who had earned himself the dubious reputation of being the man who had air-lifted a killer.

Ryan stood up with his mug of cold coffee and prowled towards the long window overlooking the car park. Streetlights flickered along the main road and he knew that a few miles yonder, the city would be coming to life. Bars and restaurants opened their doors and people flocked, despite the wolf lurking in their midst.

It was the perfect hunting ground.

"Lowerson?"

Across the room, the young detective constable looked up from his desk.

"Guv?"

"Contact the railways and the buses again. I want updated feeds of their on-board CCTV cameras."

"There'll be a delay," Lowerson warned him.

"As quickly as possible, then," Ryan said. "After you've done that, go home and rest. I want you here bright and early tomorrow ahead of the interview with that solicitor."

"Understood."

Lowerson busied himself with his task and Ryan turned away from the window to look back at Phillips, who was hunched over his desk. His suit jacket lay crumpled on the floor where it had fallen off the back of his ugly green desk chair and his hair stood out at odd angles, the product of restless fingers. Ryan couldn't recall the last time they had eaten and he berated himself for not taking better care. After a few moments spent rifling inside his desk drawer, he produced a depleted multi-pack of chocolate bars and tossed one onto Phillips' desk.

His sergeant looked up in surprise.

"Eat that," Ryan ordered. "Then go home and have something more substantial."

"I'm not hu—"

"I've got a funny feeling that he'll move tonight, Frank. I've ordered extra patrols at the mainline station in Newcastle and at the airport. I need you primed and ready when the call comes in."

Phillips looked down at the chocolate, then back at Ryan.

"In that case, I'll see if the pie van is open on my way home."

Doctor Anna Taylor yawned widely and flipped her legs up onto the sofa, crossing them at the ankle while she tried to concentrate on a tedious academic article about the Viking raids on Northumberland during the first century. The history of early pagan religion was her specialist subject but it was hard to focus on people who were long dead when you were too busy worrying about those who were still alive.

A strand of dark hair worked its way loose and she tucked it behind her ear with an absentminded hand, joggling the sheaf of papers resting precariously on her knee.

Where was Ryan?

After recent events, they had agreed he would try to be home as early as possible. Anna understood that his job was demanding and it was not always possible to stick to a schedule, especially when you cared as much about the victims as Ryan did. Besides, she had her own heavy workload at the University in Durham and the small matter of a book to write.

Still, the house was awfully empty.

She thought of Denise MacKenzie, a woman she had grown to love. Only weeks ago, they had laughed together in a bridal shop while Anna tried on an array of floaty white dresses, each more preposterous than the last. It was a moment when every woman wanted her mother beside her. Anna's was gone, but Denise had been there instead, tactfully reminding her that meringue dresses had gone out of style in the nineties. They had plotted and planned for the perfect wedding day, but now…

Anna smiled sadly and tried not to imagine where her friend might be or the terror she faced. Instead, she craned her neck to look at the carriage clock on the mantle.

Eight-fifteen.

Where had the time gone?

She was about to set her papers aside and roll off the sofa in search of coffee when her mobile phone jingled out an electronic rendition of Kenny Loggins' *Footloose.*

She snatched it up.

"Anna?"

Her entire body relaxed at the sound of his voice. Clipped, well-rounded but with just enough edge.

"Is everything alright?"

"As well as it can be," he replied. "Look, I just wanted to let you know I'm running late. Is the surveillance car still there?"

Anna unfolded her legs and walked across to the window, tugging aside the heavy curtains to look outside. A silver Ford Mondeo was parked across the street and, noting her presence, its headlights flashed once.

"Still there," she confirmed, giving the two plain-clothed police officers a quick wave before letting the curtains fall back into place.

Back at his desk in CID, some of the tension eased from Ryan's shoulders.

"Good. They have orders to stay put for another hour until their relief arrives. I'll be back by then, anyway."

Standing alone in the quiet room, Anna injected some brightness into her tone.

"No problem. I'm absolutely fine, here. Absolutely."

There was a short pause.

"You said 'absolutely' twice," he pointed out, feeling the tension creep back.

Anna rolled her eyes. It was impossible to get away with even the most well-meaning white lie when you lived with a man whose job it was to sniff them out.

"Alright, smarty-pants," she snapped. "I'm feeling a bit on edge. Does that make you feel better?"

Ryan considered the question.

"Actually, it does," he surprised her by saying. "We can't afford to get complacent. If you're scared, it makes you human and it makes you alert."

He wasn't the only one who could read nuance.

"Something's happened. What is it?"

Ryan sighed.

"Nothing...yet."

"You mean, something might happen tonight."

Ryan looked up and caught Phillips watching him across the room with dark, sombre eyes.

"Just make sure you lock the doors," he murmured. "And Anna?"

"Yes?"

"Be careful."

Keir Edwards drove confidently, his grip firm at the wheel of the old Toyota Rav 4. It had taken him a while to meander his way along the A68 leading into Durham using roads he had mapped out in advance. It would have been much quicker to take a more direct route but, as he had learned, patience was a virtue.

He supposed he had prison to thank for that. The routine and regimen had taught him fortitude, something he had never exercised before. Now that he had reclaimed his rightful place in the world, he could afford to be magnanimous about it.

Almost as soon as the thought entered his mind, it was erased by a mental image of Ryan swanning around playing the hero while he rotted away behind bars. His foot flattened the accelerator pedal and the car surged forward, edging towards eighty-five on the speedometer.

Smug bastard, Edwards thought venomously. He'd wipe that self-satisfied grin from Ryan's face soon enough. He had followed the man's meteoric rise to near-celebrity status from the widescreen television in the prison common room, when he had behaved himself for long enough to warrant recreational privileges.

Privileges.

As if any of the apes in uniform at HMP Frankland would know the first thing about privilege. They wouldn't know the difference between filet mignon at a Michelin-starred restaurant and a double whopper. In fact, if he had time, he might just go back and clean the lot of them out. The Prison Service could consider it a form of community service on his part.

Then, as quickly as it had come, the red mist receded and he eased his foot off the pedal. It wouldn't do to attract the interest of a passing traffic cop or a speed camera. No siree.

Average car, average speed.

Just another average Joe heading home to his lovely fiancée.

He met his own eyes in the rear-view mirror and grinned.

Anna spent another fruitless half-hour reading and re-reading the same paragraphs before setting her work aside. It was useless trying to concentrate when her mind was miles away, lost in memories from the past.

She remembered first meeting Ryan two years ago, on the little tidal island of Lindisfarne which lay an hour or so further north of Newcastle. Twice a day, the North Sea rolled in and cut it off from mainland Northumberland and the people who lived there could enjoy the peace and serenity of having a corner of the world entirely to themselves. Anna had been born on the island but her childhood held few happy memories, so when she had returned to assist the police with a murder investigation it had been with no small amount of trepidation. For Ryan's part, he had recently lost his sister and had escaped to the island to grieve and recover. Death had followed him there and the call of duty had been something he couldn't ignore. Neither of them had searched for the other or wanted the complications that a relationship might bring. People said it wouldn't last and that it was impossible to live with a man who gave his life to avenging the dead. But she had since come to realise that there were some things in life you just didn't fight and her love for Detective Chief Inspector Maxwell Finley-Ryan was one of them.

Anna looked again at the brass carriage clock above the fireplace.

Eight-fifty.

Time always passed slowly when you were eagerly awaiting an arrival, so she decided to try another form of distraction by taking a bath to relax her taut nerves. She selected a book from a stack of well-thumbed paperbacks and reached across to turn out the lamps.

The house felt very empty.

Anna rubbed a brisk hand across her arm to warm herself, then stole another glance behind the curtain. She was reassured by the presence of the silver Mondeo and raised her hand to wave to the police officers sitting inside it.

She waited, but this time there was no flash of headlights.

Her forehead wrinkled but she shrugged it off, thinking that they probably couldn't see her against the canvas of a shadowed room.

Yes, that would explain it.

Anna headed for the staircase but as she reached the first step, she stopped and swore softly under her breath. Then she went back and turned all the lights on again.

Edwards drummed his fingers in time to the radio as he passed through the darkened streets of Durham and was careful to keep his sunshade turned down, as an added precaution just in case an officious bystander should happen to recognise his face as he entered the city limits.

Speed cameras. ANPR cameras. Ticket inspectors. Just schemes to squeeze more money from hardworking taxpayers, he thought self-righteously.

Whatever next?

They should think about investing money in more robust safety measures to keep dangerous criminals off the streets.

He almost laughed out loud at his own joke as he passed under the shadow of Durham Cathedral, which towered like a giant over the river and the castle sitting at its feet. Edwards didn't stop to admire its architecture but continued across the bridge, slowing down to watch for the turning that would lead him towards Anna's cottage. He happened to know that Ryan hadn't been able to return to the penthouse apartment he owned on Newcastle's Quayside ever since their last interlude, and it was currently standing empty and unoccupied while he shacked up with his little tart.

Pity.

It was a shame to let a prime investment go to waste.

His attention was diverted and excitement began to fizz through his veins as he spotted the private road leading down to the waterfront.

"I'm home," he snarled. "Put the kettle on, sweetheart."

Water sloshed noisily into the roll-top bath, blotting out the oppressive silence in the empty house. Anna threw herself into the idea, lighting a row of scented candles on the window ledge and dragging an old CD player into the doorway. Upbeat music combined with the cosy warmth of the bathroom helped to create a sense of calm and she began to think that she was worrying about nothing.

Really, it was ridiculous to jump at shadows or to think that a murderer lurked behind every door. It was a waste of energy and it was probably very unhelpful to Ryan, who needed to focus all his attention on bringing MacKenzie home.

If Edwards wanted to harm her, he would surely have done it by now.

Wouldn't he?

Anna began to undress, folding her jeans and shirt neatly on top of the toilet seat. She paused to pull a face at herself in the mirror above the sink and then dipped her toe into the bathwater.

Was that a noise, downstairs?

One foot on the floor, one in the bath, she stood perfectly still, listening.

Nothing.

Laughing at herself, Anna shook her head and climbed into the bath. She sighed happily and allowed the water to surround her in a warm, safe cocoon. On the radio, the Beatles began to play and she hummed along under her breath.

Edwards parked the car half a mile away, then doubled back on foot towards the private road leading towards Anna's cottage beside the river. He kept his chin lowered, stealing upward glances now and then to watch for street cameras. When he spotted one, he zigzagged across to the other side of the road to avoid its line of sight.

Two women making their way home admired the tall, good-looking man with broad shoulders.

Edwards swept his dark eyes over them and assessed their attributes, much as he might have done a slab of meat in a butcher's window. The taller one reminded him of a pigeon: top heavy and cooing. He didn't mind the noise since he didn't care about anything she might have to say. But the poorly fitting skirt, the cheap heels? Bad taste was unforgivable.

As for the shorter one, she was fat, plain and simple. Not *curvy*, not *hourglass*, but fat. The thought of touching her left him vaguely nauseated.

He gave them both an empty, twinkling smile and a flirtatious wink, heard them giggle, then his face fell back into the hard lines of a predator.

The streets were moderately busy but that was alright. People heading home after work or dinner with friends hardly noticed what went on around them, let alone remembered specifics. He slipped into Anna's road and immediately crouched behind one of the parked cars overlooking a row of pretty stone cottages.

Then he waited.

It was nearly five minutes before he spotted it. The interior light flickered on inside one of the cars parked further along, illuminating two figures who appeared to be unwrapping sandwiches in tin foil.

Et, voila!

The police were nothing if not predictable, he thought, and retreated into the shadows to join the footpath leading down to the waterfront. If the front door to Anna's cottage was barred, he'd just have to go around the back.

Ryan tapped a finger against the steering wheel of his car as he manoeuvred through late evening traffic heading out of Newcastle. He smiled at the sound of an enormous SUV blaring its horn, dodging back and forth between lanes to get home ten seconds sooner than everybody else. Idly, he considered turning on the in-car siren just for kicks but he couldn't justify its use outside of an emergency.

Instead, he flicked on the hands-free mobile and selected Anna's number.

It rang out.

He shrugged, thinking that she was probably in the bathroom.

His finger tapped a little more energetically, then he gave in to the impulse and keyed in the number for one of the police officers on surveillance duty.

"Peters? It's Ryan…yeah, alright thanks. Look, just wanted to check everything's still quiet over there."

"Yeah, nothing stirring here, guv. Think your lady has gone upstairs."

Ryan nodded.

"Thanks. I'll be there in about twenty minutes, with a bit of luck."

"No worries. We're manning the fort."

He rang off and stared ahead at the crawling traffic. He should have felt better after that phone call. Why, then, was his heart racing?

"Sod it," he murmured, and flicked on the siren.

***

Edwards watched a student jog along the footpath next to the river, long hair swishing back and forth in a ponytail. She was tall and slim—both things he admired—and she wore a baggy sweatshirt bearing the Durham University logo. She was less than five metres away from where he hid behind one of the hedgerows separating the footpath and the grassy verge leading to the row of cottages. He could have taken her, he thought, and she would never have seen it coming with her headphones in and music blasting in her ears.

Perhaps another time.

Keeping to the hedgerow, he walked parallel to the cottages until he reached the one at the very end. Its curtains were shut but he could see cracks of light peeking between the swathes of material, indicating that somebody was home.

It was possible that *both* lovebirds were at home, but he thought not. If Ryan was in residence, he was unlikely to have enlisted a surveillance team to watch over him. That would hardly fit his heroic image, now would it?

He crept up the grassy verge until he reached the back door and wasted no time trying the handle, but found it locked.

That would have been too easy.

Sneaking glances to either side, he reached into the inner pocket of his jacket and retrieved a set of bump keys—a present from one of his pals back at Frankland. He selected a key and pushed it into the lock, listening intently for the sound of each inner pin dropping into place. Edwards paused before reaching the last pin, then took another look around him.

All quiet.

He could hear the distant sound of a neighbour's television turned up loud, but otherwise there was nobody to see or to hear. He removed his shoe and tapped the heel firmly against the key several times before twisting it fully around.

Edwards replaced his shoe and retrieved his bump key, then slicked his hair back with two shaking hands. He was tremulous with excitement, breathing hard in anticipation of a kill he had dreamed of for two years.

The door opened with a gentle *click*.

Anna sat up in the bath with a start.

"Hello?"

She had definitely heard a noise downstairs that time.

The CD player continued to blare inanely, taunting her with its buoyant melodies while her heart had frozen inside her chest.

"Hello?" she repeated, a bit louder.

She began to struggle out of the bath, water slopping everywhere in her haste to reach the dressing gown which hung on the back of the door. Her mobile phone lay just out of reach, on the shelf above the sink. Another moment and she would have it in her grasp.

The door creaked open.

"Hello, sweetheart."

CHAPTER 6

Ryan surveyed the scene in front of him and thanked whichever god was listening for having made woman. His fiancée stood naked in front of him, wet from the bath and spitting with anger.

"Ryan! For heaven's sake, are you trying to give me a heart attack?"

"Hmm?"

"Oh, for the love of…hand me that towel."

Ryan took his time selecting one, grinning unashamedly.

"It's not funny!" She snatched the towel from his outstretched hand. "I heard a noise downstairs and I thought…I thought…"

Instantly contrite, Ryan folded her against him and ran a soothing hand along the length of her back.

"I'm sorry. I tried calling you on the way here."

"I must have put it on silent," she mumbled, picking it up and clearing the notifications.

"I didn't mean to scare you." He kissed the top of her wet head, inhaling the scent of whichever shampoo she used. "I called out when I came in but perhaps you didn't hear me over…whatever the hell you're listening to."

"Enya," she said, testily.

"Of course."

Anna leaned back to make a closer inspection of his face, eyes narrowing at the sight of his swollen nose and the greenish-purple bruise blooming around his left eye.

"What happened?"

Ryan blew out a laboured breath.

"I fell onto Phillip's fist."

Anna stuck her tongue in her cheek.

"Uh-huh. Do you want me to kiss it better?"

"I've heard your kisses have miraculous healing properties."

Edwards crept through each room in the cottage but he already knew the place was deserted. He sensed it even before he saw the timers plugged into the walls, controlling the lights to give the impression that it was still occupied.

Very clever.

He stalked from room to room, dark eyes tracking over the minutiae of Anna and Ryan's life.

Cute pictures. Knick-knacks.

He swept one thickly muscled arm across the dresser in the master bedroom, scattering perfume bottles and photo frames onto the floor. Amid the debris, he spotted a pair of engraved gold cufflinks and bent to retrieve them.

"MFR," he read, with a short laugh. "Finders keepers, Maxwell."

He rifled through drawers but found nothing of interest until he reached the wardrobe.

He let out a long, appreciative whistle and selected a red dress Anna had once worn to a Christmas party. He stared at it, wondering whether her blood would run to the same shade.

All in good time.

He looked around for a bag or a rucksack and found a battered leather holdall underneath the bed. He folded the dress inside it and moved on to Ryan's clothing. Almost reverently, his hand trailed across a row of smart suits, some of them hand-made, over silk shirts and cashmere jumpers hanging next to wash-worn cotton and faded jeans.

A man of contrast.

Edwards wriggled his fingers and selected a black suit of fine wool which he paired with a shirt of the same colour. He stripped down completely and then rooted around for a pair of Ryan's underpants, chuckling to himself. He took his time getting ready in the bathroom next door and thought about taking a shower.

Too risky.

He allowed himself time for a shave, looking out a disposable razor to deal with the unwanted hair on his face. The outdoorsy look was alright for some, he supposed, but he much preferred the smoothness of a clean-shaven face.

He turned his head this way and that, checking for flaws but finding none.

With bones like that, who needed to hide behind facial hair?

Edwards blew himself a kiss and sauntered back into the bedroom, imagining how many times Ryan must have made the same journey. He pulled on the man's clothes and was unsurprised to find that they were of a similar height and build. Since his time behind bars, he had certainly put on some muscle and his arms and thighs stretched the fabric in the most *flattering* way. Turning to admire himself in the antique cheval mirror, he was delighted to find that even Ryan's polished dress shoes were a perfect fit. He ran a hand across the smooth fabric at his chest and decided that the suit definitely looked better on him.

"Time to hit the town," he decided. "I deserve a night off."

While he searched the kitchen drawers for a box of matches, he came across a keyring and could hardly believe his luck when he saw the name of the building written on the back. There was no number, but it didn't matter—he had been to that particular address before and knew precisely how to get there. He dropped the keyring into the holdall he had filled with other clothes and trinkets, struck a match and then left without a backward glance.

He was long gone from Durham, heading northbound along the A1 towards the neighbouring city of Newcastle, by the time the two surveillance officers looked up to find Anna's cottage in flames. One of the downstairs windows exploded, shattering the quiet of the street, and smoke billowed out in thick black clouds. They dashed forward to help the people who ran out their front doors to see what the commotion was about. Children screamed, men and women stood aghast as they watched the cottage catch alight.

"Fire brigade!"

"Get the fire brigade!"

By the time the first engine arrived, it was an inferno.

Ryan tossed and turned in his bed at the safe house. After the first night spent at a poky, inner-city flat with an overpowering stench of mildew and a knackered boiler system, he'd risked ridicule from his peers and thrown some money at the problem. Hell, it was his money to spend, and he chose to spend it on a decent rental house with a king-sized bed and working radiators.

But the spacious mattress wasn't helping him now, he had to admit. For the hundredth time, he glanced across at the green light of his digital alarm clock.

Ten-thirty.

So much for catching up on some sleep.

Beside him, Anna had fallen into an exhausted slumber and he watched her body rise and fall with concern. She was badly shaken and neither of them had slept much during the past six days. She missed her friend, as they all did, and she missed her home and having her own things around her. He wanted to reassure her there was nothing to worry about and it would all be over soon but it would be a lie, and that wasn't his way.

Quietly, so as not to disturb her, he got up and moved to the window. Outside, the surveillance team had changed and it was now a black Corsa parked outside. He could see the faces of two constables reflected in the light of their mobile phones and he couldn't really blame them for losing focus after six full days keeping watch. On the other hand, it only took a momentary lapse in concentration for Edwards to strike.

He would have a word with them about it first thing tomorrow.

Ryan leaned his long body against the edge of the window and folded his arms across his chest, staring blindly through the glass. He had nothing other than gut instinct telling him that something would happen tonight. But the feeling was so powerful that his stomach churned, keeping him from sleep.

Some sixth sense had him reaching for his mobile, even before it started to ring. His eyes closed briefly as he listened to the disembodied voice of Phillips at the other end of the line and when they opened again they burned pure silver.

"I'm on my way," he said bleakly.

Ryan turned, silhouetted with the window at his back, to watch Anna's peaceful breathing. He wished he could leave her to rest and that he could allow her troubled mind the escape it so desperately needed. He wished he could trust the surveillance team parked outside. But he had just been informed that Edwards had managed to slip past another surveillance team in Durham.

He had known Edwards would try to target Anna. The temptation was too great. She matched the Hacker's preferred physical type and there was the added bonus of her association with him. What better form of revenge? For that reason, the surveillance team in Durham had been appointed with only one task: to pounce on Edwards as soon as he showed up.

Instead, a killer had waltzed into their home, walked among their things, breathed the air they breathed, and then destroyed everything.

He sighed and reached down to wake her up.

Eddie's Beach Club opened its doors six nights a week, from seven in the evening till four in the morning. It occupied an enormous warehouse space on the banks of the River Tyne and, in an era of trendy wine bars and swanky, upscale eateries, it provided just the right amount of seedy appeal to students, underage drinkers and middle-aged night owls alike. Dancers dressed in skimpy beachwear occupied small podiums dotted around the nightclub, touting cheap drinks and fruit-flavoured shots of alcohol with a gyration of hips and a thrust of torso. Cheesy holiday music pumped into the club from a state-of-the-art sound system set up in strategic corners around the main hall and every hour a troupe of semi-professionals performed a sequence of dances in time to *UB40's* greatest hits.

Monday night was 'Student Night' at Eddie's and both floors of the nightclub heaved with what looked to be the entire student population of the North East. Given the beach club theme, many of them had turned a blind eye to the chilly northern weather and had come dressed in grass skirts, bikinis and board shorts. Nights such as these always presented an opportunistic hunting ground for older men and women hoping to get lucky with someone younger and more energetic than themselves, but tonight an even bigger threat loomed.

Keir Edwards strolled past two burly, meat-headed bouncers at the door of the club. One of them held out a hand for him to shake, possibly mistaking him for the owner. Edwards laughed and wandered into the main hall, pausing to accept a free drink from one of the pretty hostesses. He watched her pupils dilate—a sure sign that she was attracted—and gave her one of his best smiles as he considered her clinically over the rim of the cheap plastic cup. Young, slim, but he suspected her hair was dyed.

No dice. He liked his ladies to be *au naturel*, if there was such a thing these days.

He replaced the cup and continued towards the main throng of people, the hostess already forgotten. Hundreds of men and women shuffled in time to an old reggae classic and one of them jostled against him, holding out a drunken hand in apology. Something in Edwards' eyes must have had a sobering effect, because the young man stumbled back through the crowd, falling over himself to get out of the way.

Edwards stood still, letting the bodies move around him like cattle. He breathed deeply, raising his face to the ceiling, holding his arms out as if to invite a higher power to challenge him. But there was no transcendent, guiding hand to stop him and nor was there the strong arm of the law.

He began to weave through the crowd, his eyes scanning the face of every woman he passed. Once or twice he paused to consider one of them more closely, but ultimately he rejected those he saw and headed upstairs to continue his search. *There were so many to choose from*, he thought, and almost every one of them vied for his attention. It was thirsty work and he headed for the bar. Funds were sufficient to allow himself a small flurry but, as it happened, he didn't need to wait very long before a woman with brassy blonde hair nudged him with her impressive chest and offered to buy him a drink.

As usual, he felt nothing remotely resembling arousal and it made him angry.

Pushing away from her with a growl, he sliced through the crowd. His head was hurting now, spinning with flashing images from the past, blurring with those from the present. They all merged into one face, the one he would never escape however many times he killed her and suddenly the reek of human odour was overwhelming. He stumbled against the gallery rail overlooking the lower dance floor and tugged at the collar of Ryan's silk shirt, skin pale against the black material.

A girl noticed he was breathing hard and rested a concerned hand on his shoulder.

He reared back as if she had burned him.

"Sorry, I thought you might be unwell," she gabbled, taken aback by the chiselled face and expensive clothes.

She glanced down at the bargain dress she wore. It was white and made of cheap polyester lace, but she'd chosen it because it looked like a beach dress. Her black hair fell in an elaborate braid over one shoulder and she had thought it made her look fashionable but now she felt gauche and self-conscious in comparison.

Edwards, on the other hand, couldn't have been happier. His headache disappeared, as if by magic. This girl was the one he had been looking for, he was sure of it. Maybe her eyes weren't quite as arresting; maybe her lips were a bit too thin. But she looked to be somewhere in her early twenties and overall it was an excellent match.

"That's all right, darling, I was just taking a breather. Hot in here, isn't it?"

He gave her a big, winning smile she couldn't help but return.

"Yes…" She searched her scrambled brain for something intelligent to say. "Do you…um, are you a student?"

He smiled again, enjoying himself enormously.

"I'm a murder detective."

Her eyes widened.

"Wow," she breathed. "I bet you've seen all kinds of grisly things."

"You could certainly say that."

The girl shifted her feet more comfortably in her high heels and raised her voice above the music.

"Are you helping to track down that serial killer? You know, the one who escaped?"

Edwards gave her a conspiratorial wink.

"I'm not supposed to talk about it, but…" He affected a look over his shoulder and then leaned in closer, watching her baby-blue eyes widen even more. "I'm sure you won't tell anyone."

She nodded and he rested his cheek against hers, to whisper something in her ear.

"Guess what, gorgeous? I'm the lead detective. You can call me Ryan."

Back in Durham, the man himself stood beside Anna and surveyed the hollowed-out carcass of what had once been their home. It had taken a team of firemen an hour to quell the blaze, which had spread across to Anna's immediate neighbour but, luckily, there had been no fatalities and it had spread no further. Water collected in puddles on the street, leakage from the spray of gallons of water expended in a bid to stop the fire. Now, all that remained was a lingering smell of burnt plastic, smoke and char which carried on the air in a noxious cocktail.

Phillips stood a short distance away chatting to the Fire Investigator and Tom Faulkner, who had thrown on crumpled chinos and a lopsided jumper to haul himself down to the scene. Anna's neighbours had been re-housed for the night at a budget hotel nearby, to allow them to assess the scene with as little cross-contamination as possible. The road had been closed to ordinary traffic while forensic specialists searched the vicinity for clues, transforming what had once been a quaint riverside area into something resembling a football stadium. Enormous, freestanding film lights had been erected in a perimeter around the row of cottages and the CSIs made painstaking progress across the ground while the weather remained dry.

"I can't believe it," Anna murmured.

She looked at the remains of her home and shuffled inside her plastic shoe coverings, thinking of the years she had spent saving for her own little place, then all the time she had spent filling it with memories and mementos. The copper pots she had lugged through customs from Turkey. The Moroccan side table she had bought at a thrift shop in London. Dozens of framed pictures, some of which were one-of-a-kind, not stored on a memory stick anywhere except in the recesses of her mind.

Ryan watched the emotions flit across her face and draped an arm around her shoulder, drawing her into the warmth of his body.

"It's only bricks and mortar," he murmured.

Anna's lip wobbled but she drew in a deep breath and nodded.

"There are more important things," she agreed. "But, oh, I loved what we had there. It was ours."

She shrugged and waved away the words.

"It sounds silly."

Ryan rubbed a gentle hand against her arm.

"Far from it. But it isn't the walls that make a home, it's the people inside them and we're still standing."

Anna looked across at his hard profile, cast like marble in the artificial light.

"Do you mean that?"

Ryan gave her a sideways glance.

"I was always bumping my head against those old beams," he quipped. "And there was that leaky tap in the bathroom. *Drip, drip, drip*, all night long."

Anna's lips trembled into a smile.

"Next time, we'll look for somewhere with high ceilings," she promised.

"And a hot tub," he added.

The girl was beginning to sway, her body succumbing to the high volume of alcohol she had ingested in a short space of time. The bottle of Laurent Perrier represented a major departure from her usual alcopop or tumbler of heavily-diluted vodka and coke, and she wasn't prepared for the impact.

"Another glass of bubbly, sweetheart?"

He was so handsome.

"You're so handsome," she blurted out.

Edwards smiled.

"You're not bad yourself, darling. I'll bet all the guys are after you."

She leaned back against the booth he had found for them. Her head was swimming and the music sounded distant.

"N-nope." She hiccupped and slapped a hand against her mouth. "Besides, they're all b-boys."

She leaned forward unsteadily and gave him what she hoped was a sophisticated smile.

"I m-much prefer older men."

"Oh?"

She put her elbow on the sticky table between them and tried to rest her chin on her hand, but coordination failed her.

"Mm hmm. My last boyfriend was a l-loser," she confided, taking a generous gulp from the glass he had recently re-filled.

Edwards reached across to play with the end of her braid, stroking the soft hair between his fingertips while he looked deeply into her eyes.

"I don't like to lose."

The girl blushed hotly under his scrutiny. On the opposite side of the booth, two students dressed in multi-coloured Hawaiian shirts and flower garlands were in the throes of passion and oblivious to their audience. The girl swallowed and looked back at the man sitting beside her, watching her patiently with big, chocolate-brown eyes.

They were to die for.

"D-do you like me?" she ventured.

In answer, he leaned forward to bestow the barest, gentlest of kisses. When he leaned back, she remained in the same position, eyes closed and mouth pouting for more.

It was like shooting fish in a barrel.

Edwards topped up her glass and clinked it against his own untouched drink.

"Bottoms up," he drawled.

A combination of shock and exhaustion made sleep inevitable. MacKenzie stayed awake for as long as she could but sometime during the early hours her body succumbed and she curled up on the uncomfortable narrow bed to rest, just for a minute. Cold night air filled the room, seeping through the cracks in the window and she shivered, arms wrapped around herself to try to preserve body heat as nightmares took over.

In her dreams, she could fit through the tiny bedroom window and her body was quick and able to jump from the roof to the ground beneath, where she sprinted across the open fields like a March hare towards freedom and the people who loved her.

She dreamed of Frank's face and cried in her sleep, tears drenching the mattress as she thought of him and wondered whether they would see each other again.

From the doorway, Edwards watched her.

He moved silently, his feet criss-crossing the floor in a pattern he had learned many years ago, when he had been a boy in this room. He remembered which floorboards moved and creaked the most, and he avoided them effortlessly until he stood directly above the bed where she lay.

Edwards watched her for a while and wondered, not for the first time, why he felt nothing when he looked at her. She was an attractive woman, he supposed, taking in the mane of red hair and the line of cheek and jaw, but nothing stirred within him. The bruises marring her face and neck brought no sense of shame or guilt.

He simply felt nothing.

There was no movement or sound to alert her to his presence, but MacKenzie's eyes opened suddenly to find him looming over her. A scream welled up in her throat and came out as a strangled gasp.

And she thought: *this is it.*

Now, he would end it.

Fierce anger followed on swift wings. He would overpower her—she knew that much. But she would not go without a fight. She would inflict as much damage as she could, before the end.

Just then, the clouds shifted outside and the moon's watery light shone through the tiny window onto the tall, menacing figure standing over her. She could see that he had changed his clothes, and they were covered in blood.

She knew then that the beast had already been sated.

CHAPTER 7

Tuesday 5ᵗʰ April

Overnight, the wind swept away the smoke clouds to reveal sunny blue skies across the city of Durham, though the air still held the chill of a northern spring. Morning fog curled over the river while fire investigators worked inside the charred embers of Anna's cottage, deconstructing layers of collapsed debris to see if the arsonist had left anything of himself behind. They followed smoke trails and the soggy remnants of what had once been furniture to try to determine the fire's point of origin while Anna and Ryan watched gravely as a piece of their lives was stripped away. After a night spent canvassing for eyewitnesses and camera footage of the surrounding area, the police teams were physically and mentally exhausted but they did not pack up until their task was complete.

Ryan and Phillips exchanged words with local Durham police, who reiterated their promise to contact them again with any further news, before deciding to return to the reassuring haven that was CID Headquarters, back in Northumberland. Despite its dismal architecture and mortuary-inspired interior design, there was no other refuge to be had.

Before they departed, Ryan led Anna to one side and prepared himself for an argument.

"I don't want you going back to the safe house," he began, in tones that would brook no opposition. "It's not…safe," he finished lamely.

"That's good, because I have no intention of going back," she said, calm as you like.

Ryan opened his mouth and then shut it again.

"Well, I'm glad that's decided."

"I value my independence, but I value my life a heck of a lot more. If it's a choice between spending the day with a roomful of trained police versus a day on my own at a supposedly 'safe' house with a killer on the loose, then it's a no-brainer as far as I'm concerned. I'll take the police guard, thanks."

His shoulders visibly relaxed.

"It would give me some peace of mind to know that you're with me," he said. "Or, at the very least, with people I trust. After what happened last night, we can't leave anything to chance. I'm going to be looking for alternative accommodation today."

The thought of moving for the second time in the space of a week held no appeal, but she understood that his reasoning was sound.

"I can help with that," she offered.

"We don't know who has been helping Edwards, or how far his tentacles reach, so I don't want to use any of the houses listed on the pre-approved list. It's supposed to be secure, but…"

"I understand." She stuffed her hands into the pockets of her windbreaker as a gust of wind whipped her hair around her face. "I'll find something we can move into straight away. Leave it to me."

Ryan forgot for a moment that he should be angry because their lives were in upheaval. He found himself captivated by the sight of a woman with dark, intelligent eyes and a mane of shining hair which gleamed in the morning light. Her friend was missing and her home was ruined, but she was already looking to the future and wanting to know how she could help.

"I love you, Doctor Taylor."

Anna shoved an impatient hand through her hair, wishing she had thought to tie it back, and flashed a smile.

"Same goes, chief inspector."

From his position a few feet away, Phillips watched them like a child with his nose pressed against the window of a sweet shop. He couldn't expect them not to love each other, nor to forego the simple pleasure of being together simply because his heart had been ripped from his body. It was not their fault that a madman had taken the woman who represented the other—better—half of himself.

But it hurt to watch them, so he turned away to look out across the river. Sunshine bathed the skyline in golden light, trailing across the stonework rising majestically from the banks of the river. Normally, the sight of it would have lifted his spirits, but not today. He felt around his pockets for an emergency cigarette and looked at it for long moments, tempted to lose himself in the old addiction he had fought for nearly two years. Nobody would blame him in the circumstances, and if ever a man deserved a tab, it was now.

Except, Denise wouldn't like it.

The cigarette fell to the blackened earth and he crushed it methodically with the toe of his boot.

Northumberland was an overcast grey when they arrived back at CID Headquarters, and the dreary light seemed to accentuate its ugly, rendered walls. Their subdued mood was improved slightly by the news that they had arrived in time to enjoy the police canteen's legendary Full English breakfast or, as they preferred to call it, the 'Full Geordie'. Food had a wonderful way of lifting the spirits and, with their stomachs suitably lined with an excess of caffeine and tomato ketchup, Phillips took Anna under his wing while Ryan accompanied Lowerson to the interview suite on the lower ground floor, ahead of his interview with the Hacker's former solicitor.

Elaine Hoffman-Smith was on a period of suspension from work pending criminal and disciplinary action.

She looked distinctly uneasy, crossing and then re-crossing her legs underneath the wooden table inside Interview Room A. Her mousy brown hair was dishevelled and she wore no make-up; a far cry from the glossy picture on her firm's website. It must be embarrassing for a solicitor to find herself on the wrong side of the law and requiring a solicitor herself, Ryan thought, as he watched her from the observation room next door. Then again, if you decided to make a deal with the devil, a little workplace awkwardness was to be expected if everything went tits up afterward.

"I'm sorry about Anna's cottage," Lowerson offered, coming to stand beside him.

Ryan continued to assess the solicitor with unmoving, icy-grey eyes.

"Nobody was hurt—that's the important thing."

"Yeah, but Edwards probably rifled through your things, sniffed your undies and all that." Lowerson gave a shudder. "It gives me the creeps."

"I don't care whether he had a full-blown orgy on my bed, Jack. He's shown himself and that's the mistake we've all been waiting for."

"Why?"

"He's not superhuman," Ryan said, watching the solicitor squirm on the other side of the glass. "We all leave a trace of ourselves behind, a trail that can be followed. That's how we'll find him—and MacKenzie, too."

Lowerson looked away, thinking of his mentor. Throughout his time as a murder detective, MacKenzie had taught him how to look at the worst of humanity and come away with his own still intact. It was a rare skill to bestow on another person.

"I owe so much to Denise," he said.

Ryan heard the catch in the younger man's voice and gave him a bolstering slap on the back, then nodded towards the woman chewing her fingernails.

"Get in there, Jack. I think we've kept her sweating long enough. Show me what you've learned and remember who you're doing it for."

Lowerson straightened the lapels of his slim-fitting suit before giving Ryan a calm nod.

"Rely on it, guv."

As the door clicked softly shut behind him, Ryan smiled. "Atta boy."

Despite the attack on Anna and Ryan's home—or perhaps because of it—the Incident Room buzzed with renewed energy. People spoke in urgent tones, exchanged notes and added details to the burgeoning stack of intelligence that was being filtered and assessed by two reader-receivers tasked with logging each and every piece of data as it came in. That, in turn, was checked against information already in their possession and eventually passed on to more senior officers for evaluation. In the case of Denise MacKenzie, every officer worth their badge was giving it their undivided attention.

There was no unused space anywhere to be found, so Phillips requisitioned an overstuffed chair from the broom cupboard and positioned it at the end of his own cluttered desk for Anna to use while she was with them.

"Thanks, Frank."

She settled herself down to try to work on the Viking raids.

"No bother, pet. There's a kettle full of limescale over there, probably a box of soft hobnobs—and you can get coffee that tastes like watered-down mud if you travel to the vending machine on the second floor."

Anna grinned. "I'm spoilt for choice."

"Never let it be said that Northumbria CID doesn't know how to push the boat out."

She chuckled, then laid a gentle hand on his arm. "How are you holding up?"

Phillips' desk chair wheezed as he sat down heavily and thought about how to answer. She wasn't a woman to accept empty platitudes and, besides, he didn't have any to give.

"Most days, I try not to think about what's happening to Denise. I just try to keep busy because I know that's the best way. Crying isn't going to bring her home," he said, gruffly. "It's just...everywhere I look, there's something to remind me. I keep thinking she's going to walk through the door."

He took a deep breath and said something he hadn't had the courage to say before.

"It feels like she's dead already."

Anna had lost her entire family and was no stranger to grief, but this was different.

"I can't imagine how you're feeling, Frank. It's a terrible purgatory you're in—but you're never alone. We're walking beside you, every step of the way, and we all miss her so much. In my heart, I believe she's still alive."

Phillips rubbed a calloused hand against hers and gave her fingers a quick squeeze.

"It means a lot to hear that," he managed. "In this business, there isn't a lot in the way of hope going spare."

Anna nodded and kept her hand on his arm.

"Come and stay with us," she said, impulsively. "We're moving into a new place tonight, just as soon as I've found one."

"Eh? No, lass. I wouldn't want to impose…"

But the thought of returning home to an empty house was terrifying.

"It makes sense," she argued. "That way, you and Ryan can work after hours, as well as getting some sleep when you can. If you play your cards right, I'll even throw a roast dinner in the oven."

Phillips was embarrassed to find sentimental tears pricking his eyes and he cleared his throat loudly.

"Aye, all right. Never could say 'no' to a Yorkshire pudding."

"That's settled, then."

Phillips turned to fire up his computer, which had been resting with a screensaver whizzing around its black screen.

Anna watched his stubby fingers fly across the keyboard with surprising dexterity, then a series of grainy, black-and-white video images of street scenes popped up. All thoughts of Viking raids and roast dinners forgotten, she leaned closer to peer over his shoulder.

"Is that Durham?"

"Aye." Phillips pursed his lips, took a swift look around the office, then motioned her closer. "I don't s'pose it'll hurt to let you come and take a look. Just don't tell the boss."

Anna made a sound like a raspberry and wheeled her chair around beside him.

The screen was split into a series of separate images, each representing the footage from a different CCTV camera within a half-mile radius of her cottage. Phillips selected the top left, which showed traffic moving down one of the main shopping streets in a southerly direction. With a quick click, the image zoomed to full size.

"This one's a good bet," Phillips said. "Whether Edwards drove into Durham from the north or the south, he would have to pass along this road at some point to get to your house."

Anna nodded, watching the flashing images.

"What timescale are you looking at?"

"The Fire Investigator reckons that the blaze started sometime around nine-thirty. If we say that he arrived up to an hour before then and left just before it started, that gives us a window of between eight-thirty and ten o'clock."

Anna shifted in her seat as the images start to roll.

They stayed like that for a while, scanning slow-motion traffic for a face they recognised until Phillips let out an irritated sigh.

"The footage is so dark, it's hard to make out any faces, and that takes us well past ten o'clock," he said, dejectedly.

"Let's go over it again," Anna suggested.

Another forty minutes passed while they re-watched the same footage. A few times, Phillips paused the screen but once again the reel came to an end.

"I've made a note here of a few vehicles where the driver looked tall and male," Phillips said. "I'll send it on to the techies, who can clean up these images a bit. It's also worth checking out the registration plates to make sure we haven't missed anything."

"Hmm. You're sure it was Edwards who started the fire?"

Phillips rubbed at the stubble on his chin reflectively.

"No, can't say that I'm sure. Could be whoever set him up with money and transport also went out on a limb for him again, last night. The question is, who? Lowerson's interviewing the Hacker's old solicitor right now but she's on bail at the moment, so she'd have to be bloody stupid to risk it."

"D'you think anybody else would have helped him?"

Phillips let out a long breath which hissed between his teeth.

"Thing is, the bastard's so bloody charming, he's always had a way of manipulating people. Keir Edwards could have wrapped anybody around his finger and we wouldn't know about it until it was too late."

"What about his communications while he was in prison? Have they checked his letters and phone calls?"

"Aye, lass. It's one of the first things they did. Durham CID went over his old cell with a microscope looking for contraband or anything that might give us a lead on how Edwards managed to break out. There are a bunch of letters from pen pals—mostly lonely people with a bit of a fascination about serial killers—and they've been eliminated already. As for phone calls…" Phillips shook his head. "They record incoming and outgoing phone calls from the prison telephones, but they can't keep track of mobiles which are smuggled in all the time. That's probably how he arranged everything."

Anna nodded thoughtfully. "I didn't realise things were so accessible, especially in a maximum-security prison."

"The staff do their best," Phillips said. "They're having to contain a bunch of hardened, violent criminals. If they manage to get through a week without riots or GBH, they're doing well. It'd be easy for me to blame them for what happened and, God knows, I want to. But the fact is, there's a handful of them against a bloody truckload of dangerous men. The odds don't stack up, especially when the prisons are overrun."

"I still can't believe a helicopter managed to land inside the yard."

"It's been done before," Phillips said. "It was quite popular in the eighties and the prisons started putting up wire barriers to prevent anything landing, but that sort of thing takes money. It comes down to brass tacks again, love. The prisons just don't have the cash to fit fancy wire netting when they're having enough of a job trying to retain staff and pay to house all of them."

Anna leaned back while she thought of the road network in Durham city centre.

"How about checking the footage across Prebends Bridge, as you drive across it from the direction of the cathedral? The side road leading to my cottage is almost directly after that."

Phillips was unconvinced. "I thought Prebends was a footbridge?"

Anna nodded. "It is, usually, but sometimes they use it for vehicle traffic if another bridge is closed, or if they need an alternative route. It's wide enough to allow cars to cross and I was just thinking it's been open for the past week during the Easter holidays."

Phillips made a low, rumbling sound in his throat.

"It wouldn't make much sense for Edwards to have driven into Durham via the motorway, then to have gone across one bridge and through the tourist centre, just to cross back over another bridge to get to your cottage. He'd want to get in and out again, as quickly as possible."

"You're assuming he drove into Durham via the A690," Anna argued. "What if he took a coastal route? Or, what if he came off the motorway earlier, then took the quieter ring-road and circled into Durham from the east? If he came in that way, he would have to drive through the tourist centre to get back to the right side of the city."

With a new light in his eyes, Phillips turned back to the footage and began to search.

"I don't know what visibility will be like," he mumbled to himself. "Aha! Here we go, this is the view overlooking Prebends Bridge. I only have it in one direction, but hopefully we'll catch something."

They put their heads together again and watched the cars move with comically slow speed across the screen.

"Wait," Anna murmured, and pushed her nose to the screen. "What's that?"

Phillips shook his head.

"I don't see—"

"Why would anybody be driving with a sunshade down, at night?"

Anna tapped her index finger against the shape of a small SUV with both sunshades lowered as it passed across the eighteenth-century, stone-arch bridge.

"I always said you were a goodun," Phillips declared happily, and turned to bestow a smacking kiss on her cheek.

"Do you think it's him?"

"I think you've got a bloody good nose for this business," he said. "Because I'm damned if I know why anybody would keep a sunshade down at night unless they didn't want the cameras to pick up their face."

Phillips zoomed into the image even further and could make out a pair of strong male hands on the steering wheel and some kind of dark jumper. He might not be able to see a face, but he could see a registration plate.

"Bingo."

———

An hour into the interview, DC Lowerson could feel a light sweat breaking out beneath his impeccably-pressed shirt and wondered why he had never noticed the lack of air conditioning before. Probably because no interview had ever seemed so vital, and the weight of expectation weighed heavily on his padded shoulders.

A fraud inspector from Durham Area Command was seated to his left, wearing the slightly dull expression of one who would rather be back on his own home turf, and had a habit of checking his watch with annoying frequency. Opposite him, a lanky man with a pinched expression and a gold pinkie ring was scribbling notes in a pale blue legal notepad, while his client fidgeted in her seat beside him.

Despite her obvious anxiety, Elaine Hoffman-Smith was a stubborn woman. After nearly an hour of determined questioning, she remained adamant in her refusal to discuss any details of her relationship with Keir Edwards.

"That's privileged," she said, mulishly, for the fiftieth time. "As I've told you, discussions between a legal professional and their client are subject to legal professional privilege."

Lowerson could feel himself beginning to lose patience. The woman's career as a legal professional was already in tatters and she was being prosecuted separately for aiding and abetting criminal harassment alongside a string of unrelated fraud charges.

Why didn't she make a clean breast of it and disclose what she knew?

"In the first place, professional privilege does not apply to communications which you knew constituted, or intended to constitute, a criminal offence," he said coldly and, behind the glass partition, Ryan smiled in approval. "In the second place, privilege only applies to communications pursuant to litigation or where you have been asked to give advice."

Lowerson tapped the top of a stack of papers.

"These e-mail exchanges with Edwards, dated as recently as two weeks ago, don't have any connection with ongoing litigation and they were not responding to a request for advice. Were they, Elaine?"

Her solicitor looked up from his notepad and fixed Lowerson with a patronising stare.

"Detective, as you are well aware, my client has not been found guilty of any criminal offence relating to her former client, Keir Edwards. In *this* country, we prefer to allow the courts to determine guilt and persons are presumed innocent until proven otherwise. It is quite clear from Ms Hoffman-Smith's statement that she formed a genuine, if mistaken, belief that certain e-mail communications were subject to legal privilege—"

Lowerson cut through the spiel.

"I'm not interested in her 'mistaken beliefs'. I want to know why she thought it was acceptable to hand-deliver threatening notes from a known serial killer to Detective Inspector MacKenzie's home address in the days leading up to her kidnap by the same man."

There was an uncomfortable silence around the table.

"My client reiterates that she genuinely believed those messages to contain pertinent information relating to an offence—"

"And she failed to pass it on to the police through the proper channels?" Lowerson scoffed. "Give me a break."

The woman's face fell into worried lines and she darted a glance towards her solicitor, who took his cue and tried again.

"At worst, my client acted *rashly*, detective." He spread his hands. "Hardly worth all of this fuss."

Lowerson felt something snap and he leaned forward, every inch the man in charge.

"*Fuss*?" He laughed shortly. "Is that what you call a nationwide manhunt? Or the kidnap of a police officer? The attack on a man and his family? *Fuss*?" He turned back to Elaine and pinned her with a hard stare. "What did he tell you, Elaine?"

His voice lowered almost to a whisper, inviting her confidence.

"Did he tell you he'd changed, Elaine? That *you* were the woman who changed him?"

He caught a flicker in her eyes and knew that he'd stumbled onto the right track.

"Maybe he told you he loved you," Lowerson said, with a trace of sympathy he didn't feel whatsoever. "Is that it, Elaine? When you visited him in prison, he told you all about his remorse...or, better yet, did he tell you he was a wronged man? That it was all a terrible mistake?"

The woman flushed a dark shade of red and her lips trembled.

"That's right," Lowerson murmured, holding eye contact. "Edwards told you he could never have harmed those women. That he was a doctor, a man who had devoted his life to saving others. One day, he vowed to clear his name, he just needed someone to believe in him, to help him—am I right?"

Her solicitor gave him another pitying look.

"Detective, do you have any relevant questions to ask or are you planning on telling these fairy tales for the remainder of the interview?"

But Lowerson didn't look away.

"It isn't a fairy tale—is it, Elaine? You fell in love with Keir Edwards."

She said nothing, but he caught the sheen of tears in her eyes.

"Listen to me, Elaine." He leaned forward to try to convey the importance of what he was about to say and took out a photograph of MacKenzie. "This is Denise. She's forty-three and a good person. She has people who love her and who desperately want her to come home. Please help us to bring her home."

Elaine looked resolutely at the wall but, after a few humming seconds, her eyes strayed to the photograph.

A woman not dissimilar to herself, she thought.

"You think he took her," she said, huskily. "What if she ran away with him?"

At first, Lowerson thought he had misheard. Was this woman so deluded? But, looking closely, he could see the tell-tale signs of jealousy.

Unbelievable.

He took a sip of water to give himself a few precious moments to consider his next words. Handled correctly, he might be able to use her emotions to their advantage.

"What makes you think that?"

Her solicitor interjected.

"I need a moment with my client—"

"Why do you think she would have run away with him, Elaine?" Lowerson overrode the interruption.

The woman ran shaking hands through her hair and, under the grey, energy-saving light bulbs, her face was haggard.

"Elaine—" The solicitor tried again to warn her, but she had reached tipping point.

"It was all in those love notes!" she burst out, and spittle flew from her mouth in a perfect arch to land on the desk between them. "To think I *believed* him. I *delivered* them to that *bitch*."

Her hands were shaking now and she clasped them together in her lap. Lowerson frowned at her choice of words, thinking back to the sinister notes MacKenzie had found stuffed inside her letterbox and beneath the doormat.

"What makes you think they were love notes, Elaine?"

She bristled. "I don't know for *sure*, but it's obvious that's what they must have been."

"You didn't read them?"

She shook her head. "They...I..."

Her solicitor watched their defence go flying out of the window, set his pen to one side, and resigned himself to professional embarrassment.

"Keir...Mr Edwards wrote the notes while I was visiting him in prison. I brought the stationery with me and I took the notes away when I left. I never read them because he told me they contained details of someone the police should investigate, something he'd heard inside prison about the man you were looking for in connection with the Graveyard Killer. He said that, if he helped the police, they might agree to look at his case again."

"And you believed that?"

"I..."

Tears began to fall.

"You never reported it."

"I trusted him," she said, as if that explained everything.

Lowerson ran his tongue along his lower lip.

"What else did he ask you to do for him, apart from delivering these notes?"

"I wouldn't give him another thing!" she shouted. "No more phones, no more money! *Nothing!*"

Then Elaine was completely lost, crying loud, snivelling tears that ran through her mascara and smeared black tracks across her puffy face.

———————

At precisely eleven o'clock, Lowerson concluded the interview and re-joined his chief inspector in the observation room next door. Ryan said nothing at first but held out a cup of lukewarm coffee and waited until the man had taken a long gulp to quench his thirst.

"I'll make it a pint, after all of this is over."

Lowerson nodded and rolled his shoulders.

"Was it alright? I could have pushed her harder at the end."

Ryan took a swig of his own coffee and remembered Jack Lowerson on his first, stumbling days in CID, compared with the self-assured detective standing before him today. Pride welled up inside him and he wondered fleetingly if he would feel a similar emotion one day as a father.

He took another hasty slug of coffee, coughed as it promptly went down the wrong way, and dragged himself away from that worrying line of thought.

"Your handling of the interview was spot on. If you'd pushed any harder, she would have clammed up. I might have appealed to her better nature," he mused, tipping his head towards the woman being ushered from the interview room next door by her irate solicitor. "But I would have been wrong. You were exactly right to prod her jealousy, because Edwards is her weakness. It sounds like she was completely taken in by him."

Lowerson was relieved.

"I appreciate that, sir. I only wish I'd been able to get more out of her."

Ryan gave him a keen look.

"We've got plenty," he said. "For starters, we know who wrote those threatening notes, where they were written, and how they got to MacKenzie's door. That was a confession of guilt on her part, and it'll do her court case no good."

"That's true," Lowerson acknowledged.

"Then there's the small matter of providing Edwards with contraband while he was inside." Ryan gestured with his coffee cup. "She brought him mobile phones and money, which helped him to escape and do God knows what else. What did you think about her claim that she wouldn't help him anymore, once she found out that he had 'run off' with an attractive redhead?"

Lowerson stuck a hand in his pocket, unconsciously mirroring Ryan.

"I think that it still wouldn't rule out the possibility that she provided Edwards with a vehicle for him to pick up at the Styford Roundabout. He might have told her it was a getaway car for himself, in which case she was happy to provide it. Once she found out he'd used it to transport another woman—she doesn't see it as a kidnapping, no matter what we say—it would have been too late."

Ryan crumpled his plastic cup and lobbed it into the bin in the corner of the room.

"I agree. There's still every possibility that Elaine Hoffman-Smith drove a car up to that roundabout. There's only one vehicle registered under her name and that's the one she's still using. But she could easily have picked up some old banger and left it there for him to find."

"If only we knew the model," Lowerson replied.

"Toyota Rav 4, late 2008 model in dark blue, registration number SX08 0DW," Phillips pronounced, as Ryan and Lowerson entered the Incident Room.

"How the hell did you find it?"

Phillips leaned back in his chair and winked at Anna, who had her nose stuck in an enormous history textbook.

"Solid police work," he said, casually.

Ryan wasn't fooled but he decided to overlook any minor contraventions of strict police procedure in favour of calling an urgent briefing.

"Alright everybody, stop what you're doing and listen up!"

Anna had to admire the speed at which conversation died.

"We've had a breakthrough. I want you to focus all attention on locating a Toyota Rav 4." He rattled off the registration and particulars. "Last seen crossing Prebends Bridge in Durham—"

Ryan paused mid-sentence as one of the traffic analysts raised his hand.

"Well?" he demanded.

"Sorry to interrupt, sir, but I think I've located the vehicle in question."

Ryan's eyebrows flew into his hairline.

"And?"

"A dark blue Toyota Rav 4 with that registration plate was reported on the system after being impounded, sir. It was found parked obstructively across the entrance to the Copthorne Hotel late last night."

Ryan's eyes flew to the map on the wall of the Incident Room and pinpointed the Copthorne, which stood on the bank of the River Tyne, on its bustling Quayside. There were countless bars, clubs and restaurants in that area, but it was also within easy reach of the city centre. He should know, since he used to live there.

"Did they locate the driver?"

The analyst shook his head.

"That's just it, sir. The registered owner is listed as a Mr Reginald Farley, but he died more than two years ago and there's no record of any new owner."

Ryan considered the information and felt his heart begin to pound. There was only one reason why Edwards would risk exposure by returning to the city, and that was to kill.

He turned quickly to Phillips, who was already running a check on the missing persons database.

A sickly feeling began to creep through his body, a foreboding of things to come.

"If we assume the driver of this Toyota was Keir Edwards, we know that he drove from Durham to Newcastle late last night. He dumped the Toyota across the entrance to a major hotel in what must have been a deliberate and calculated move to draw attention."

"He's peacocking again," Lowerson put in.

"Yes. What I want to know is where he went after dumping the car. Get me footage from every CCTV camera in the area. Frank?"

Phillips looked up from his computer screen and Ryan knew the answer before he had even asked the question.

"Tell me," he said shortly.

"Girl reported missing this morning," Phillips said softly. "Bethany Finnegan, goes by 'Beth'. Five feet seven inches tall, long black hair."

Ryan looked away and into Anna's dark eyes, which were full of understanding as she listened to the description of a woman who sounded remarkably like her.

They both turned with crestfallen faces to hear the next part of the missing persons report, which Phillips read out in a low, monotonous voice.

"Beth is due to have a birthday next week. She'll be sixteen."

CHAPTER 8

"I'll never forgive myself."

Those stark words hung in the air while Bethany Finnegan's mother continued to rock in the armchair of her sitting room, on the twelfth floor of a high-rise block of flats overlooking St James' Park football stadium.

Ryan and Phillips perched on a small sofa opposite, hands clasped between their knees. Long experience had taught them that there was no 'better' way of speaking to the parents of children who were missing. It didn't help to sit or to stand; to accept a cup of tea or to use a certain tone of voice.

It simply hurt to do it, and each time was as painful as the first.

"Ms Finnegan," Ryan began gently. "The most helpful thing you can do is tell us exactly what happened yesterday, in the hours leading up to when you reported Beth missing this morning."

Kelly Finnegan scrubbed the top of her hand beneath her nose, then dabbed at her eyes with the sleeve of her navy cardigan. She was still wearing yesterday's clothes and they could see the logo of a cleaning company on her crumpled polo shirt. Mid-length black hair was drawn away from her face in a neat ponytail, which had unravelled so that wisps of hair fell across her forehead. Her face was pale and devoid of make-up, except for the remnants of mascara which had long since been washed away by tears shed throughout the course of the morning.

She sniffed loudly and Ryan reached inside his jacket pocket to offer her a small packet of tissues, which she accepted with shaking hands.

"Beth was a good baby," she said, staring off into the distance. "I was seventeen when I had her."

She raised her chin, ready to fend off any judgmental comment that might follow, but Ryan and Phillips continued to listen with attentive, compassionate faces.

"Her father was just a lad from school. I knew it was stupid and he wouldn't stick around, but I didn't want to get rid of her. I wanted to keep her, right from the start."

Her voice wobbled and she raised one of the tissues to her eyes to stem a fresh flow of tears.

"Like I said, she was a good baby."

They nodded, letting her talk it out. Ryan had already skim-read the file and he knew that life had been hard for Kelly Finnegan. Long before she'd become a mother, she'd spent a childhood in care and had no family to speak of. Her juvenile history read like a textbook on shoplifting and petty crime but, since the birth of her baby, he'd seen nothing but a solid track record of full-time, low-paid work that must have been back-breaking. Almost sixteen years later, she'd worked her way up to the position of supervisor for a corporate cleaning company and she kept a tidy, polished home, even if it did belong to the state.

On the main wall above the sofa there was a blown-up, framed image of Kelly and her daughter and Ryan assumed it had been taken in the soft-focus light of a local photography studio. He was struck by how much older Beth looked than her sixteen years and, taken together, mother and daughter could easily have been mistaken for sisters.

"We're really close," Kelly sniffled, almost reading his thoughts. "We were always close, right from the start, and she told me everything. All about her friends at school, boyfriends, all the gossip—you know?"

She appealed to them and, dutifully, both men nodded.

"Did Beth tell you where she was going last night?"

Her mother drew in a shaky breath and looked down at the tissue twisted in her hands.

"She said that one of her friends, Emily Mallen, was having a party at her house. I know the family, so I said she could go. They live down in the rough end of Walker but"—Kelly lifted her chin once again—"you can't judge people on where they live. They're a nice family."

"We understand," Ryan murmured. "You felt confident about letting her go."

She nodded. "It's the Easter holidays, and to be honest she was starting to climb the walls," Kelly confided. "They're back to college on Monday but with a whole week to fill and me working most days, I worry about what they all get up to when they're bored."

"Aye, that's kids for you," Phillips put in, and she smiled.

"Beth is responsible." She wanted to make that clear from the start. "She has one hundred per cent attendance at school and good grades. She doesn't get into trouble."

She stopped and looked pointedly at both of them.

"I s'pose you know I was a bit of a tearaway?"

Diplomatically, they remained silent.

"Aye, well, things changed after Beth was born. Some people probably thought I was too strict but I swore Beth would have a better life than me. She wouldn't have to worry about where the next meal was coming from or whether I would be coming home at night. I want her to finish school and get her A-levels. I don't care what she wants to be, so long as she works hard and gets her schooling."

Phillips listened to her proud words and was transported back in time to thirty-five years ago, when his own mother had made a similar speech.

"Frank," she'd said. *"Your father doesn't work six days a week at the factory for you to throw your life away. Now, you just think about it, my lad."*

"I trusted her," Kelly was saying. "I trusted Beth to tell me the truth about where she was going last night. I had a late shift at work but she texted me all the way until about ten o'clock. She told me the party was great and that she was planning to stay over at Emily's house."

She fumbled around to find her mobile phone and hurriedly found the text exchanges.

"Look, it's right here." She offered the phone to Ryan, with a look of appeal. "Maybe her phone is still working and you can find her that way."

Ryan took a cursory glance down at the messages and saw that things were exactly as the woman had described.

"That's what we're doing right now," he assured her. "We're liaising with the telephone company and they'll come back to us, very soon."

Kelly clutched the phone, clearly hoping it would ring.

"And you'll tell me?"

"Of course. You'll be the first to know, Ms Finnegan. But to return to events last night," Ryan continued, steered her gently back to the facts. "You were telling us that Beth was supposed to be staying with her friend, Emily. She wasn't there, after all?"

The woman drew in a shuddering breath and looked across at the tall, good-looking man with the sad, serious grey eyes. She wondered what he thought of a woman like her; she wondered whether he heard the same old story every day, or whether he really cared.

He seemed genuine, but you could never tell.

"I couldn't get hold of her after ten o'clock and I started to worry," she said dully. "I went straight to Emily's house after work and knocked on the door—"

"What time was that?" Ryan interjected.

"About ten-thirty. I thought that I could always use an excuse if it turned out everything was fine. But when I got there, Emily's mum told me she thought the girls were all *here* for the night"—she gestured to the living room— "so we knew straight away something was up and we rang around all the girls' houses. Turns out they were planning to stay at their other friend's house—Hayley, she's called—after a night on the town."

"On the town?"

She rubbed at her eyes and felt her heart break.

"Fake ID," she said. "Apparently, they all have it, but I never knew. I never thought that Beth—"

"Kids," Phillips said again. "They're like moths to a flame. Tell 'em they can't do something, and that's exactly what they want to do."

"I thought that," she said. "And that's why I let her have the odd glass of wine, at home. I know they're only fifteen or sixteen," she said defensively, "but I felt better knowing that if they experimented with drink, they did it under my roof where I knew about it."

"A lot of parents feel the same," Ryan offered, as if he knew what he was talking about. "What happened after that?"

"I wasn't too worried," she said, voice muffled by the sodden tissue she held to her face. "I thought Beth had snuck out for the night to have a bit of fun and she would come home with a hangover the next day. I knew she was with a group of friends and I *know* my daughter, detective.

She's normally so sensible. I was angrier about the fact she'd lied to me."

Ryan swallowed and prepared to ask the next question.

"When did you become seriously concerned?"

"I had a message from Emily's mum, joking about how Emily was in the doghouse for telling lies. She asked me how Beth was doing, but I couldn't answer because she still hadn't come home and she wasn't answering her phone. I was beside myself. I rang every one of her friends and then rang the police."

"What did her friends say?"

Speaking to the girls who had been with Beth the previous evening was next on Ryan's list, but it never hurt to get a story from all angles.

"They said Beth told them she was going to get in a cab and go home early. They were drunk themselves, so they left her to it."

Kelly's lips shut so tightly they turned white at the edges.

"Ms Finnegan."

She turned dazed eyes towards him and he knew that she was starting to shut down, so he asked the most important question as far as they were concerned.

"Did her friends remember seeing her with a man? Any man in particular?"

Kelly lifted shaking fingers to her temple as the ramifications of his question began to unfold. A man had recently escaped from prison, a serial killer who liked young, dark-haired women.

Oh, God. My baby.

"A-a man?"

"Yes."

Snatched memories of conversations with her daughter's friends replayed in her mind and she tried to sort through her jumbled recollection.

"I…I think Emily said that she'd seen Beth talking to a man. She didn't say much, because—well, I'm her mother," she finished inadequately.

Phillips made a note on his pad and circled it twice.

"Is it…is it him? That man from the news?"

"We don't know for sure that your daughter is missing." Ryan forced the words through stiff lips and felt like a fraud. "We'll be searching for her, but let's not jump to any conclusions."

Silent tears rolled down her face and his jaw clenched hard.

"What happens now?"

Her eyes darted between them, wide and searching. Ryan retrieved two small white cards from his pocket and handed them to her.

"These are my contact details and those of the family liaison officer," he explained. "If you need to get in touch, if you remember *anything* important, call either one of us on these numbers. All right?"

She clutched the cards in a tight grasp and gave him another searching look. Something in his face must have reassured her because she seemed to relax against the back of her chair, finally giving in to the tiredness which laid claim to her body and mind.

"You'll find her. Won't you? Please," she added, "Beth is all I have."

Ryan did what he rarely did, and dropped to his haunches so that they were face-to-face. He rested his hand on top of hers, in a silent gesture of support.

"I'll find her," he promised, but he could promise nothing more.

They spent half an hour rifling through the contents of Beth's bedroom but found nothing except the usual flotsam and jetsam of a teenage girl. With nitrile-gloved hands, they checked in all the usual, secretive crevices that a mother might overlook and still found nothing to suggest that Beth Finnegan had been groomed by Keir Edwards before his escape from prison. There were no letters stashed away, no suspicious, expensive gifts and the girl hadn't owned a computer or a tablet. Faulkner's team of CSIs would likely go over the room again but their instincts told them that, if Beth was indeed missing, she had not been complicit.

They said their goodbyes and took the creaking lift down to the ground floor, inhaling the unfortunate scent of stale urine and marijuana as they went.

"Impressive woman," Phillips offered, as they stepped back out into the midday sunshine.

Ryan kept stride with him as they headed back to his car, parked nearby.

"Yes, she was."

Phillips caught the note in his voice.

"We'll find her, lad. Mark my words."

Ryan stopped and raised his face to the sky, trying to clear the emotion swirling inside his head. A magpie swooped to land on the rusty green climbing frame of a children's play area up ahead and he admired its colours, taking the time he needed to recover himself.

"The question isn't whether we'll find her, Frank. He wants us to find her so that we can admire his handiwork. The question is whether I'm going to be able to stand it when we do."

Phillips tugged at his lip and wondered what he could possibly say, but Ryan beat him to it.

"I guess we'll find out the answer to that soon enough."

With that, he stalked towards his car.

CHAPTER 9

As a light afternoon drizzle began to fall, MacKenzie watched Edwards perform a series of semi-acrobatic moves from the window of her cell. She had ceased calling it a bedroom and had reverted to a more accurate description of the dingy box room that had now been her prison for over a week. Outside, Edwards completed a set of fast press-ups on the grass, then lifted a heavy log up and down in place of gym weights, pushing his muscles to the limit. He did the same thing every day, come rain or shine, and always with the same intense look of pleasure on his face.

It was sickening.

Last night had been a watershed moment for both of them. The sight of Edwards covered in human blood and wearing the same look of pleasure he wore now had brought horror but also the understanding that an invisible seal had been broken. She was reminded of an old nature programme on great white sharks, where David Attenborough had spoken in dulcet tones about the shark's ability to smell blood up to a quarter of a mile away and to detect one single drop of blood among a million drops of water. The thought of it seemed too fantastic to be true, but watching Edwards on the lawn outside, she was not so sure. There was an animal inside him, she thought, one so close to the surface that it took very little to break free from the constraints of ordinary, decent behaviour. She had seen it in his eyes last night, more so than ever before.

MacKenzie recognised that she was starting to change too. She felt like one of those caged animals you see at the zoo, and probably looked similar with her bare feet and unkempt hair to match the wild look in her eyes. Her body was constantly poised for battle and when a fresh surge of adrenaline flushed through her, she paced the room like a tigress and would have sharpened her claws if she had any.

Instead, she focused on mending her ankle. Her ribs would have to make do with the splint she had fashioned from thin wood and strapped against her midriff using the dirty covering from her mattress. She couldn't wear it when he was around, which admittedly could be at any time of the day or night, because the longer he believed her to be incapacitated, the greater the advantage she might have in the end.

She rolled her ankle and winced. It was still tender following her escape attempt yesterday and she had probably put back its healing process. For much of the day, she had forced herself to lie on the bed, using the upturned bucket as a stool to keep the ankle elevated. Hopefully, by tomorrow it would be good enough to use again.

It would have to be.

There was no other choice, she thought, watching Edwards dispassionately. She must try to find a way out. The animal had been given another taste of blood and it wouldn't be long before he would go in search of his next kill.

Bethany Finnegan was immediately classified as a 'high risk' missing person and, after a short conversation with Chief Constable Morrison, it was decided that the investigation into her whereabouts would be managed by Ryan's existing task force because of the potential link to Operation Ireland. If Beth's body was found, it might provide a trail leading back to her killer and they needed all the help they could get. Still, it did not remove the dirty, unspoken truth that, to find one woman, the police were relying on another having lost her life.

Supposition and instinct played a disproportionately large role in their decision-making. However, the timing of her disappearance, Beth's physical attributes and the fact that her behaviour was so out of character were also strong factors in the escalation of her case. The Missing Persons Bureau acted as a national and international point of contact for all missing people and would usually be informed after seventy-two hours had passed, but Ryan took an executive decision and called them himself, the same day.

Meanwhile, Ryan's staff worked to trace the last movements of the Toyota Rav 4 and its driver. Although they were swamped and understaffed, Faulkner spared two of his CSIs to go over the vehicle, which had been recovered from the entrance of the Copthorne Hotel and impounded on the premises of one of CID's authorised contractors. Dave's Motors was a small but perfectly formed operation, nestled in a tin-pot garage between two car rental giants less than five minutes' walk from the railway station in Newcastle. The yard was crammed with cars of varying shapes and sizes and in a range of conditions, but the Toyota had been given pride of place in the covered garage area. Not a soul but Dave himself had touched it before the CSIs arrived and it took less than two hours for them to perform a thorough sweep of the vehicle.

While they waited for further reports to trickle in, Ryan and Phillips spent their afternoon in the west end of Newcastle holding lengthy discussions with a series of distraught teenage girls, some of whom had overcome their distress at losing one of their friends to stare in frank admiration at the chief inspector and with considerably less interest at his beefy sergeant. Such behaviour elicited embarrassed apologies from their parents and a degree of impatience from Ryan, who was in no mood to find humour in their raging hormones.

"I need a drink," he fumed, once the last interview was concluded and they had returned to the safety of his car.

Phillips rubbed at his chin, to hide a smile. "Bit nervy, are we?"

Ryan ran an agitated hand through his hair. "I'm sure I was never that bad," he said, emphatically. "I swear, when I was their age, I had more…"

"Decorum?" Phillips said sweetly. "Respect for your elders?"

"Yes!" Ryan said. "Their friend is missing—dead, for all they know—and that kid in there"—he jerked a thumb over his shoulder in the general direction of the house they had just left—"spent half the bloody interview asking me whether I liked Coldplay and if I would come over and show her some self-defence moves!"

"The cheek of it!" Phillips chuckled. "At least I was there to chaperone."

"I'm old enough to be her father!"

"Nah," Phillips said. "You're still the right side of forty, which makes you fair game."

Ryan sent him a fulminating glare and then leaned his head back against the headrest, allowing the irritation to seep out of his system before he spoke again.

"Their stories essentially match," he said, feeling calmer than before. "We've got four teenage girls, all of them underage drinkers wanting to go to the student night at Eddie's Beach Club, down on the Quayside."

"Aye." Phillips unrolled a stick of nicotine gum and began to chew rhythmically. "That lass—Hayley—seemed to be the leader of the pack."

"Pack?"

"They all move in packs," Phillips said, sagely.

Ryan held out a hand for the gum and shoved some in his mouth, irrespective of the fact he had never been a smoker, because Phillips was right. He was feeling downright nervy.

"Hayley's parents weren't around last night, which is probably why the girls decided to use her house as a base for their little deception. The parents were, incidentally, out getting drunk themselves."

Phillips made a sound like a *harrumph*.

"What day is it?"

"Tuesday," Ryan answered. "I must be getting old."

"You and me both, son."

"Anyway, the girls headed straight to Eddie's, not long after the place opened. They managed to talk their way into the club using some fake ID. Apparently, nobody remembers how they came by them," he added, with a roll of his eyes. "But that's the least of our worries. Beth's best friend, Emily, says she remembers seeing her speaking to a 'really fit bloke' at around ten-thirty, but she can't be sure of the time. About twenty or thirty minutes later, Beth told them she was going home early and would get in a taxi."

"That alone would ring alarm bells for me," Phillips said. "What schoolgirl can afford a taxi home on her own?"

Ryan nodded.

"They were all too far gone by that stage to care. They waved her off and Emily thought that maybe Beth was heading off with the aforementioned 'really fit bloke.'"

"She couldn't say for certain it was Edwards, when we showed her his picture," Phillips cautioned.

Ryan stared at the felt ceiling of his car.

"It was dark, she was drunk, and Edwards might have changed his appearance again," he said. "D'you know what the worst of it is, Frank? The kid says that she wasn't worried about her friend heading off with him because he was well dressed and *didn't look dodgy*."

Ryan propped his elbow against the window and leaned his head against his hand, only to be disturbed by the shrill ringtone of Phillips' mobile phone. They exchanged a look before he answered it, and everything changed.

"Phillips."

Ryan heard the distant voice of Lowerson at the other end of the line, but couldn't make out what was said.

"They're absolutely sure?"

Ryan turned to Phillips with an enquiring look, which was ignored.

"This goes no further until I say so. Meet us there in ten minutes." He risked a quick glance at Ryan, then away again. "No, lad. Leave it to me."

Phillips hung up and his mind worked quickly, thinking of how best to deliver the news he had just heard, while Ryan watched him with growing alarm.

"Spit it out, man."

"That was Lowerson," Phillips said finally, taking his time about returning the mobile phone to his inner breast pocket. "Apparently, Beth Finnegan's mobile phone provider has pinpointed her last known location, down to a radius of twenty feet."

Ryan began to smile, but Phillips hadn't finished.

"They say her phone is still switched on and transmitting, right now, from the same address."

"Well?" Ryan began to reach for the ignition key. "Tell me where we're headed."

Phillips gathered the courage to look him in the eye, before delivering the final blow.

"It's your old apartment building at Wharf Square, down on the Quayside."

CHAPTER 10

Ryan declined Phillips' offer to drive and manoeuvred through the streets of Newcastle as if in a trance. His eyes were open and his hands and feet went through the motions of operating the car, but he didn't respond to Phillips' quiet pleas to reconsider and his face wore the ashen, shocked expression of someone who was reliving a nightmare. As they turned onto the Quayside, Ryan no longer saw a spring afternoon in April, but the early hours of a summer morning in 2014. He visualised himself as he had been that morning, exhausted from another endless day searching for the Hacker and begging for sleep. Phillips had driven him home to Wharf Square sometime after midnight, telling him to get some kip and start afresh the next day. His sister was staying with him and would probably be asleep already. Ironically, his parents thought that some company would be good for him; somebody to take his mind off work and help him out for a couple of weeks.

But in all the hours he had laboured, Ryan hadn't thought to protect what lay under his own roof, and he would live with the guilt for the rest of his life.

"*Ryan!*"

Phillips' sharp voice cut through the reverie and Ryan slammed his foot on the brakes to prevent the car running through a red light. His hands clutched the steering wheel as he struggled to get his bearings, feeling light-headed.

"Son," Phillips' gravelly voice was filled with concern. "Pull over."

Ryan gave a small shake of his head and put the car in gear as the lights changed again.

"You don't have to do this," Phillips tried again. "I can tell Morrison it was too much of a conflict and you decided to step back. It's good sense, lad."

"I need to see her," Ryan said. "There's always a chance."

He tried to keep his mind focused on the road, until the courthouse appeared on their left. Its salmon-pink brickwork had aged badly in the years since it was built and it was fast becoming an eyesore compared with the glistening glass concert halls and classical townhouses surrounding it. The car slowed to a crawl as they passed and Ryan remembered the day he had given evidence at Edwards' trial, when he had recounted every hideous detail of his sister's murder so that twelve jurors could agree that her killer deserved to be locked away from the world. He saw their faces in his mind's eye, with their eyes downcast so that they wouldn't have to look at him while they listened to the unpalatable truth he had to tell. Ryan remembered the look of denial on their faces, the same disbelief he had seen earlier today in the innocent eyes of a teenage girl.

Not Doctor Edwards, they thought. *Not him.*

For it was only sinister-looking individuals who murdered people in the movies, not well-dressed, well-spoken men from the 'right' background who saved lives at the hospital. It wasn't possible, they thought, even when faced with overwhelming evidence to the contrary.

Thankfully, justice had prevailed and Ryan remembered how he had felt after it was all over, stumbling down the steps outside the courthouse and through the crowd of reporters, running until he found somewhere to expel the acid rolling inside his gut.

Behind him, a car honked its horn and he snapped back to the present, urging his car the remaining distance until they arrived outside a smart, glass-fronted apartment building overlooking the river. It looked innocuous, just another quietly expensive block on the redeveloped waterfront with bars and coffee shops surrounding it, appealing to the young professionals who lived there.

But then Ryan noticed DC Lowerson standing beside a team of CSIs, already suited and ready to enter the building, and he knew that history was repeating itself.

Ryan parked in his allocated space in the residents' car park at Wharf Square and switched off the engine. He looked up at the apartment building with bewildered eyes and wondered how it was that he felt so much a stranger here, when he had lived on the top floor apartment for nearly three years, not counting the last two he had spent with Anna at her cottage.

Then he remembered that was gone too.

"I can take care of things," Phillips said, urgently. "It doesn't take three murder detectives to go over a scene—"

"If that girl is lying dead in my apartment, I have to ask myself how she got there," Ryan said, in a voice so quiet that Phillips struggled to hear him.

"If—and only *if*—we find Beth Finnegan upstairs, it's because that maniac killed her. You had nothing to do with it," he replied.

Ryan continued to stare out of the window.

"Edwards must have found the spare set of keys," he said to himself. "I left them in the drawer at the cottage. He must have found them before he set the place on fire."

"So what if you did? It wasn't an invitation for him to drive up here and help himself."

"Don't you *get* it?" Ryan demanded. "He brought that girl here so that I would find her, so that I would see how *bloody* brilliant he is. Why did he do it? To prove that he's better, stronger."

"And killing some helpless young lass proves that, does it? The man's a raging nutter. There's no reason behind his actions."

"I disagree," Ryan said, blinking a couple of times to shake off the hazy feeling clouding his head. "What Edwards really wants is another shot at finishing what he started the last time we were inside that apartment," Ryan continued. "This time, he doesn't want to lose—he wants to win. He wants to see me beaten and preferably dead on the floor at his feet. But he doesn't want to make it easy. Oh no," he laughed shortly. "He wants to draw it out, to drag me down inch-by-inch until we're on a level."

Phillips swallowed a hard lump in his throat, wishing he could wipe away the hurt and the grief.

"If he's killed that girl, you don't have to be the one to see it," he tried one last time to persuade him, but Ryan shook his head.

"I made a promise to her mother."

With that, Ryan summoned the strength to step out of the car and face his demons.

Dressed head-to-toe in polypropylene suits, they moved in a silent procession through the gleaming entrance foyer, past the wall of post boxes and polished steel doors of the lifts, which Ryan bypassed in favour of taking the stairs. It was a desperate attempt to delay their arrival, to give himself more time to…he didn't know what. To prepare, he supposed.

But nothing could have prepared Ryan for what he saw beyond the bland white-painted front door leading to his penthouse apartment. His hand shook as he tried to insert a brass key into the lock and it took several attempts before the door swung open.

Ryan simply froze, staring at the scene which awaited him. His back was ramrod straight and his face was utterly expressionless as he forced himself to look at the remains of what had once been a girl. Behind him, Lowerson paled and looked away to allow his system time to adjust to the sight and smell of violent death. Faulkner turned 180 degrees and braced his hands against his knees, taking deep breaths in and out until the urge to vomit subsided.

"Dear God," Phillips whispered, throat working. He was not a religious man, but he sent up a silent prayer all the same.

"Faulkner," Ryan said, in a queer, flat tone. "Are you ready?"

The man was breathing hard and had to swallow his own bile, but he pulled himself together and nodded queasily.

"Phillips," Ryan turned to his sergeant and seemed to look straight through him. "Contact Pinter down at the mortuary and tell him to expect a delivery within the hour. Lowerson?" He turned the same vacant gaze onto the young man whose pallor now matched his white polypropylene suit. "Stay here."

"But, sir—"

"Stay here," Ryan repeated, with finality. "You don't need to see this."

With that, he took the first step inside.

Immediately, the stench of death assaulted him, penetrating his nostrils with its sickly-sweet odour. The line between past and present blurred again and he saw the living room as it had been two years ago, before he'd called in a team of decorators to re-paint and replace every scrap of furniture, even down to the kitchen units. He saw himself injured on the floor, crawling towards his sister who was seated in a chair in the centre of the room, bound and gagged.

He saw Edwards sitting beside her, brandishing a scalpel.

Ryan shook himself, breathing hard through his teeth as memories swarmed his mind.

Blood was everywhere. It coated the floor and spattered the walls, concentrated in the centre of the room. But the body of the decapitated girl lying in an overturned chair was not his sister. He would not have to make another phone call to his mother, for it was somebody else's daughter he had failed to save this time.

In a daze, Ryan scanned the room and found the girl's head sitting grotesquely on the countertop of his open-plan kitchen. Blood pooled in a wide circle around it and had dripped into a congealed puddle on the floor, leaving the flesh on her face an ashen grey.

His breathing was becoming erratic, shuddering in and out as he began to hyperventilate, but Ryan wasn't aware of it. He took another shaking step into the room and looked back at the girl's body.

Memories flooded in now, engulfing him in a maelstrom of colour and sound. His head began to pound and he felt dizzy, black spots dancing in front of his eyes. He groped around for something, anything to take his mind off the horror of that day, but it was too late.

All at once, the dead girl was his sister, Natalie. He saw her looking at him with big, grey eyes the same shade as his own, full of terror.

Ryan let out a cry and stumbled forward, arms outstretched to prevent the first cut from Edwards' scalpel, but before he could collapse to the floor, two pairs of strong arms shot out to break his fall.

"There, lad," Phillips soothed. "We've got you."

Anna had just booked a short-stay holiday rental in the pretty, rural village of Blanchland on the border of Northumberland and County Durham when she received the call from Phillips. She needed no further bidding and, after making a grab for her coat and bag, she took a taxi from CID Headquarters to the Royal Victoria Infirmary, arriving less than fifteen minutes later. She exited the cab at a run and made directly for the main entrance to Accident and Emergency, where she was directed along a long, narrow ward containing a number of small consultation cubicles separated by patterned curtains in a jarring shade of turquoise.

Even if she had not known the cubicle number, she could have found Ryan simply by following the sound of his raised voice.

"I don't need an MRI scan!"

"Ryan?" she called out, and a curtain was promptly swished back to reveal her fiancé standing next to a flustered Phillips and an equally flustered junior doctor.

She took a quick survey, noted that he was resting a hand on the wall for support, then exchanged a meaningful look with Phillips.

"I hope you're not being difficult," she said, sternly.

Ryan scowled at her. "I'm merely trying to explain that it's completely unnecessary for me to be here."

"Oh?" Anna affected an air of confusion. "Because I heard that you'd blacked out for five minutes and were totally unresponsive."

And she'd been worried sick, from the moment Phillips had told her.

Ryan pushed a restless hand through the black hair falling across his forehead, then let it fall away again.

"Probably because I haven't eaten today," he improvised. "We've been on the go for days and I forgot to eat, that's all."

They all knew it was a lie and it was so out of character that it surprised all of them, especially Ryan. He decided to try a different tack and turned his considerable charm towards the young female doctor hovering beside him, making a valiant attempt at doing her job.

"Doctor, I really appreciate your help but I feel I'm wasting your time. There must be many more serious cases—"

"Knock it off," Anna snapped, and Phillips held back a laugh. "You're wasting the doctor's time by trying to argue your way out of a check-up. Don't think you can charm your way out of it, because I'm not budging from this spot until I know you're all right."

Taking her cue, the doctor placed a none-too-gentle hand on Ryan's arm and nudged him towards the edge of the bed where he was deposited unceremoniously.

"Follow this light, please," she instructed him, and Ryan had no choice but to obey or run the risk of looking like a prize moron.

Anna was true to her word, standing guard at the entrance of the cubicle until the check-up was complete and he was pronounced fit and well. Having received a brief summary of the circumstances, the doctor gently suggested that Ryan might be suffering from post-traumatic stress and that he should consider talking therapies to help him get through it. After she left them to write up her report, Ryan pushed away from the bed and yanked the curtain back.

"The only talking therapy I need is one where I tell Keir Edwards to burn in *hell*," he gritted out, before striding down the corridor towards the exit.

Phillips turned to Anna as they followed behind him at a slower pace.

"Edwards killed a girl, the same way he killed Natalie Ryan. He staged the room to look similar, knowing that Ryan would look at it and remember what happened before. He walked in there and relived it all, then just blacked out."

He snapped his fingers, to signify a light switching off.

"I don't know what to do for the best," he confessed. "What happened today pushed him to the limit, took him right back to a place he's been trying for two years to escape. He needs time to recover."

"I thought he had," Anna murmured.

"Aye, I know. If Morrison hears about it, she'll take him straight off the case."

Anna watched Ryan's retreating back and gnawed at her inner lip.

"Then don't tell her," she said, taking an enormous leap of faith. "Don't tell her, Frank."

Phillips searched her face and nodded slowly. "If he doesn't see the investigation through, he'll always know that Edwards beat him. He has to carry on, for his own wellbeing."

"Exactly."

"That's good enough for me," Phillips decided.

Anna smiled and reached across to plant a kiss on his ruddy cheek. "Thanks. Give us a moment."

While Phillips lagged at a discreet distance behind, Anna found Ryan prowling around the waiting area of the A&E department, which was teeming with people considering it was a Tuesday afternoon.

She took a deep breath. "Are you alright?"

He opened his mouth to say something dismissive, but one look at her quelled the impulse. Instead, he simply pulled her into his body, wrapping his arms around her so that they were welded together.

"I feel better now."

"What can I do?" she asked.

"You're doing plenty," he said, then let out a shaky laugh. "I needed you with me, Anna, just to remind me that there's still some good in the world."

"It's all around you," she pointed out. "You have a good friend in Frank, and in Jack."

"Lowerson?"

"Who do you think helped Phillips get you to the car?"

Ryan said nothing but made a mental note to thank him later.

"I told him to stay out of there," he muttered. "I didn't want him to see what was inside."

"You can't protect him from the world. He chose to become a murder detective, just like you. It comes with the territory."

Ryan rubbed his cheek against the top of her head, then drew away to look at her. "I know you're right."

"Sorry, I missed that. Can you write it down on parchment, for posterity?"

He chuckled, and it was the most reassuring sound she had heard from him all day. It lit up his eyes and his face creased into a quicksilver smile that floored her, every time.

She rested her hand against his chest, feeling his heart beating strong and sure beneath his cotton shirt.

"Now," she said. "Stop loafing around and get back to work."

"Yes, ma'am."

CHAPTER 11

Ryan summoned a patrol car to deliver Anna safely back to CID Headquarters and then he and Phillips headed towards the service stairs leading to the basement mortuary at the Infirmary; the province of Doctor Jeffrey Pinter, Chief Pathologist.

Their heels clicked against the concrete steps as they descended to the lower level and entered a long corridor leading to a set of secure steel doors at the end. The temperature in the corridor was suffocating, thanks to a series of fans expelling hot air in an effort to keep the mortuary consistently cold. As they neared the double doors, Ryan entered a four-digit code into the security pad on the wall and, after a few seconds, they let out a long *buzz* and opened automatically. The two men stepped into the large, open-plan mortuary space and shivered as the temperature dropped immediately. Banks of metal drawers lined one wall and a state-of-the-art, electronically-controlled immersion tank had recently been installed next to the existing row of gurneys placed at intervals in the centre of the room. They detected the unique aroma of formalin and natural gases, which no amount of bleach could ever quite remove and they would forever associate with death. Noses wrinkled, they busied themselves with the task of shrugging into the visitors' coats hanging on a peg beside the door. Ryan scrawled their names in the log book and they took a moment to don plastic shoe coverings and hair nets to complete their ensemble.

"Very fetching," Phillips said.

With the formalities complete, they sought out the man in charge and found him in his office, annexed just off the main area. Jeffrey Pinter was tall, gangly and comfortably middle-aged. His hair was thinning around a gaunt, hollow-eyed face and when he stood up to reveal an over-large lab coat flapping around his legs, he bore an uncomfortable resemblance to the Grim Reaper.

Then his face broke into a welcoming smile and the likeness dissolved.

"Ryan, Phillips! Good to see you."

He gave them both a firm, fist-pumping handshake and didn't seem to notice when both men rubbed their hands against the back of their lab coats immediately afterward. In a place like this, you could never be too careful.

"Have you had an opportunity to look at the body?" Ryan asked, not bothering with any small talk.

Pinter's face fell back into solemn lines and he clutched the lapels of his coat.

"Only briefly," the pathologist replied. "It'll take quite a while to perform a thorough post-mortem, given her condition."

There was something horribly prosaic about describing the decapitation of a not-quite-sixteen-year-old girl as a 'condition' but Phillips tried not to let it bother him. He supposed that Pinter needed to remain objective, just as they did.

"Do you want to take a look at her?" Pinter continued, as if he were inviting them to test drive a new car. "I've had her body laid out in a private examination room, just next door."

"Tempting, Jeff, but we had a good look earlier," Phillips said, before Ryan had time to react. "Have you been able to confirm her identity—medically, I mean?"

"I've sent off the blood work for analysis, but once we cleaned her up a bit, we could see a clear physical match with the profile of the missing girl you sent through—Bethany Finnegan."

It was no more than he had expected, but Ryan felt grief wash over him all the same.

"I don't want her mother brought in until you've taken care of her." He would not budge on that. It was the least he could do for the woman who had lost the most loved and important thing in her life; the only thing that had given it meaning. "I would rather she didn't come in at all, but I don't think she'll listen to our advice, so just…do what you can for her."

Pinter nodded judiciously.

"I, ah, don't know whether it will bring much comfort to her mother, or to any of us, but I don't think the girl was alive when her killer removed the head. It's most likely she died from major cardiac arrest brought on by the severity of her other injuries. Every major artery has been severed, as far as I can see, and blood loss on that scale would have weakened her system to such a degree that her heart failed. There is some evidence of clotting around certain sites at her knees and elbows, so it would appear he performed those incisions ante-mortem."

There was a short silence in the room as both detectives thought of the pints of wasted blood seeping through the floor of Ryan's apartment. It didn't help that the loud *tick tock* of an industrial white clock on the wall seemed to mimic the sound of blood hitting the floor.

"How about the murder weapon?" Ryan asked.

"Oh, I'd say it was almost certainly a large, serrated knife. I'll be able to give you more specifics after the lab has examined the incision marks around the neck area, but it wasn't a single, clean blow with an axe or anything like that. I'm afraid that, if she had been conscious at the time, it would have been excruciating because it would have taken some time to saw through—"

"We get the picture." Ryan did not allow himself time to dwell on that prospect. "How about time of death? We were the first on the scene—we found her just before four o'clock."

Pinter let out a theatrical *whoosh* of breath, causing the two other men in the room to regard him with thinly-veiled irritation.

"Well, this is only a very rough estimate, but I'd say that the post-mortem interval was anywhere up to fifteen or sixteen hours, by the time you found her."

"Which would put her death at around midnight last night," Ryan murmured.

"Yes. Her body is already in quite an advanced stage of rigor and her core temperature was ambient when she was brought in to us. Bearing in mind that the body cools at a rate of around one and a half degrees Celsius per hour and factoring in variables like her size, the likely drop in core temperature as she suffered cardiac arrest…it's difficult, but I'd still say roughly fifteen hours."

"That would tie in with what we already know about her movements," Phillips observed, thinking of the statements they had taken from Beth's friends.

Pinter rocked back on his heels, waiting to deliver the most exciting piece of information he had discovered. It was another one of his little habits that they had come to expect over the course of their working relationship and it was fortunate that they could offset his many idiosyncrasies against the fact that he happened to be the most experienced and capable pathologist within a hundred miles.

"There's something else and you're not going to like it." He gestured them towards the computer screen on his desk and brought up a recent photograph taken of the girl's body. "Take a look at this."

And there, written in plain black ink on the palm of Bethany's left hand, was an eight-letter word:

INVICTUS

Phillips leaned in to inspect the photograph and then turned back to the other two men in the room with a look of consternation on his face.

"What does it mean? I feel like I've heard it before."

"It's Latin," Ryan explained. "It means, 'unvanquished.'"

Phillips raised a single bushy eyebrow.

"Latin lessons twice a week when I was at school," Ryan elaborated.

"Oh, aye. I forgot you went to one of those posh gaffs. I bet you never thought it would actually come in useful, though."

"For a dead language, it's a remarkably popular choice for a certain brand of egotistical serial killer," Ryan agreed.

Phillips had to smile. "Why can't these fruitcakes use plain English? They always have to have the last word and it always has to be melodramatic."

"It's completely in keeping with his character," Ryan said. "He wants to be noticed, admired and feared. Latin allows him to project a veneer of intelligence. *Unvanquished.* Is it a show of supremacy or defiance?"

Phillips considered the psychology of the man they hunted. "Everything about this girl's death was a show of supremacy.

It was all staged especially for you to find." He nodded at Ryan. "The way I see it, he's sending out a challenge."

A muscle ticked in Ryan's jaw as he looked at the image on the screen.

"In that case, I accept."

MacKenzie heard the soft tread of footsteps on the stairs and hurriedly stripped off her support splint, stuffing it underneath the bed before he entered the room. She sat meekly on the edge and waited for him to unlock the door.

"Dinnertime, Ruth," he sang out, holding out a cracked plate with a meagre portion of what looked and smelled like tinned anchovies.

She accepted the plate with demure thanks and immediately began to force it down her throat, hating the salty taste of fish that had been embalmed in brine for too long. She chewed methodically, reminding herself that her body required fuel and silently reciting Yeats to take her mind off its rancid flavour:

Though I am old with wandering
Through hollow lands and hilly lands,
I will find out where she has gone,
And kiss her lips and take her hands.

The poetry reminded her of Frank, and she wondered where he was and if he thought she was dead already.

Then Edwards clicked his fingers in front of her face, demanding her attention.

"Ruth? Pay attention when I'm talking to you. Rudeness is most unbecoming."

MacKenzie didn't bother to point out the obvious fact that he was hardly qualified to comment on manners or much else relating to the human condition.

"I beg your pardon."

Edwards seemed to accept her apology at face value or else decided to ignore the sarcasm leaking from every pore.

"That's better. If you'd been listening, you'd have heard me telling you that I'll be going out again tonight. Now, I know what you're thinking…" He wagged his finger at her and dropped down on one knee so that his face was less than five inches away from hers.

MacKenzie recoiled and the plate clattered to the floor.

"*Tsk tsk,*" he said. "Look at the mess you've made."

"S-sorry," she muttered. "I'll clean it up."

"Yes, you will," he said patiently. "When I return, I'd like to see this room spick and span, and you sitting right here where I left you. Is that understood?"

MacKenzie's lips trembled. "Yes."

He sighed dramatically and flicked a finger across her nose in the kind of casually intimate gesture that made her stomach turn.

"I can read you like a book," he said, with a malicious smile. "I know that, as soon as my back is turned, you'll be thinking of how you can scamper away across the hillside to find your knight in shining armour." He paused and cocked his head. "Incidentally, where is the good sergeant? Surely, if he really cared, he would have come to save you by now?"

MacKenzie told herself not to react. His words were calculated to hurt and to undermine her resolve. She must not react.

"I don't need anybody to save me," she surprised them both by saying, and Edwards bared his teeth in something resembling a smile.

"Feisty! I do like that about you," he confessed. "Practical, too, because—and let's not beat around the bush—it's no use hoping for a saviour. I could kill you very easily, whenever I choose."

He said it so nonchalantly that it took her breath away.

Suddenly, Edwards sighed again and rose to his feet, raising an arm to stretch out the muscles across his back. She watched him stroll to the window and look down at the patch of ground he had designated as an exercise yard.

"I hope you've been enjoying the view." He threw a wink over his shoulder.

MacKenzie looked away, feeling bilious. It could have been the anchovies, but she suspected it was the thought of Edwards attempting some form of mild flirtation with her, for some malevolent reason known only to himself.

"You know, Ruth, if you're feeling lonely at night, you can always just tap on the wall and I'll be happy to oblige," he continued, watching the changing expressions on her face. Fear came first, followed by some other emotion he didn't understand, nor had any particular inclination to try to decipher. Frankly, the effort of feigning ordinary human empathy was something he no longer felt obligated to do.

Then she surprised him again.

"Perhaps you're the one who's lonely," she said, turning her cat-like green eyes on him.

MacKenzie felt her stomach quiver as the silence stretched on and she worried she had gone too far. During the long hours spent on her own, she had considered the possibility of striking up a rudimentary connection with her captor, to test whether anything remained of Keir Edwards, the man. Now, she could see aggression warring with curiosity and she assumed aggression would be the natural victor, so she prepared herself for further injury as punishment for her audacity.

The silence thrummed for long seconds, then he relaxed his frame against the wall and crossed his arms across his chest in a manner that reminded her unnervingly of Ryan.

"And what makes you think I'm lonely, sweetheart?"

Her skin itched at the sound of another endearment from the lips of a killer, but she concentrated on saying the right things and providing him with a response that would be acceptable.

"It must be…difficult," she said, searching for the words to convey the right amount of implied sympathy for a man she considered no better than a wild animal. In fact, he was worse. At least animals killed to defend themselves or to survive. He took lives for the sheer joy of it.

"It must be difficult—" she tried again.

"To do what? To be me?" he offered, pointing a finger at his own chest.

He threw back his head and laughed, long and hard.

"Let me tell you something about myself," he said conversationally, once the laughter dried up. "I look just the same as other men—other *exceptional* men. I have arms and legs, two ears, ten fingers and toes."

He wriggled his fingers and moved towards her again. MacKenzie's heart hammered against the wall of her chest as he drew nearer and she felt his rage growing stronger with every step.

"This body"—he gestured to himself—"is nothing more than a superficial shell. I like to hone it, to keep it running smoothly, but it's just the suit that I wear every day. Underneath it, there isn't a single thing that connects me to the rest of you. Nothing remotely resembling 'emotion'; at least, not in the way you mean. I look at you, sitting there shaking with fear, and I feel nothing. Do you understand? Not an inordinate sense of achievement, or even the kind of pleasure I was hoping for. I feel *nothing*, Denise. Not love, not hate, not pity, not pain. The only thing I feel is an urge to find out what your insides look like and how long it would take your pretty green eyes to die. The urge is getting stronger every day, so much so that I barely see you as a person. You're just a mass of flesh and bone."

He came to stand in front of her and dropped back down so that she could feel his warm breath against her face.

"So," he said, very softly. "Why don't you ask me again if you think I feel lonely?"

MacKenzie could not move from her position on the bed for a long time after he left. Partly, she was fearful that he would return and remember the reason he had visited in the first place: to incapacitate her somehow and remove her ability to walk or run. The other reason was the degrading knowledge that, at some point during his introspective monologue, she had wet herself.

Tears leaked from the corners of her eyes, but she dashed them away because she had achieved a small success, whether he realised it or not.

Edwards had not attacked her and he had also called her 'Denise' for the first time, unconsciously reinstating an aspect of her identity that he had tried so hard to remove.

She wondered if he was even aware of it.

Outside, night had fallen and a light rain pattered against the roof above her head, filtering through the open window so that the room was not only cold but damp. She raised herself from the bed, cleaned herself up as best she could, and when she heard him leave—whistling to himself as he rounded the side of the house—she trained herself to fight again.

CHAPTER 12

Ryan found Jack Lowerson hovering outside the back entrance to CID Headquarters, sucking deeply from an apple-flavoured e-cigarette. He stood beneath the smokers' canopy listening to the sound of rain hitting the plastic roof, while he looked out at the unappealing vista that was the staff car park. Ryan tucked his hands into the pockets of his jacket and walked across to stand beside him.

"I wanted to thank you, Jack."

Lowerson took a long drag of his cigarette and it bubbled like a shisha, emitting a faint aroma of Golden Delicious. Ryan smiled to himself, thinking that the man had certainly learned a thing or two about the value of silence in drawing people out.

"I wasn't myself earlier today and I know you and Phillips were there for me when I passed out. I appreciate it, and I want you to know the reason I didn't want you working the scene had nothing to do with your capabilities."

Lowerson maintained his silence and Ryan supposed he should congratulate himself on having taught him so well, but he hadn't anticipated that his own methods would be used against him one day.

"Alright, you're angry. You've a right to be," Ryan bit out, and watched surprise flit across the other man's face. "I was wrong to shut you out but I won't apologise for wanting to protect you from the worst damage one human being is capable of inflicting on another."

Lowerson took a final drag of his e-cig and then tucked it into the breast pocket of his suit jacket, which still carried a lingering scent of death from earlier in the day. He imagined he would continue to smell it, long after the suit was dry-cleaned.

"I understand why you wanted to keep me out. But you need to understand that I chose this job for the same reasons as you. I can't get any better at it if you wrap me up in cotton wool."

Ryan inclined his head.

"Just one last thing," Lowerson said. "Next time, if you're going to fall like a redwood, give us some bloody warning. I nearly put my back out making a dive for you."

"Noted."

Phillips ended the call and let his mobile fall onto the desktop in disgust, replaying the conversation he'd just had. Durham CID re-interviewed the helicopter pilot,

Andy Hayworth, and his wife earlier in the day but hours had passed without any update. Feeling impatient, he had taken matters into his own hands and put a call through to the detective in charge. Detective Inspector Bill Rodgers was close to retirement, with nearly forty years on the force. He knew how to run an investigation and didn't appreciate being taught how to suck eggs, even by someone he respected as much as Frank Phillips. Was it his fault, if the pilot's wife couldn't remember any more details about her attack? The woman was traumatised, for heaven's sake.

In truth, Rodgers knew the real reason Helen Hayworth refused to talk. It had nothing to do with trauma and everything to do with fearing that her life, or the lives of her husband and son, might be in danger if she blabbed. He'd seen it dozens of times before and said as much to Phillips.

"You and I both know what's happened here, Frank, but we've tried pushing the wife and she's not budging an inch. As far as she's concerned, it was a muscular man of average height and mid-brown hair who turned up on her doorstep, pretending to be selling steam-cleaning services. He talked his way inside under the pretence of needing to use the loo, following which he got hold of her little boy and told her to pack a bag. He threatened to hurt the boy if she didn't do as he said, so she hopped to it and got inside his blue van. She thinks it had a white steam-cleaning logo on the side. He took her and the boy for a long drive during which time they were kept in the back, out of sight. He kept driving and didn't stop except to let her hunker down beside the road and relieve herself a couple of times, then dropped them off the morning after it was all over beside the junction at Scotch Corner, and the rest you already know. That's all she will say."

"She must be able to tell us something about his accent, his name, his clothing," Phillips gabbled. "Have you shown her some photos of the usual suspects?"

At the other end of the line, Rodgers rolled his eyes.

"Aye, Frank, we have. She claims that none of them are the man who abducted her and the littlun."

"Give me strength," Phillips had muttered. "What about the pilot?"

"As for the pilot, he only saw Edwards in person and you know all there is to know about that," Rodgers pointed out. "If the wife has told her husband anything about her mystery abductor, he's keeping schtum as well."

"Bill, please. This could mean the difference between finding Denise and losing her."

At the other end of the line, Rodgers pinched the bridge of his nose. "I know it, Frank. But if we push that family any harder, anything they tell us won't stand up in court. We'll have some snotty little defence barrister quoting chapter and verse from the Police and Criminal Evidence Act about intimidation of witnesses and that'll be all it takes to throw everything to the wind. Besides," Bill said, "there's a very real danger of harm. It's a small community, up here in the North East. If Helen Hayworth points the finger at who's responsible, whoever was the money and brains behind it all will find out pretty quickly, and the repercussions for that family could be devastating.

"Truth be told, Frank, I might do the same thing myself, if I were her."

With Rodgers' words ringing in his ears, Phillips had hung up the phone and resigned himself to a process of elimination. He turned his mind to the question of who was responsible for helping the Hacker break free. Whose reputation generated enough fear to prevent the Hayworths from giving a clear description of their attacker? It could only be somebody well known in the area as being a dangerous entity. According to the National Criminal Intelligence Service, there were about forty organised criminals operating in the North East, but he would have said the number was closer to fifty or sixty, most of whom belonged to two or three ruling gangland families operating in Newcastle, Gateshead, Sunderland and Durham. They mostly ran protection rackets and facilitated drug trafficking through the control of pubs and clubs throughout the region, but one or two of the more sophisticated outfits were branching out from the kind of traditional, enterprising crimes that Phillips remembered in the old days, towards financial crimes like counterfeiting and fraud.

He picked up his biro and spent some time drawing a detailed network of what he already knew to be in operation, in Newcastle and Durham particularly. Keir Edwards had been careful in his communications with his solicitor, Phillips thought, and had only slipped up once by sending an e-mail setting out MacKenzie's address and when the notes should be delivered to have maximum impact. There were no telephone recordings to the solicitor's firm and no other written communications to give so much as a hint of who was funding Edwards' escape.

If Edwards had money squirreled away somewhere waiting for him, he might have made a promise of payment to his mysterious benefactor in exchange for services rendered. But with three significant criminal families operating in the region, all of them with the means to intimidate witnesses and procure a helicopter, it was going to take more than a prayer to flush out the rat.

He was going to have to make some house calls.

Phillips was nowhere to be seen when Ryan called his final briefing of the day at seven-thirty. His core staff were all present and even Anna had been smuggled into a seat in the corner of the Incident Room under heavy camouflage, in deference to the fact that Chief Constable Morrison was liable to pay them an unexpected visit at any time and would not be impressed if she found a civilian among their number.

"Jack? Have you seen Phillips?"

Lowerson shook his head. "Not for the last half-hour. I think he mentioned something about getting a bit of fresh air."

Ryan thought it was unusual that his sergeant hadn't informed him of his movements, considering the mountain they still had to climb, but he supposed he shouldn't begrudge the man a break. He was going through hell and was handling it in a more dignified fashion than most.

"Fair enough," he said, to the room at large. "Let's crack on."

Ryan rolled up his shirtsleeves and folded his arms while he collected his thoughts.

"Alright, here's the round-up. As of this morning, we have Edwards' second vehicle impounded and the CSIs have gone over it already. We're waiting for the lab results to confirm a DNA match, but it's looking very likely that the Toyota Rav 4 was left at the Styford Roundabout—we don't know when or by whom—and picked up by Edwards in the early hours of last Tuesday after he dumped MacKenzie's Fiesta. They drove to an unknown destination, where Edwards has been holing up until finally rearing his ugly head again last night."

Ryan paused to take a swig of coffee, buying himself enough time to prepare for the next part of his round-up.

"As you can see, there's a new photograph on the wall," he said quietly, and watched their heads turn to look at the colour photograph of Bethany Finnegan, provided by her mother when she thought her daughter was merely missing.

"This is Beth, and she was a week away from her sixteenth birthday when she died sometime around midnight last night."

He let his gaze travel around the room, burning them.

"Beth was decapitated and her body mutilated, but not in any kind of frenzy attack. Her injuries were inflicted with the steady, knowledgeable hand of someone with advanced anatomical knowledge, using something like a common bread knife."

There were quiet gasps around the room as some of his staff flipped the pages in their printed packs and stumbled across images taken from the crime scene earlier that day.

"The pathologist is performing a post-mortem this evening and will get a report to us as soon as possible but it will likely be days before the CSIs have completed a full sweep of the crime scene."

It would take them that long to wade through the blood.

"Incidentally, Edwards chose to use my old apartment as his first kill site after unleashing himself back into society."

There were some who already knew about it, but for those who hadn't yet heard it on the police grapevine, their faces registered shock.

There was also a healthy degree of curiosity, as Ryan had anticipated.

"Needless to say, his choice of location was a meaningful one." He kept his voice firm and was relieved that it didn't waver. "I don't need to go over old ground, but this is the second time Keir Edwards has chosen my digs for his dirty work. After we've kicked the prison door shut on him for the second time, remind me to forward him the cleaning bill," he added, dryly.

The unexpected touch of dark humour came as a welcome relief to his staff, who were glad to find something to laugh about, if only briefly. As for Ryan, he was tired of feeling like a victim and didn't need or want their pity.

"Our working theory is that Edwards drove into Durham to attack my fiancée at her cottage. Since we have temporarily relocated to a safe house, he found the place empty and had to settle for ransacking it instead. There were no signs of forced entry at my apartment at Wharf Square, so we have to assume he found the spare set of keys whilst he was rummaging through drawers at the cottage and was able to let himself in later on. After he finished looting, Edwards started a fire at the cottage at ten o'clock or thereabouts and took a drive into Newcastle. When he arrived, he parked obstructively across the entrance to the Copthorne Hotel on the Quayside and we have CCTV footage of him exiting the Toyota at 22:24. He then proceeded to walk the short distance to Eddie's Beach Club, where he met Beth Finnegan and lured her away from her friends by eleven o'clock. We have footage of them walking along the Quayside heading east, arriving at the front entrance to my apartment building at Wharf Square at quarter past eleven."

Ryan felt his stomach muscles tense and he reached across to pick up a paperclip, to give himself something to cling to while he covered the necessary ground.

"There are several points to note. Firstly, Edwards is unconcerned by the fact that we now have an updated image of his physical appearance, which clearly shows he is feeling brazen, not to mention opportunistic."

Ryan pointed to another photograph tacked to the wall, which showed Edwards clean-shaven, wearing what looked to be dark clothing. He felt the breath catch in his throat as another thought struck him, and he wandered across to the murder board to take a closer look at the man's clothes.

Oh, please, no.

He turned back to his audience with a face like thunder.

"A detailed description of the crime scene, including Beth's injuries, has been included in your packs. For now, let's just say he acted with extreme violence, as with all his previous victims. Furthermore, her body was deliberately staged to resemble the death of Natalie Finley-Ryan—my sister."

Nobody spoke, and the air seemed suddenly so still that he couldn't breathe.

"Ah, can I ask a question?"

His grateful eyes sought out the source and when he found it, he smiled into Anna's eyes, drawing strength from their strength.

"Go ahead, we'll say you're an honorary member of the team for the duration."

"In that case, can you tell me how Edwards managed to get back out of the city? Wouldn't he have been covered in blood?"

Ryan felt the constriction in his chest begin to abate.

"We don't actually know for sure that he has left the city," Ryan pointed out, and his voice carried a warning.

"Likewise, he might have stolen a change of clothes whilst he was at our house in Durham. However, it's likely that he either found somewhere nearby to hide out, or he managed to procure another vehicle."

"We're checking for vehicles reported stolen in the area," Lowerson put in. "I'll let you know when we have something."

Ryan nodded. "Start with the residents," he said. "The CCTV beside the entrance to Wharf Square captured Edwards coming inside with Beth, but there's no record of him leaving again. If he was covered in blood and wanted to keep a low profile, it would make sense for him not to wander too far. I noticed today that there was a camera overlooking the residents' car park at the rear of the building, so I want to know why I don't have that footage on my desk."

Some of the support staff exchanged worried looks.

"It's been vandalized," Lowerson explained. "So we don't have any footage of the car park for the relevant period."

"Of course it has," Ryan said darkly. "Find out when that camera was broken, because I'll take odds that it went down sometime around midnight last night. I want to see any remaining footage prior to the breakage—see which cars were parked outside and check them all to see if they're still with their respective owners."

Lowerson wrote a hasty note.

"On it."

"Like many killers with narcissistic tendencies, Edwards has chosen to leave a calling card with his latest victim.

The word 'INVICTUS' was written in black marker pen on Beth's left palm. Translated from the Latin, it means 'unvanquished'. We can only assume that Edwards intended it to be a defiant gesture, once again part of the staging of his victim."

There were murmurs of disgust around the room.

"Trace his mode of transport and we'll be able to trace him," Ryan reminded them, and waited a beat before clapping his hands together. "Let's go."

As they were galvanised into action, Ryan checked the time on the clock on the wall against his watch. Both read eight-fifteen and there was still no sign of Phillips.

CHAPTER 13

The streets were dark and soaked with rain when Phillips returned to Buddle's Boxing Gym. Unlike Ryan, he didn't have any trouble finding it among the rows of identical streets on the borders of Benwell and Elswick, in Newcastle's West End. It had been many years since he'd played on these streets as a boy, and perhaps too many since he had been back to pay them a visit, but there was still a sense of homecoming. There was nowhere else in the world he could be himself, or at least the version of himself he used to be when he'd been a scrapper, a stocky kid with no direction and plenty of time on his hands.

Nowadays, he had no family to bring him back to Benwell. His father died years ago and by the time his mother passed away, he'd already moved out of the area with his late wife, Laura. He'd been on the way to passing his detective's exam and they'd moved so that he could be closer to work. They never had any children but life became busier all the same, and there had been less time to drive across town for an early morning sparring session at Buddle's. When Laura had become ill with the cancer that eventually killed her, he hadn't wanted to be away from her any longer than necessary and he had no time for boxing matches and pints down at the Pig and Whistle.

But his body remembered the old feeling of being in the ring, even if he was a bit out of condition. It had felt good to come back yesterday, not only to rid himself of some of the grief and frustration of his present nightmare but simply to feel *alive*.

This time, though, he hadn't come to fight.

Phillips walked through the main entrance into the gymnasium and shook hands with some of the boxers stretching on mats or training with pads. He didn't stop to chat but continued past the ring where he and Ryan had recently gone a round, to a small office area bearing a plaque that said 'MANAG-R'. The letter 'E' had been missing for as long as he could remember and he'd been coming on and off since it first opened in the early seventies.

The door had been left open to reveal a group of four men sitting in front of a high-end flat screen television, watching the recording of a recent fight. He glanced at the screen and recognised both fighters as local champions.

"Knock-knock," he said, stepping into the room.

"Y'alreet, Frank," one of them replied, without turning around. Phillips waited patiently until the fight was over and the recording came to an end. These men took their boxing seriously, and the presence of a detective sergeant from Northumbria CID wasn't enough to divert their attention.

Only when it had finished did they turn and greet him properly, faces creasing into smiles.

"Frank! Y'old bugger, where've you been?"

They exchanged hard, back-slapping hugs and handshakes, some token words of sympathy about Denise and then three of the men left following a swift jerk of the manager's head, closing the door behind them.

"Frank. I was sorry to hear about Denise."

Harry Donnelly Jr was a man of diminutive height but enormous local stature. He owned several investment properties in upmarket areas of Newcastle but preferred to live in the same house he had grown up in, not far from the gym. He was in his mid-fifties, like Frank, but instead of a dark grey suit, he wore a pair of straight-legged jeans and a tight white t-shirt which stretched over a muscular beer belly. His arms were hairy and tanned almost to leather from his twice-yearly holidays to a timeshare in Marbella and there were deep crow's feet around his astute blue eyes. His father, Harry Sr, had founded Buddle's sometime in the early seventies after the closure of Manors Hall, a legendary boxing venue which had been open since the 1920s right up until its demolition to make way for a new Metro station in the late 1960s. In his heyday, Harry Snr had trained some of the local boxing greats and had even sparred with Cassius Clay.

Harry Snr had gone on to found the new Buddle's Boxing Gym in a notoriously downtrodden area of town, to give the men who had lost their livelihoods a healthy escape. It had since become an institution in its own right under his son's careful management and its doors stood open to men—and women—from all walks of life. But its main clientele was, and always would be, men and boys from the local community.

And, as Phillips was aware, some of them made their living operating on the wrong side of the law. What he intended to find out was whether any of them were involved in Edwards' escape.

"Evening, Harry." He accepted one of the worn oak chairs sitting at right-angles to a basic desk pushed against one wall. Behind it, there was a long window looking out into the gym area, so that Harry could keep an eye on things.

"Heard you went a round or two, yesterday," Harry said, reaching for a cup of herbal tea resting on the edge of the desk. He held it up and grunted, which Phillips understood to be an invitation to have a cup himself.

He waved it away. "Aye, I came in on Monday morning," Phillips replied, not wanting to rehash it. "Felt better after."

Harry grunted again and took another slurp of his lemon and ginger tea.

"What brings you back so soon, if it's not to put a pair of gloves on?"

Phillips swiped a hand across his face and looked away, then back again.

"Look, Harry. We've known each other for—what? Fifty years?"

"Must be something like that," the other agreed, waiting to see where the conversation was headed. "Used to spark you out, even back then."

He grinned, showing a mouthful of bright white caps.

"In all that time, you know I've never bothered with the odd bit of funny business going on in this place—"

"Wait a minute—"

"Hear me out, Harry," Phillips overrode the automatic defence because they both knew the score. "I loved coming here when it was your da' at the helm, and I've missed coming back more often. You've got a good, solid thing going here and some of the lads have gone on to do great things."

Harry smiled proudly because it was true. Ryan had worried about a lack of safety measures when he'd seen Phillips punching the living daylights out of the punters, but that wasn't the norm under Harry's watch. He'd made an exception for his boyhood friend, but anybody else who had stormed into his gym demanding a fight without headwear or mouth guards would have been kicked out.

"For all that, we both know that a lot of traffic comes through these doors and not all of it is law-abiding."

Harry said nothing but lifted the mug to his lips again.

"I pick my battles," Phillips went on, looking him dead in the eye. "And, God knows, I've no wish to start a battle with you. But, so help me, I mean to find out who financed the man who's taken Denise."

Harry listened with a sinking heart, hearing the note of desperation in Frank's voice. A desperate man would stop at nothing until he got what he wanted, but there were other things to consider. Important things that could cost lives. He looked out into the gym, watched a pair of young lads sparring, and when he looked back into Frank's tired brown eyes, he remembered when they had been youngsters together, picking fights on street corners just for the fun of it.

"Alright Frank," he said, and reached across to flip the blind down. It fell in a heap of clattering plastic against the window frame and they were enclosed for a moment, just two old friends. "But this didn't come from me. Understand?"

Phillips nodded.

"One of my lads sometimes trains the blokes who come in for a white-collar fight. Makes them feel better about themselves when they're stuck behind a desk playing with spreadsheets." He let out a short, rumbling laugh. "Takes all sorts. Anyway, they stick with the same trainer for six months ahead of the fight but, about a week ago, some chump comes into the gym asking for a new trainer because his old one has buggered off. My lad agreed to step in, and that's how they got chatting."

"Go on," Phillips urged.

"As I say, these two got chatting over the past week and it turns out this toff's old training partner disappeared without so much as a by-your-leave. I thought nothing of it"—Harry shrugged—"until, the very next day, I hear one of the other lads talking about a job opening down at the All-American Diner. That's Moffa's place—"

"I know it," Phillips growled, as the pieces began to fall neatly into place. The Moffa family was one of the notorious gangland families written in bold blue ink on his notepad. Originally from Manchester, the three brothers had migrated further north to claim their own patch of turf. Considering there were older, more established claims to the lucrative drugs industry in Newcastle, it was a testament to their innovative methods that they had been able to muscle their way in.

The All-American Diner was a trendy, all-day hotspot near the railway station in Newcastle, decked out to look like the set of *Pulp Fiction* with a long bar, red leather booths, a chequered dance floor and an enormous Cadillac in the middle of it all. Behind all that, Jimmy 'The Manc' Moffa kept his office, both literally and figuratively.

Phillips turned his attention back to Harry, who continued his story.

"Aye, well you probably know the lad wasn't talking about a job opening as a waiter. One of Moffa's best men has gone AWOL and that means there's an opening in the firm."

"Who's left—and is he still alive?"

Harry scratched the side of his bulbous nose.

"Couldn't tell you whether he's alive and kicking on the Costa Brava or whether he's making friends with the fish at the bottom of the river. But his name was something weird," he muttered. "Made me think of a board game."

"Like Cluedo?" Phillips offered, without needing to rack his brain.

"Aye, that's the one. It rhymed with that, I reckon."

"Ludo," Phillips said. "Moffa's right-hand man is called Ludo, on account of his close and personal relationship with Quaaludes back in the day."

"I remember him, now." Harry nodded. "Big lad, built like a brick shithouse, pock-marked face."

"That's him."

It was little wonder that Helen Hayworth had been too frightened to describe the man who had abducted her. She would have known that he was so physically distinctive that any police officer within four county command areas would have identified him immediately and, in doing so, would have signed her own death warrant.

Phillips found that he was now faced with a new dilemma. He had a solid suspect but doing anything about it might endanger a young family.

But doing nothing would endanger Denise.

He rose from his chair and held out a grateful hand to his old friend.

———

Ryan tried calling Phillips' mobile for the tenth time and, when it went straight to voicemail, he swore loudly and to nobody in particular. Anna raised tired eyes from her own laptop computer and took that as her cue to shut it down for the day.

"I don't have time to be running around looking for him," Ryan said, tersely. "We've got enough on our hands trying to hunt down a murderer before he kills again. I'd have thought Phillips would want to pitch in, instead of disappearing off into the night."

Anna hitched herself up onto the edge of his desk and crossed her ankles, letting him rant.

"Perhaps he's found a new lead," she suggested.

"If he had, you'd think he would damn well share it with the rest of us," Ryan bit out. "Now isn't the time to be galloping off, playing the hero."

"You'd never do a thing like that," Anna said, ever so smoothly.

Ryan's next words died on his tongue and he sent her a withering look, which slid like water off a duck's back.

"Those were very different circumstances," he argued.

"Mm, going after the people who endangered my life," Anna mused. "Yes, I can see how that's different to Phillips' situation."

"There's no need to be sarcastic."

"Then climb down from your high horse, detective," she shot back. "You're the boss, but this is Frank's city. He knows it, and he's probably speaking to other people who know it, too."

He gave her a searching look. "What did he tell you?"

"Now, don't get mad."

Ryan's eyes darkened to an ominous, stormy grey. "Anna."

"Alright, don't shoot the messenger." She held out both hands in appeal. "He asked me not to mention it for an hour or so because he had a couple of things he wanted to take care of alone. He said he was heading out to speak to some old friends but he'd be back by nine-thirty."

Ryan looked again at the clock and saw that it read 21:20.

"Why didn't he want me with him?" he asked, and Anna was sorry to see a flicker of hurt in his eyes. "I would have gone with him, anywhere he needed. Does he think I'm a liability after what happened this afternoon?"

"I'm sure he doesn't think anything like that," she tried to reassure him. "Frank knows that this afternoon was a one-off and nobody could blame you for it. I'm sure there's another explanation."

But Ryan looked unconvinced. "I hope he knows what he's doing," was all he said.

CHAPTER 14

Phillips sat in his car for a while after leaving Buddle's, considering what was the right and proper thing to do. He was in a quandary; one half of him bound in conscience to a family who had not asked to be part of the Hacker's evil game, the other half bound in love to the woman who had come to mean everything to him. Eventually, he settled on a course of action that would satisfy both sides. He fiddled with his smartphone and forwarded an e-mail to DI Rodgers over at Durham CID with an attached image of Paul Evershed—the man known more commonly as Ludo—taken from his police file. He typed only one request, which was that Rodgers show the photo to Helen Hayworth and watch for her reaction.

After his phone made a tinkling sound to signify that the e-mail had sent, Phillips ignored the red notifications telling him Ryan had been trying to get in touch and turned his phone off. He started the car engine and steered it back towards the centre of town, slowing as he passed the house he had grown up in. There were net curtains in the windows, which was something, but the front door had a scrap of plywood nailed across it following an attempted break-in. He felt a weight of sadness settle on his chest but he shoved it to one side and accelerated through the darkened streets.

It wasn't his home anymore.

Back in the centre of town, the All-American Diner was busy, even for a Tuesday night. Waitresses dressed in candy striper uniforms buzzed from table to table and men dressed to look like John Travolta flipped cocktails behind the bar. Groups of twenty-somethings laughed, enjoying the kitsch feel to the place with none of the discomfort that came from knowing how it managed to stay in business while so many other new bars and restaurants dropped like flies in the overcrowded market. The Diner managed to affect a cheerful atmosphere thanks to its bold colour scheme and classic power tunes pumping out of the jukebox in the corner, but Phillips hated everything about it.

It was a curse of being in his line of work, he supposed, but with his trained eye, he was able to see beyond all the gloss, stripping it away to uncover what was buried beneath the surface. And what he saw was a brawny bouncer with bloodshot eyes thanks to a reliance on cocaine and a generous helping of steroids, a bar-restaurant fronted by unscrupulous men, and an awful lot of *pink*.

As he approached the doors, the bouncer began speaking into a microphone at the lapel of his cheap black suit. Phillips gave him an easy-going smile.

"Alright, lad? I was just after a quick pint and a burger. Is there a problem?"

He couldn't have been more than thirty, Phillips thought, and his face was too smooth, too clean to have had much experience. He was just muscle, intended to intimidate the weak.

"We're closing."

Phillips stood on his toes to look over the man's shoulder at the bustling crowd beyond and gave him a disbelieving look.

"Doesn't look that way to me, son."

The bouncer took a menacing step forward and grabbed hold of Phillips' jacket, thrusting him away from the door so hard that he stumbled and hit his head against the doorframe.

"Bugger off home, pig," he spat. "You're not welcome here."

Phillips brushed a hand over his jacket to set it right again, checked his tie, then gave the man a disapproving, fatherly look.

"If there's one thing I can't abide, it's rudeness," he said, before planting his fist in the man's face.

The bouncer crumpled to the floor, unconscious. Phillips rubbed at his knuckle, stepped around the man's bulk and headed inside the Diner, ignoring the shocked faces of nearby staff who ran to the telephone, presumably to call the police.

Phillips set his jaw and decided to worry about that small complication later.

Phillips knew exactly which door led to the executive offices of Jimmy Moffa, having had the misfortune of visiting the man on several occasions, always in connection with serious crimes. When you were party to as many shady deals as Jimmy, you could expect regular visits from the police. Phillips ignored the shouts from one of the barmen and tugged open the side door which led to a long corridor painted in a tacky shade of red. At the end, a young man was guarding Jimmy's office, wearing a brand-new black suit with his hair brushed back from a boyish face. He had a wiry, muscular physique which seemed to tense as Phillips stomped down the corridor towards him.

"Tony, what would your da' say if he could see you now?"

The younger man shrivelled inside his suit.

"Aw, howay, Frank. I'm just filling in for a while, that's all."

Phillips gave him a beady-eyed glare. "Aye, that's what they all say in the beginning. Stand aside, son, this doesn't concern you."

"Frank, you know I don't want to get into anything with you, but…"

Phillips continued to stare him down.

"I can't let you in," he finished, lamely.

Phillips watched the young man's eyes flicking upward and to the right. He repeated the action two more times and he realised that there must be a camera watching their every move.

"I understand what you're telling me," Phillips said, then shifted his feet to give the man time to prepare himself. A moment later, Tony gave an almost imperceptible nod and Phillips swung the first blow. There followed a scuffle between the pair of them that any thespian would have been proud of, and after they both felt that a sufficient effort had been made to bar Phillips' entry, Tony fell against the wall.

"Thanks, lad," Phillips gave him a wink and pushed open the door to Moffa's inner sanctum.

Jimmy Moffa watched the altercation from the comfort of his leather desk chair via a live CCTV feed linked to the gigantic flat screen television dominating one wall of his office. In fact, the entire room was modelled on a Vegas hotel suite, from its monochrome colour scheme to the expensive photographic prints blown up on large canvases dotted around its walls. Top of the range technology was everywhere, vying for attention with expensive antiques chosen to give the impression of affluence rather than good taste.

Amid all the glitz, it was easy to miss the man sitting behind the super-sized black desk in the centre of it all. The youngest of the three Moffa brothers was, at first glance, an average-looking man in his early thirties. He wore an expertly tailored suit of fine charcoal grey with a crisp white shirt and a fashionably skinny tie. At his cuffs, he wore a pair of diamond encrusted cufflinks to match the stud winking in his right earlobe and the Cartier watch on his left wrist. His hair was closely shaven, drawing more attention to his face, which was a mixture of sharp cheekbones and the palest blue eyes Phillips had ever seen.

When Phillips entered, he was waiting for him with a mobile phone in his hand, poised to dial.

"Well, if it isn't Scrappy Doo," he rasped. "Have you lost your way?"

Phillips stayed near the door but faced him down.

"I've got plenty of bite left in me yet, especially for a common little prick like you."

Moffa bared his teeth in the semblance of a smile. "Big talk, old man. You might have caught the bouncers off guard, but you'll not have the same luck with me, so watch your step."

He jiggled the mobile phone he held in his hand.

"Guess who I'm about to call?"

"Your mum?"

Phillips happened to know that Moffa's mother had died after an accidental overdose and, sure enough, a dark red flush of anger crept along the man's neck and he thrust upward to slap both hands on his desk.

"You'd better turn around and walk back out of that door before I lose my temper," he snarled.

"Aye, remind me to shit my pants later," Phillips shot back. "In the meantime, I want to know where he is."

Something like surprise flickered across Moffa's face, quickly masked.

"Who? Your boss? Maybe you should try looking in the loony bin." His laugh was gleeful. "I heard the Big Man took a right funny turn, earlier today."

And there must be a rat in the department who told him all about it, Phillips thought, but that was a problem for another day.

"You know exactly who I'm talking about. Keir Edwards."

Moffa walked around to the front of his desk and pressed 'dial' on his mobile phone.

"Let's put this on speakerphone," he said.

The ringing tone was replaced by a click and then an operator's voice, asking which emergency service he required.

"Police," Moffa gasped, theatrically. "I've been attacked. He's gone mad, attacking everyone. Come quickly…"

He turned and threw the mobile into the corner of the office, where it smashed against a crystal decanter laid out for his more discerning guests.

Phillips looked on aghast as Moffa strolled around to the other side of his desk and swept the contents onto the floor. His laptop fell with a crash, followed by several heavy desk ornaments. As a final pièce de résistance, he selected a large crystal tumbler which had partially broken against the polished floor and brandished it in front of Phillips.

"What the—?"

Moffa merely laughed. "Now for my final trick, ladies and gents."

He crossed the room and Phillips braced himself for a confrontation, fists clenched and ready to throw the first punch. But Moffa took him by surprise. He grasped one of Phillips' fists, shoving the broken tumbler hard into his palm and driving the jagged edge of glass into his skin. Phillips cried out as Moffa continued to crush the glass against his palm, then suddenly he withdrew it.

Phillips realised then what he planned to do and tried to make a grab for the glass, but Jimmy had been born on the same kind of streets as him and knew all the right moves.

"You're screwed, mate," he spat, and brought the glass down hard against the side of his own head, once, then twice. The third time, he brought it down hard enough to dig an inch-long cut into his own scalp.

Phillips watched in horror as blood began to trickle from Jimmy Moffa's skull and, behind him, there came the sound of running footsteps down the corridor as the local police arrived. Raw, helpless anger rushed through Phillips' system as he looked into the smug, self-satisfied face of the man who had been responsible for hurting so many people.

"Don't you ever feel it?" he whispered.

Moffa frowned his confusion. "Feel what?"

The door burst open behind them and, all of a sudden, the room was filled with voices.

Ryan ruminated on what could have taken Phillips away from the immediate task of following the leads generated by Beth Finnegan's murder. It was probable that they would be able to trace Edwards' new vehicle and, after that, there would be every chance they could track his movements.

Then again, they might not.

He let out a long sigh and felt a pair of slim arms wrap around his neck.

"Stop worrying," Anna said, then yawned until her jaw cracked.

"You need some sleep," he said. "We all do."

"It doesn't matter. I've sorted out a new place for us, just for the next few days. It's a holiday rental, so we can pick up the keys whenever it suits."

"Where?"

"A little village called Blanchland," she said, pulling up a chair beside him.

"I know it," he said. "It's over in the North Pennines, off the A68 west of Durham. It's a bit rural, don't you think?"

"It's equidistant to Durham and Newcastle," she explained. "Your investigation seems to be split between the cities, so I thought it would make sense to choose somewhere in the middle. It's off the beaten track and not an obvious choice for anybody trying to find us."

"Which makes it safer," he finished for her.

"Yep."

"I like it," he said succinctly.

"It comes with a small addition to the property spec," she added, and Ryan's eyes brightened.

"A hot tub?"

"Ah, no, sadly not. It comes with Phillips, since I asked him to come and stay with us."

Ryan pulled her around so he could look at her. "Thank you," he said quietly. "It's a kind thought, except that he appears to have done a runner."

Anna pulled a face.

"I'm surprised he isn't back by now," she admitted. "I wonder what's keeping him."

Just then, Ryan's mobile phone began to vibrate and he slapped his hands against his pockets until he realised it was sitting in his direct eyeline, on top of his desk.

"Ryan."

Anna watched his face transform into a forbidding expression.

"Right. No, don't do that, I'll come and pick him up."

He jabbed a finger to end the call.

"*Damn!*"

"What is it?" she asked worriedly. "What's happened?"

"It's Frank. He's being taken into custody for GBH on Jimmy Moffa. They've got him inside a squad car parked outside the All-American Diner."

"I don't believe it," she whispered. "What on earth was he doing there?"

Ryan shrugged into his jacket and waved goodbye to any prospect of sleep in the near future.

"That's a very good question."

He started to make for the door, stopped, then doubled back to bestow a lingering kiss.

"Don't go anywhere," he said. "There'll be staff on site here throughout the night—I'll be back as soon as I can."

She watched his long legs eat up the floor and a moment later he was gone.

CHAPTER 15

Edwards looked inside the room where MacKenzie slept soundly and was satisfied that the barbiturates he'd sprinkled into her water had served their purpose. She was in no fit state to run very far, but the sedative would serve as an added precaution.

So peaceful, he thought.

He stared at her for a while and felt lethal, like a cocked rifle ready to discharge. His hands began to shake with the effort of holding back, when he could so easily see her blood soaking into the mattress as life drained from her body.

No, he warned himself. *Not yet.*

He forced himself back from the brink but it left him feeling restless and dissatisfied. It would be imprudent to kill another one tonight because the streets would be rife with uniforms and they'd likely trace the car soon enough and start making connections. Even the mentally challenged rejects down at Northumbria CID would eventually begin to add the corresponding numbers together to make four.

Which was why he needed to tie up some loose ends tonight.

But not before making a quick search of MacKenzie's bedroom. There weren't many places to hide weapons in the barren space, but he expected her to be resourceful. She had tried stabbing him, knocking him out, and running away, none of which had worked so far. That didn't mean she had given up trying to find new, increasingly innovative ways to escape—not that he minded that. If it came to it, he much preferred his targets to make him give chase, because there was nothing remotely exciting about having one's prey already cooped up and ready to eat.

Aha!

When he dipped his head to look beneath the bed, he was amused to find a rudimentary splint, consisting of strips of wood held together by the stained elastic covering torn from the edge of the mattress. He held it up and assumed she used it to support her broken ribs. They were probably painful, he thought, without much interest.

Should he confiscate the splint?

She should know better than to try to cheat him, but perhaps it would be more diverting to let her go on believing that she had outwitted him.

He left her sleeping and headed out into the silent night, to hunt.

Jimmy Moffa wore the most elaborate head bandage Ryan had seen since he had visited the Ancient Egypt exhibition at the British Museum a few years ago. The man could give King Tut a run for his money, judging by the yards of clinical strapping tape wound around his head, no doubt to ham up the extent of his injuries. Ryan drove the car slowly past the entrance and watched in utter dismay as Moffa was led from the All-American Diner by his greasy solicitor—who had probably hot-footed it down there faster than you could say 'ambulance chaser'.

"Bloody hell," Ryan muttered, as he recognised two local news hacks running up the street with hungry looks in their eyes. "That's all we need."

Lowerson grunted his agreement from the passenger seat of Ryan's car and glumly observed another local patrol car arriving, alongside more passers-by and media.

"What was Frank thinking, coming down here on his own?"

Ryan gave up trying to find a legal parking space and swerved up onto the pavement, flipping on his hazard lights.

"God only knows," he replied, as they opened their doors and made for the circus developing nearby. "He must think that Moffa is responsible for backing Edwards' escape."

"I thought the Hayworths refused to confirm or deny who threatened them?" Lowerson panted a little trying to keep up with Ryan's long strides as they rounded the corner.

"That's right. But Phillips went off and did his own detective work this evening and something obviously turned up to lead him down here."

"He should have come to us, rather than charging in like a bull in a china shop."

Ryan stopped just before they turned the corner and gave Lowerson a hard stare.

"I seem to remember a time, not so long ago, when you went into a dangerous situation guns blazing and without proper back-up. You were in a coma for months afterward, but nobody crowed about it when you woke up. We were all happy to have you back because that's all that mattered."

Lowerson had the grace to look away.

"We're only human, Jack, especially where our loved ones are concerned. Just remember that."

"I—"

Lowerson found himself talking to Ryan's back because a moment later he was striding off again to face down the people who sought to tear down everything he had built.

"Chief Inspector Ryan!"

He ignored the jostles and shouts from the local media, blinking as a camera flashed in his face. In reflex, he swiped out a hand and managed to snag its strap from the intrepid reporter's neck, where it fell to the concrete floor and shattered.

"Hey! That's private property!"

Ryan stared down his nose and smiled wolfishly. "Oops," he said.

He ignored the stream of verbal abuse which followed and barged his way through the crowd until he found the blue-and-white police barrier, behind which there stood a young and slightly harried-looking police constable from Tyne and Wear Area Command.

Ryan produced his warrant card and checked that Lowerson had caught him up.

"DCI Ryan and DC Lowerson, Northumbria CID," he said, dipping beneath the barrier. "Where's your commanding officer?"

The constable pointed them inside the Diner, where they found a woman they recognised as one of the local sergeants talking to a thick-skulled bouncer with another enormous bandage hanging from the side of his face.

"Aye, he was totally out of control," they heard him say. "Turned up at the door effin' and blindin', proper rude like, all up in my face."

"Do you remember precisely what was said?"

The bouncer nodded vigorously.

"Aye, no bother. Well, I said something like, 'Good evening, sir,' and he started ranting and raving. Called me a twat, or something like that." His eyes frittered away, up and to the left while he fabricated the next part of the story. "I tried to be polite, right, an' I told him he sounded drunk and should probably head home, like."

"Uh-huh," she said, making a cursory note on her pad. "Then what?"

"He just came for me, like, out of nowhere. Just thumped the side of my head and left me for dead," the bouncer finished, with dramatic effect.

Ryan waited until the man loped off before cornering the sergeant.

"DS Thomas?"

She turned to him with tired brown eyes, which brightened immeasurably when she spotted who had arrived. Lowerson watched her reaction with long-suffering acceptance and thought that, if he didn't like the man so much, he might resent being consigned to the role of Ryan's 'less attractive wingman'. Some of his colleagues had begun to call it the 'Ryan Effect', but the man himself seemed totally unaware of the impact he had on people, which was probably for the best.

"Yes. And you're DCI Ryan." She held out a hand and wished she'd had time to run a brush through her hair.

"What happened here? All I've heard is my sergeant was involved in some kind of minor incident—"

She snorted inelegantly. "I don't know where you got your information but it's not minor from where I'm standing. I've got four waiting staff and over twenty diners who confirm that your pal forced his way inside after flooring that hapless-looking bloke back there." She nodded towards the bouncer who was now talking to Moffa, bowing his head like a Labrador about to have his belly rubbed.

"He must have been provoked," Ryan insisted, raking his gaze over them both with contempt.

"Phillips admits to knocking him unconscious after being denied entry," she said, in a tone that invited him to argue at his peril.

Ryan's lips firmed. "He must have had a good reason."

"That's not for me to say," she pointed out, fairly.

"I know one thing for certain. Phillips is never, *ever* drunk on the job, so that bouncer is full of it."

DS Thomas told herself to remain patient in the face of six-feet-two-inches of angry male, particularly one used to being in command.

"I already know your sergeant is sober." She was casual, but firm. "Do you think I came in on the banana boat? We breathalysed him straight away, and there wasn't so much as a whiff of booze."

Ryan was relieved to hear it. "Alright. What's Moffa's valuable contribution to all this?"

She smiled, appreciating his humour. "He claims that Phillips accosted the doorman outside his office and then entered shortly afterward, threatening to inflict bodily harm if he didn't admit to being involved in the escape of Keir Edwards and the abduction of DI MacKenzie."

"Which Moffa denies?" Lowerson asked, and she nodded.

"Profusely. He claims that Phillips is a man on the edge and was seeking revenge for perceived injustices of the past. He's a cool one," she added, thinking of those unnerving blue eyes. "Moffa says he told Phillips outright he wasn't involved and advised him to go home to sleep it off, otherwise he would call the police. He says Phillips just lunged for him, upset the desk and hit him around the head with a glass tumbler."

"Frank wouldn't do that," Lowerson burst out.

Thomas shrugged. "Phillips has a bloody hand which he admits came from cutting it on the same glass tumbler, but he says Moffa forced the glass into his hand and then used it to whack himself around the head. Sounds far-fetched, if you ask me," she finished.

"If he says that's what happened, then it did," Ryan retorted.

"We'll check out the swabs, any CCTV, and piece things together."

"I'm giving you my word," Ryan said quietly, and she had to admit his voice was compelling. "There's another side to this. The CCTV will show who threw the first punch, I'm sure of it."

She swallowed. "Look, I've told you we'll be looking at any footage. Until then, all I have is one hell of a spectacle, which is getting bigger all the time."

They followed the direction of her gaze and watched as Jimmy Moffa was led, hobbling and clutching at his bandage for the benefit of the paparazzi, towards a black Porsche Cayenne.

Ryan's whipped back around.

"You're letting him *go*?"

DS Thomas gave him a warning look. "I've taken a statement from Mr Moffa and he has seen a medic. He's free to go home, subject to his voluntary attendance at an interview tomorrow morning. If you want to speak to his solicitor, he's still hanging around somewhere."

Ryan wished it didn't sound so damn reasonable. "Where?"

She scanned the crowd outside and eventually nodded towards a portly man in a three-piece suit with a mop of blond hair falling across his forehead in a foppish style that wouldn't have looked out of place in a BBC period drama.

"I might have guessed," Ryan said, and shook her hand again. "There must be more to this," he started to say again, but she interrupted him with another mild, knowing smile.

"I wasn't born yesterday. Moffa's on our radar and we'll be taking everything he says with a massive dose of salt."

Ryan told himself to be content with that, for now. He thanked her and motioned Lowerson in the direction of Moffa's solicitor, who was holding court with several prominent journalists, his rounded baritone projecting out into the night air as if he were on stage at the Royal Albert Hall and not a street corner in Newcastle City Centre.

"It would be unwise for me to pass any comment at this stage of an active investigation," he said, in a serious tone to be expected of legitimate legal counsel. "Except to say that my client, James Moffa, has asked me to convey his sympathy to Detective Sergeant Frank Phillips, who he considers to be deeply unwell following the sad news of his girlfriend's abduction, which has been widely publicised. He, like all of us, wishes and prays for her safe return."

He paused, to ensure they had made a good note of his soundbite.

"However, Mr Moffa's sympathy does not extend to forgiving unprovoked attacks on his person and his staff, at his place of business. It is behaviour unbecoming of a detective sergeant of experience and rank, and Mr Moffa is fortunate not to have sustained more serious injuries. As it is, he is being driven directly to the hospital to have stitches."

He held up both hands theatrically, fending off any more questions.

"Really, that's all I can say." He began to walk towards his own chauffeured car, where Ryan was waiting with a sneer and a slow clap.

"Ever thought of changing profession? You deserve an Oscar, after that little performance."

"Detective Ryan—"

"Chief Inspector," he corrected.

"Whatever. Get out of my way."

"I'd like to ask you some questions. Here, or at your office, it makes no difference to me."

The man started to reach for the door of the dark Audi but Ryan put a restraining hand on his shoulder.

"Careful, inspector," the solicitor warned him. "You'll end up being sued alongside your mate."

"I want your name," Ryan ground out.

"Why? Do you think you'll be needing representation?"

The solicitor chuckled and produced a heavy cream business card, thrusting it into Ryan's hand. A minute later, he and the car were gone, speeding off into the night.

Lowerson stumbled through the crowd to where Ryan stood, tall and commanding amid the throng.

"Well? What did he say?"

"The usual," he replied, tapping the card against his palm. "But look at the name of his firm, Jack."

Lowerson took the card and glanced down at the fancy gold-embossed lettering on the front. "What a coincidence that a notorious gangster and a prolific serial killer share the same firm of solicitors."

"What do I always say about coincidences, Jack?"

"There's no such thing."

CHAPTER 16

Edwards leaned back against the bonnet of his newly-acquired car and watched the moon shining in the heavens. It dwarfed the people and houses far beneath, who continued their ephemeral lives, watching television and talking about the latest celebrity gossip as if any of it mattered. He cast his eyes upward, past the cloudy ring of light pollution above the city, higher and higher, hoping that somebody would be watching him.

"Talk to me," he commanded, closing his eyes to blot out the sound of mankind, hoping that it would be replaced by something ethereal and beautiful.

But, as always, there was a deafening silence.

He opened his eyes and considered the sky again, resplendent with stars. Pegasus and Ursa Major dominated and he was reminded of a time, long ago, when he had been gifted a telescope. What had been his most prized possession was forever lost to him now, hidden beneath the earth by years of dirt and overgrowth.

He wouldn't think about that now.

All those massive burning balls of gas were named after mythical gods to inspire awe in ordinary, simple-minded people. One day, his name might join theirs, alongside Hercules and Jupiter. The Hacker would shine its fiery white light and the people would stand in awe of it. They would speak of the man who had risen above ordinary men.

He heard the rumble of an approaching vehicle and spotted the glimmer of headlights along the single-track lane. Quickly, he retrieved his rifle and melted into the shadow of a tree until he could see the car and its driver. When the familiar lines of a black Porsche Cayenne came into view, he lowered the rifle and emerged back into the moonlight.

Jimmy Moffa would have preferred an army of heavyweights to accompany him to meet a man like Edwards but he was suffering a temporary staffing problem made worse by the fact that his right-hand man was taking a necessary leave of absence from the public eye. The young lad standing in his place looked the part, with a scar running across his neck and thick, gym-honed muscles after six years of boxing at one of the best rings in the city. However, Tony's scar came from a childhood fall and he was yet to prove himself a fighter outside the ring, judging by his failure to put down Frank Phillips earlier. In the ordinary way of things, Tony would have been given his marching orders after that display.

But good men were hard to come by and he needed somebody he could mould into the kind of creature he wanted. One thing that could certainly be said of Tony was that he wasn't exactly the sharpest tool in the box, so he had high hopes that it wouldn't take too long to train him.

"Door," he ordered.

Tony jumped down from the driver's seat to open his master's door without needing to be told twice and Moffa stepped down from the back seat of his car, motioning for his driver-cum-bodyguard to follow him.

"You're late," Edwards remarked, resting the rifle in the crook of his arm.

"You're a fugitive," Moffa replied, as his feet squelched in the mud underfoot. "Put the rifle on the floor."

Edwards tapped his hand against the butt.

"I don't want to get it dirty," he said.

"Tony."

The bodyguard nodded and reached into his breast pocket for a smaller handgun, which he held awkwardly in his sweaty palm.

"Don't forget to take the safety off," Edwards advised him.

Moffa's jaw hardened and the whites of his eyes gleamed.

"You've caused quite a stir."

"I'm nothing if not flamboyant," Edwards agreed. "What happened to your head?"

Moffa swore viciously and stripped away the excess bandages, leaving only a small square surgical plaster to cover the butterfly stitches on his scalp.

"Evasive measures," he explained. "I had an unexpected visit from Ryan's lapdog this evening."

"Phillips?"

Moffa inclined his head. "He wants to know where you are."

Edwards' face registered no emotion whatsoever but his mind came to an immediate decision. If the police were on to Moffa, dominoes would start to fall and it was too soon for that. There was no loyalty between them and nothing to secure his position other than the promise of money which he was in no position to fulfil. It was a precarious situation, whichever way he looked at it.

"What did you tell him?"

Moffa laughed, and it was a rusty, grating sound. "I don't know nothing, *guv*," Moffa parodied. "That was my end of the bargain. Transportation, supplies and silence. In exchange, you would finish Ryan and provide full payment for services rendered, at a heavy discount, I might add."

"You'll get your money," Edwards lied. "And Ryan will get his just deserts."

"You're playing for time," Moffa rasped. "But you won't play me. Let me make myself perfectly clear, so we know where we stand. If you fail to provide the money within three days, I will tell the police all about your dirty, *dirty* little secrets. I'll tell them all about the real Keir Edwards. I'll tell them about the escape plan and I'll say that you threatened to kill members of my family if I didn't help you.

I'll tell them about your solicitor, all about how she passed messages between us. I will spill my guts and I'll have a steak dinner while they chuck you back in prison, love, but before then I'll ask Tony here to pay you a little visit, with my compliments."

Edwards didn't like his tone. No, not one little bit.

He cast a cursory glance towards the man standing half a step behind Moffa, categorised him instantly as lightweight and looked back at Moffa with a mocking smile.

"I don't like it when we quarrel," he crooned, placing the rifle gently on the ground. He held both hands up, palms facing outward in a non-threatening gesture.

Both men braced themselves as he moved towards them, his dark eyes twinkling like stars through the dusky evening.

"That's far enough," Moffa snapped, but he found himself mesmerised.

Edwards was an expert at reading certain types of behaviour. He might not be able to empathise with his fellow man, but he could read them like a book and this one had just become a lot more interesting.

Jimmy Moffa, a hardened gangster feared by many, was hot under the collar. He was breathing quickly, his chest rising and falling beneath his tailored suit and Edwards could almost smell the pheromones. If night hadn't fallen, he was sure there would be tell-tale signs of sexual attraction written all over his face.

"Well, well," he murmured. "This is a delightful surprise."

Tony watched the exchange with wide eyes and wondered whether he should have stepped in by now. Neither man said much, but there seemed to be plenty of conversation flowing in other ways and the young man flushed with embarrassment and surprise.

Moffa could only think that it was like being hypnotized by a snake. He had seen and done many things in his short life, few of which he could be proud of. He ran one third of a growing criminal empire but he would always be the youngest brother no matter how many times he proved himself. Faces of the men he had killed often haunted him at night but they did not frighten him, or fascinate him, half as much as the man standing in front of him right now. With the possible exceptions of Ryan and Phillips, every other man he met was intimidated by his reputation. But not this one. Edwards stood in front of him without any pretence about the fact he was a murderer, a killer, an assassin.

Equals.

And it made him feel like a fumbling, rock-hard teenager again. A part of him wanted to roll the dice and see where they would fall; to play Russian roulette with his own life, if it meant having one taste of the utopia he could see with this man.

"I said, that's far enough," he repeated, but even to his own ears his voice sounded weak.

"Oh, I don't think so," Edwards purred. "Why don't we talk about it back at your place?"

There was a short, tense silence before Moffa spoke again and, when he did, his voice shook with excitement.

"Tony, get the car started."

―――――――

Ryan and Lowerson found their friend sitting listlessly in the back of a squad car. The knuckles on his left hand were grazed and his right hand was completely bandaged up. There were a couple of smaller nicks and cuts on his face and his shirt was speckled with blood that wasn't his own.

In short, he looked awful.

"Jack, do me a favour and grab us a couple of coffees, will you?"

Lowerson read the meaning in Ryan's eyes and nodded.

"No problem."

Ryan opened the car door and rapped his hand against the roof.

"Time to go, champ."

Phillips moved as if in slow motion, not saying a word. Ryan put a firm hand in the small of his back and propelled him onward, not stopping to talk to the stragglers hoping to catch a final quote for the early morning edition.

Only when they were safely ensconced in his car did Ryan put both hands on the wheel and turn to his sergeant.

"Tell me you had a good reason to go in there, Frank. If there's anything you need to get off your chest, do it now and do it *quickly*."

Phillips lifted his chin and then did something that Ryan had not expected.

He covered his face with both hands and began to weep.

Ryan stared at him much as he might stare at a carnival oddity, and if Phillips had been his usual self he would have bellowed with laughter. Ryan wore an expression falling somewhere between constipation and panic, as he wondered what the hell to do. He had cried himself—of course he had. But it was always in private or, very rarely, in front of Anna. Over and done with quickly and not spoken of again.

Well, it wasn't encouraged, was it?

Boys were supposed to keep a stiff upper lip and the story was no different when they grew up to be men. People said there was no shame in it, that it was a healthy expression of emotion and all that, but life experience had taught him differently.

Cry baby. Wimp. Pussy.

Maybe life had taught him the wrong lessons, Ryan realised, and pulled the man in for a hard hug.

"All right, Frank. It'll be all right."

Phillips let himself be held by a friend and poured out the heartache he'd tried so hard to contain.

"Denise is gone. I know it. She's gone."

Ryan clutched him in a bear grip and didn't move a muscle when Lowerson returned with three steaming hot cups of coffee.

"No, she's not. She's a born fighter, just like you."

Chief Constable Morrison was waiting for them when Ryan finally turned his car back into the car park at CID Headquarters. It was late, past eleven, and they had lost track of the last time they had eaten—or slept in their own beds. Phillips had purged himself, pouring out the whole sorry tale of what had happened to take him into the viper's nest, but the damage was already done and it was written all over Sandra Morrison's face. Her tired eyes passed between them and she didn't smile; she didn't even say a word.

She simply led the way upstairs to her office.

Once the door closed behind them, she didn't sit down, nor did she invite them to do so. Her voice was remote, impersonal, and her words fell like a death knell.

"Detective Sergeant Phillips, I am formally placing you on suspension pending a full disciplinary inquiry into allegations of gross misconduct and serious breaches of professional standards of behaviour. Your behaviour this evening has discredited our department, the police service, and may have damaged public confidence in the service that we provide. You have not been issued with a police caution but an investigation is ongoing. In the circumstances and until further information comes to light, I am ordering an immediate suspension until further notice."

Ryan vibrated with anger but it was no more than Phillips had expected.

"This is bollocks!" Ryan stabbed a finger in her general direction. "Take a look at his hands. Just *look*! Moffa has an injury on the right side of his head but Phillips is left-handed for God's sake! The man pushed a broken glass into his palm to smear it with blood and then smashed it into his own head. He's deranged!"

"And the bouncer at the door?" Morrison enquired, without rancour.

"Threw the first punch!" Ryan said. "And the CCTV will prove it, unless that mental defective has wiped it."

Morrison turned to Phillips and felt a tug at her heart strings, but she hadn't climbed the police hierarchy with a reputation for being a soft touch. She believed in good practice, in order, and in fairness. If she made exceptions for old friends, she would lose the respect of her staff.

"Frank? What do you have to say?"

Unlike his younger friends, Phillips had seen more of life and had developed a certain realism to temper his natural idealism. It meant that he was unsurprised by her decision, and had prepared himself for this outcome hours ago when he had sat quietly in his car outside Buddle's. He had no regrets; his violence had been controlled and, in his opinion, it had been necessary to obtain the information he now had in his possession. Given the choice, he would do it all over again. But he understood there was a price to pay for everything and it was Morrison's job to collect.

There was no price he wouldn't pay to bring Denise safely home, and that included sacrificing a career he had spent over thirty years building. What was a job, compared with the woman he loved?

"I've nothing else to say, ma'am. I've given a full statement to Tyne and Wear Area Command and I place my trust in them to complete a thorough investigation. I went to the Diner to speak to the man who financed the Hacker and I walked away having achieved that."

Morrison waited while she swallowed the lump in her throat, until she was sure that her voice betrayed nothing of her inner turmoil.

"Very well." She nodded, while Ryan rocked back on his heels in shock and Lowerson stared at Phillips in dumbfounded confusion.

Morrison directed her parting comments to them.

"I hardly need to add that there are strict protocols regarding information sharing. If I find out that any of them have been breached, I will not hesitate to instigate further investigations of misconduct. I now have the task of re-building confidence in this department, while the public is already terrified that a killer is on the loose. To say I'm disappointed would be an understatement. Don't give me reason to be even more disappointed.

"You have been warned."

CHAPTER 17

Jimmy Moffa preferred not to shit in his own backyard. He made a habit of conducting business in the city and commuting home in the evenings, where he could pretend he was an upstanding member of the community and play golf at the weekend. He lived in an elite neighbourhood known as 'Darras Hall', on the gentrified western edge of Newcastle and a mere stone's throw from Northumbria Police Headquarters. It brought him an odd sort of comfort to know that the blues were so close at hand and that his high-tech panic alarm system was rigged up to their offices. They would have to come running if he so much as accidentally tripped the switch, which was a source of endless amusement to him. It thrilled him to know that he walked among the pigs, taunting them with his presence.

So near, yet always so far away from lock-up.

In the seventies and eighties, Darras Hall had bloomed into a colony of sorts, where the nouveau riche could help themselves to a taste of the good life. Footballers, career criminals, their wives, their husbands, their mistresses and their children mingled with entrepreneurs, doctors, lawyers and property developers.

A *lot* of property developers.

Not that he minded the blokes who over-extended themselves on bad credit. He'd picked up a brand-new, neo-classical mansion with an acre of manicured gardens thanks to a slump in property prices and the greed of one such local businessman, and he wouldn't have it any other way. Moffa's home was his showpiece, his retreat and most importantly the physical evidence of how successful he had become. He was still young enough to remember the two-up, two-down where he'd been born in Manchester. He remembered the hand-me-downs, the threadbare carpet and the cheap food. The house was always cold and everything had seemed to be an ugly shade of grey; the kind of sepia hue that filmmakers used in artsy films about poverty, written from the comfort of a panelled study.

His father did what he could to better himself and his family, but the old man had been careless. He'd taught his boys how to hate, how to steal and how to kill, then he'd promptly gone and got himself killed instead.

Careless old bugger.

Jimmy could see that same carelessness in his elder brothers. They snorted too much powder and it made them sloppy and arrogant. They lived off the fat of the land, their men grew lazy and mistakes were made while they looked the other way and partied on a yacht in Ibiza. But that wasn't his way. He never touched anything other than sparkling water and milky coffee. He was known for it, but nobody would dare mock him within earshot and expect to leave without two broken legs.

Yet, after so many careful, cautious years, he found himself ready to open the enormous lead gates of his new-build mansion to a man who threatened the equilibrium he had worked so hard to maintain. They sat side-by-side in the back seat of his Porsche while Tony pulled into the driveway and Moffa could feel sweat beading his face and neck, for the first time in years.

What was he doing?

Keir Edwards was adept at exploiting people's weaknesses. Since it was a talent they both shared, that made it easy to recognise. Moffa didn't flatter himself that Edwards wanted him. He was under no illusions that the man hoped to talk his way out of payment or talk his way into a different kind of partnership, perhaps to squeeze him for more money or a ticket out of the country. He suspected the man wasn't even gay or at the very least bisexual like himself; Edwards was just an opportunist who wasn't fussy either way.

But when he looked into those deep midnight eyes, all doubts and sense of self-preservation flew merrily out of the window. He needed to know what it felt like to be with someone of his own distinction. Just once in his life, he wanted to be on equal terms with a man who wasn't there because he was too frightened to refuse.

He supposed that made him careless, too.

Anna drove along winding country roads towards the picturesque village of Blanchland, beneath a sky that was speckled with stars. The task force assigned to Operation Ireland was buckling under the strain of an ever-increasing workload, even though much of the grunt-work had been farmed out to neighbouring divisions. It was not just that they hunted a dangerous man who seemed proficient at staying beneath the radar, or that they were tasked with investigating the death of a teenage girl who had found herself in the wrong place at the wrong time. They faced a loss of public confidence, internal politics within the police hierarchy and the constant knowledge that one of their number was still very much missing.

Against that backdrop, Ryan remained at the helm to work throughout the night, for the second night in a row. Exhausted and wrung out, Anna had volunteered to drive Phillips home to the temporary accommodation they would all share. She knew that, despite everything that had happened, Ryan trusted nobody more than Phillips and he could rest easy in the knowledge that she would be safe in his hands. Anna had almost given up trying to convince Ryan that she didn't need protecting or that she was more than capable of fending for herself. It wasn't a question of gender, or about being a mere civilian. It was a question of survival against an unpredictable foe and she was intelligent enough to know that two heads were better than one when dealing with a threat like that.

Even better yet, several heads with specialist firearms training.

"Almost there," she said quietly, blinking through the darkness to remain alert as she swerved and braked for the hefted sheep that roamed freely through the hills. She had read somewhere about sheep that had never known the indignity of a pen, but had been reared through the generations to keep to a certain patch of land. Sometime over the years a road had been built, cutting directly across the North Pennines, but the sheep didn't seem to mind the encroachment on their turf.

"Aye," Phillips mumbled, lost in thought.

"What are you going to do now, Frank?"

Phillips watched the passing landscape and felt insignificant in the universe, a tiny speck in the enormous fabric of life. What would he do? Everything that he could.

"I've been taken off the investigation," he reminded her, for appearances' sake.

"Mm, but nobody said anything about where you could, or couldn't live. Did they?"

Phillips rubbed a hand across the stubble on his jaw and the bristle snagged against the bandage on his hand, reminding him of how he had come by it.

"I don't reckon they did."

"That being the case, it would hardly be your fault if you, let's say, *accidentally* stumbled across some files that Ryan left out. On the kitchen table, for example."

Phillips grinned at the passing fields and turned to cast an appreciative look in her direction.

"I'm sure it happens all the time," he agreed.

"And, if you were to read them, it wouldn't prejudice the investigation because you wouldn't be obtaining evidence or anything like that, now would you?"

"You're a crafty lass," Phillips said. "I've always liked that about you."

Anna chuckled, then reduced her speed as they passed a signpost telling them they had reached Blanchland. They admired the shadowed houses and ancient church lit by powerful uplighters, keeping a comfortable silence until Anna pulled up in front of a stone cottage with a burgundy-painted door to match all the others in a neat row.

They got out of the car, stretched their aching muscles and Anna walked around to open the boot.

"Frank? Give me a hand with this, will you?"

Phillips loped across and glanced down into the boot, which was filled to the brim with copies of the old case files relating to Keir Edwards, alongside newer files pertaining to the current investigation.

"When did Ryan get time to swipe these?"

"*He* didn't," Anna corrected him. "But he did ask me to run up some copies. Luckily for both of you, I wasn't in the mood for reading about Viking raids today."

"Thank Odin," Phillips declared.

Pizza boxes and empty cans of sugary pop were piled high in the corner of the Incident Room, next to a bin overflowing with rubbish accumulated over the last twenty-four hours. Ryan knew he was already expecting too much of his team to continue working indefinitely; to expect them to do it on an empty stomach would be adding insult to injury. He therefore put a call through to the pizza delivery shop and ordered ten extra-large stuffed-crust, fully loaded. It might not be the healthy or nutritious option but when one was engrossed in the task of finding a killer, salad just didn't cut it.

Lowerson looked up from his desk when the scent of baked cheese carried across the room, sniffing the air like a hungry wolf.

"Did you order a veggie pizza?"

Ryan gave him a pitying glance from his position a couple of desks over.

"Jack, we've been through this before. Can I help it if you refuse to eat normally?"

Lowerson rolled his eyes. "Let me rephrase the question. Which pizza has the least meat on it, so I can pick it off?"

Ryan pointed towards a small margherita he'd kept apart from the others. "Only joking, kiddo. I know how much you care about the cute little animals."

Lowerson's face lit up and he shovelled half a slice into his mouth, chewing blissfully while his arteries clogged with cholesterol.

"If I die, I'll die happy," he muttered.

"What's that?"

"Never mind. Where are we?"

Ryan leaned back in his desk chair and ran both hands through his mop of black hair, in an automatic gesture while he ordered his mind.

"Phillips is going to stay with us for a while." He decided to begin with the most recent emergency and work backward. "He's going to look after Anna."

"Or is she going to look after him?" Lowerson reached for another slice of pizza.

"Let's say it's an even exchange," Ryan admitted, lowering his voice a fraction. "I've left them with copies of the files to look over. I want to know about any locations Edwards mentioned in his statements over the years, including all past addresses. We already know about his old house in Jesmond, but I want to go back—all the way back—to see where else he has roots."

"Mmmffh," Lowerson agreed.

"Faulkner has sent through the forensics report," Ryan continued. "He confirms the Toyota that was abandoned on the Quayside had been driven by Edwards and that spots of MacKenzie's blood were found in the boot space. They found mud on the tyres, which they're analysing as a priority to see if it can tell us anything about where he's been, or where he might still be hiding. How are you getting along with tracing his new vehicle?"

Lowerson gargled with full-fat coke and dug his heels into the carpet to propel his desk chair across the short gap between his desk and Ryan's.

"First of all, you were right about the CCTV overlooking the car park at Wharf Square. It went offline from 01:17 this morning." He paused to check the clock on the wall and was relieved to see that it was still Tuesday. "Yes, in the early hours of this morning. We can make an educated guess that Edwards was responsible for that—"

"Sounds like another one of those coincidences," Ryan put in.

"Yeah, it is. But get this, we've traced the registered owners of every car that was sitting in the parking bays before then and all of them are in possession of their vehicles—except one."

Ryan just smiled, letting Lowerson have his moment.

"Please tell me Edwards is swanning around in a battered old three-wheeler, like Del Boy."

"No such luck. The missing car is a metallic grey Mercedes sports coupé—"

"Sounds similar to mine," Ryan observed. "He must have been delighted to find that."

Lowerson cleared this throat awkwardly.

"It's actually the same car as yours, guv, except it's a newer model."

Ryan lifted his chin.

"Not all of us are concerned with keeping up with the Joneses," he said, in dignified tones. "How far have you traced it?"

Lowerson flipped the page of his notebook.

"Here's the interesting part. We've got it travelling through the city centre and along the West Road until it joined the A69 at 01:32. The last sighting we have is just before the slip-road that would take you to the airport, and we know it didn't come off the motorway at that point, which means it must have travelled further along the A69. We also know it didn't go as far as Hexham or even Corbridge because there's no footage outside either town. You know what that means?"

Ryan knew exactly what it meant, but he didn't want to ruin Lowerson's flow.

"Tell me."

"It means that the Mercedes would have come to the Styford Roundabout at some point on his journey and benefited from the same lack of recording devices as before."

Ryan steepled his index fingers and rested them against his lips.

"It has to be Edwards, following the same route back to whatever rock he's been hiding under for the past week. I want every police officer in the North East to be on alert for that vehicle, or vehicles matching the same description, if not the same number plate. Get a description out to the press and tell them to offer a reward for anybody who can offer a genuine sighting of that Mercedes."

"Already done," Lowerson said, a bit smugly.

"Then go back over all the footage on the roads leading from the Styford Roundabout during the relevant timescale when MacKenzie was taken. We didn't have a chance before, but now we know that Edwards exchanged her red Fiesta for a dark blue Toyota. Hundreds of possibilities just got whittled down to one."

"The analysts are going over it now." Lowerson nodded towards a small group of three crime analysts with their noses pressed to the screens of their respective computers, rolling through hours of CCTV footage. "They'll let us know the moment they spot it, then we'll know the direction and—hopefully—the destination it was headed towards."

"Good. Good," Ryan repeated, thinking of the million other plates he had spinning in the air. "I heard from Pinter, down at the mortuary. He's sent through an updated report on Beth Finnegan's post-mortem but I'd advise you to digest your pizza before reading it."

Lowerson had a flash memory of Bethany's headless body and felt cheesy tomato repeat on him.

"How about her mother?"

Ryan rubbed the heels of his hands against itchy, bloodshot eyes.

"Devastated," he said shortly, not wanting to think back to that painful conversation. Of all the people he had met, he would remember Kelly Finnegan as one of the strongest, as well as the most vulnerable.

Lowerson rubbed his hands on a paper napkin, feeling at a loss.

"I spoke to the Solicitors Regulation Authority," Ryan changed the subject. "I've asked them for a complete list of Elaine Hoffman-Smith's clients, aside from the Hacker. They won't agree to send it without an appropriate warrant, which I've already put in motion. With any luck, we'll have a magistrate sign it off first thing tomorrow. After then, we'll be able to confirm whether Jimmy Moffa and Keir Edwards shared the same solicitor. If they did, I'll be asking for copies of all communications. If Frank is right, she was the one who put the two of them in contact and passed messages between them."

Lowerson nodded thoughtfully, thinking back to the woman he had interviewed that very morning, which felt like a lifetime ago now.

"Yes, I think she would be capable of that."

"If she was, she's responsible for facilitating the deaths of—" Ryan caught himself before saying *two* women. "At least one woman, since Edwards broke free."

"He could be out there now, killing another one." Lowerson turned towards the window.

Ryan followed the direction of his gaze and saw their tired faces reflected in the darkened glass. He looked away and began to call up the next document on his screen, this time a summary from one of the reader-receivers containing a log of telephone calls received following a *Crimestoppers* reconstruction that had aired on national television a couple of days earlier.

"Whoever it is, they don't deserve what's about to happen to them."

Jimmy Moffa employed a daily housekeeper called Irene, who began work just before seven a.m. so that she could be on hand to prepare a healthy breakfast and take care of his immediate needs. She stayed all day to ensure the house was kept to his exacting standards of cleanliness and then departed in her three-door Mazda on the dot of four-thirty, in time to miss the traffic on her way home. Irene was a woman in her mid-fifties with a sharp eye for dust and grime, and a selective eye for all other things. If Jimmy's clothes were often stained with blood, she reasoned that he must have been walking through a rough area of town. She tutted and fussed and baked pies that he never ate but enjoyed having for their homely scent. She chose to deceive herself about the true nature of her employer's business in exchange for the generous wages he paid, and she slept like a baby every night.

Irene was the only person granted entry into Moffa's home, except on very special occasions. His bodyguards were required to sit or stand outside the exterior doors.

On their first day at work, he walked them through the house so that they knew its layout and where to come running in case of an emergency but, for the most part, he relied on high-spec radio devices to communicate with them. Moffa kept his home and his business strictly separate and all negotiations or meetings were conducted at the All-American Diner, never inside the suburban bubble he had created for himself. Jimmy's reputation was so fearsome that nobody had ever tried to gain access to his home, so he had never lived to regret the lack of security inside his house, or his own complacency.

Until now.

When his driver-cum-bodyguard took up his position beside the front door, Moffa was tempted to break his own rule and ask Tony to come inside and hover around somewhere within shouting distance. But to do so would mean losing face in front of Edwards, who was leaning against one of the pillars and watching him with growing amusement in his enigmatic black eyes.

"Shall we?" Edwards motioned towards the front doors, which were polished oak with grandiose plaster pillars and had miniature potted conifers to either side. "Or did you forget your key, sweetheart?"

"I'm wondering whether you're worth the effort," Moffa replied, with an air of challenge.

Edwards merely smiled. "I'll leave that for you to decide."

Meanwhile, Tony was sweating inside his new suit as he watched their exchange. He was painfully aware of the fact that he was way, way out of his depth. What had started out as a temporary gig—just something well-paid to tide him over—was spiralling into a nightmare beyond his control and Phillips' words replayed in his head.

What would your da' say, if he could see you now?

Tony swallowed and tugged at the collar of his shirt, wishing fervently that he hadn't lied about his past exploits to get the job in the first place.

"Ah, Mr Moffa?"

"What?"

"I, ah…" His eyes darted across to where Edwards watched him like a spider. "Do you need me to stay all night?"

Edwards laughed heartily and pursed his lips. "I'm not as young as I used to be," he admitted. "But I'm sure I could give it a go."

Moffa ignored him, feeling like the butt of a private joke.

"He'll be leaving in a couple of hours," he replied, tersely. "I expect you to drive Mr Edwards back to his car. Stay here until then and let me know immediately if anybody approaches or if you hear from the boys at the Diner. Rory is around the back and Kieron is on the side gate. You're not alone," he lied, keeping one eye on the man who listened intently.

Tony felt much better. The Hacker might be one of the country's most dangerous men but nobody had ever said he was stupid and he wouldn't try anything when the odds were stacked against him, four to one. But Moffa turned away with a sick feeling in his stomach because he knew that Rory and Kieron weren't manning the doors tonight at all. They were probably sitting in front of their television sets without a care in the world as they enjoyed a night off.

It was time to roll the dice and see where they fell.

CHAPTER 18

An hour passed slowly for Tony, who stood shivering beneath the glow of a faux nineteenth-century gas lamp outside Moffa's lavish front door. April was a cold month in the North of England and the night air billowed against his bulky frame, whipping roses into his cheeks so that he appeared much younger than his years. He'd forgotten to bring an overcoat and gazed longingly at the Porsche sitting on the driveway, imagining the warm gust of a heated air conditioning system, but he daren't risk leaving his post. One of the other guards might wander around the house, grass him up and that would be the end of *that*.

Funny that he hadn't heard them talking on the radio, he thought suddenly, and tapped the earpiece tucked around his left earlobe.

There was no sound from the other guards, but Moffa's broad Mancunian accent carried clearly through the airwaves. Tony tried not to focus on the words but on the tone. So long as Jimmy sounded happy enough, he wasn't needed. He didn't want to focus on the details of Moffa's conversation with Keir Edwards, for the same reason that he didn't particularly want to hear about anybody else's sex life; it was like listening to his parents going at it or, worse still, his *grandparents*. Everybody knew it happened but the least said about it, the better for all concerned.

Tony winced as the conversation became more explicit and he felt like the worst kind of voyeur. He was starting to wonder if there was a volume control on his earpiece, when the voices stopped.

Just like that.

Tony tapped his earpiece again and wondered if there was a problem, caught in an agony of indecision. Jimmy had made it very clear that the house was out of bounds unless there was an absolute emergency.

Was this an emergency?

His boss might have turned off his radio communicator so that he could enjoy some private time with his guest. It would be mortifying if he barged inside the house and interrupted them. It would be the end of his career and who knows what else Jimmy might inflict as punishment for his stupidity?

On the other hand, Keir Edwards was a serial killer.

Killer being the operative word.

Tony picked up his heels and jogged around the side of the house to seek advice from the other guards, feet crunching against the gravel. Bright, motion-sensor spotlights flickered on as he moved, shining through the windows of the shadowed house and helping to pinpoint his location to anybody who might be watching from the interior.

He rounded the back of the house and skidded to a halt. The wide, semi-circular terrace was completely in darkness except for a weak, greenish-yellow glow from three more old-fashioned lamps that served as a design feature rather than an effective light source. Solar-powered lighting dotted the expansive lawn and he could see low-lying mist swirling over the grass as night dragged into a new day, but he couldn't see any other security guards. The chair positioned beside the rear patio doors where Rory should have been sitting was empty and there was no sign of Kieron manning the side gate.

Tony's stomach lurched and he stood there for a moment, frozen.

Should he go into the house to help his boss? Something was very, very wrong and there was still no sound from the radio in his ear.

His body made the decision before his brain caught up, and his feet edged backward. With panting breaths, he turned and sprinted back around to the front of the house, towards the car sitting on the driveway ready to take him back to safety. The lights flamed into life again as he flew across the ground and grasped the door handle. He cast furtive glances behind him, at the big oak doors with their ridiculous knockers in the shape of golf sticks and felt a moment's guilt at the prospect of abandoning Jimmy to his fate.

Then it was overtaken by a much stronger survival instinct.

He wrenched open the car door and threw himself inside, slamming it behind him and fumbling with the interior locks. He risked another glance towards the house and was relieved to see that nobody had come to stop him.

He reached down to grasp the ignition key but his fingers clawed the air instead.

"Wha—?"

He caught a flash of movement in the rear-view mirror but it was already too late. The blade sliced a clean arc from ear-to-ear, severing his jugular and blood began to pump from his neck in an ocean of red, staining the cream leather seats.

PC Paul Cox had been a dispatcher at the Northumbria Constabulary Control Room for nearly three years and he was growing weary of the monotony. It went against his natural circadian rhythms to be up so late at night and he was seriously considering putting in for a transfer. His wife was expecting their first child and he didn't want to be working such unsociable hours, dealing with the dregs of society, when he could be at home with her and their new bundle. He smiled at the prospect, then his face fell as an alert came through from one of the local alarm monitoring centres.

He recognised the address of the so-called emergency straight away. It was the fourth time this year that Jimmy Moffa had cried wolf, just because he enjoyed seeing hardworking police officers running around after him.

Sick bastard.

Well, not this time, Paul decided. Three false alarms and the official guidelines permitted him to refuse a police response, and that's exactly what he was going to do.

With a superior smirk, he moved on to the next emergency.

MacKenzie had developed hearing like a bat over the past seven days spent in captivity. The instant she heard Edwards' soft tread on the grass outside the front door, she sat bolt upright and moved quietly to the bedroom window. She stood with her back flush to the wall and inched forward so that she could peer through the tiny gap. It was dark outside and the moon was hidden behind a blanket of thick cloud, providing little relief.

Even in the darkness, she knew that he had sensed her watching him.

"Hello, Ruth," he called up to the window, and she plastered herself back against the wall, angry to have been found out so quickly. "Have you missed me?"

She heard his soft laughter carrying on the night air, then the jingle of a key turning in the lock downstairs. A moment later, the front door slammed and she squeezed her eyes shut, listening for the sound of his tread on the staircase. There hadn't been enough time to recover her strength, she thought desperately, but she hurried into position anyway.

Her legs trembled as fresh adrenaline coursed through her body, pushing through the leftover groggy feeling from the sedative he had given her. She realised what he had done when she'd first woken up with a throbbing headache and a dry mouth but she hadn't been surprised or angry. In fact, she was relieved it hadn't been anything worse.

Now that the grogginess had worn off, she readied herself for action, arms poised and feet placed in the spot she had earmarked as being the perfect distance to strike.

Feet coming up the stairs.

She stood perfectly still in the silent room, eyes accustomed to the darkness and trained on the locked door. Then, at the top of the stairs, she heard him turn in the opposite direction towards the bathroom. A moment later, there came the sound of a bath running.

"Goodnight, Ruth!"

MacKenzie felt hot, angry tears flood her eyes and course down her cheeks. After all the build-up, he'd denied her another opportunity to break free. It would have to be the morning, now, but she didn't know how long her courage would last and a lot could happen in the small hours of the night.

"Gotcha!"

Lowerson bellowed across the breadth of the Incident Room and did a funny little victory dance on the spot. Ryan watched him indulgently and then crooked a finger.

"Jack, stop pretending to be Shakira and get your arse over here."

"It's often been said that my hips don't lie."

"Among other things," Ryan muttered, with a raised eyebrow towards the freshly printed papers Lowerson was clutching in his hand.

"These are screen shots of the Toyota." Lowerson waved them triumphantly. "We've got it heading south along the A68 from the Styford Roundabout on the night MacKenzie was taken, as far as Carterway Heads." He named a small village where the road once again became a crossroads. "We checked it against footage for the missing Mercedes and—guess what? It took exactly the same route during the early hours following Beth Finnegan's murder. We've traced the Mercedes as far as Carterway Heads again, thanks to a CCTV camera at the petrol station which is angled to face the road. It seems to take a right turn, bearing west towards the North Pennines and Weardale."

Ryan was less familiar with that part of the countryside, which was the usual province of Durham Constabulary. He rose from his chair to walk across to the enormous map on the wall so that he could get his bearings and one of the first things he noticed was that the village of Blanchland lay only a few miles west of Carterway Heads.

His heart began to pound.

"What about after then?" he asked, already reaching for the phone in his jeans pocket to put a call through to Anna. "Where did the cars go after Carterway Heads?"

Lowerson tried not to feel deflated. It was progress, just not quite enough.

"That's all we've got so far. That whole area is like a black hole—for mobile signal, for CCTV, you name it. Edwards probably chose it because he knew it would act like a force-field."

Ryan gave him a look.

"This is the twenty-first century. Edwards can't survive indefinitely without using modern conveniences. He'll need to go to the shop, access money from somewhere, fill up on petrol. Actually, there's a thought," he said. "Call the petrol station at Carterway Heads and see if he's been in."

Lowerson nodded and made a mental note.

"I'll speak to Faulkner and ask him to focus his attention specifically on the soil samples usually found in that part of the world. We might be able to narrow the field even further."

Lowerson flicked a finger against the papers he held in his hand.

"There's something else," he added, before Ryan hit 'call' on his mobile phone.

"What's that?"

"We've got the Mercedes heading back north through Carterway Heads at 21:17 this evening. I've got the analysts working to trace the other checkpoints, to see where it went after then. But…"

"He went hunting again," Ryan concluded, wrapping his fist around the mobile phone in his hand. "What he did to that girl wasn't enough to sustain him so he came back for a second helping."

Lowerson looked down at his shoes, trying not to think about what could be worse than decapitation.

"I don't understand how it wasn't…wasn't…"

"What? Enough for him?" Ryan put in, then shook his head. "That's because you're thinking like a normal person, Jack, and you need to remember that Keir Edwards isn't normal. He's barely even a person."

He could hear them going at it again on the other side of the wall, and it was the same sound every time.

Thud, thud, thud.

The sound of the bedstead hitting the wall, mingling with the sound of her gasping cries. It didn't sound like pleasure, he thought. It sounded like the keening wail of an animal in pain or the awful whine of foxes mating in the night. He often heard them, from his bedroom window.

And still, the noises continued.

Thud, thud, thud.

At first, he tried holding his hands against his ears or burying his head beneath the bedclothes, but nothing drowned out the sound. The partition walls in the old house had been added sometime after it was first built and they were cheap and thin, providing no sound insulation at all.

After another minute, the banging stopped and he heard other sounds. The groan of floorboards in his mother's bedroom as the man stepped from her bed, followed by the creak of the bedroom door opening. Three heavy steps to the bathroom next door and the sound of a tap running and water sloshing onto the floor. A moment later, the tinkle of piss hitting the porcelain and the toilet flushing.

Three steps back to the bedroom.

The sound of her pleading with him to stay with her, *just for a little while*. His curt response in the negative, then clothes rustling as the man tugged on his trousers and prepared to leave.

More pleading.

Please, Charles.

He heard her tugging at the man, pawing at him to stay with her and he felt sick with disgust. His body jerked in reaction as he heard the unmistakable sound of flesh hitting flesh, followed by her whine.

Footsteps clattered down the stairs with indecent haste and there came the dim sound of the front door opening and slamming shut again.

He froze in his bed and waited for the final, inevitable sound that would lull him to sleep. He was not disappointed, for his mother began to sob harsh, gut-wrenching tears that carried through the wall and filled the air of his room, flooding his young mind with the sound that would haunt him for the rest of his life.

MacKenzie woke with a start, covered in sweat. Her first thought was that she had not meant to fall asleep. Her second thought was gratitude that she was still alive and he hadn't stolen into her room to murder her while she slept. Anything was possible when you were dealing with a disordered mind like Edwards'. She cast dazed eyes around the room, seeking out the source of the sound that had woken her, creeping softly from the bed to stand in the centre of the cracked wooden floor.

It came again, a long wailing cry.

The sound of it tore through her, piercing the silent night air like a banshee. She stumbled to the window and shivered against the night air, peering through the gloom to see if an animal had come to harm. But she realised that it had not been a fox, not this time. The cry had come from the room next door, where Edwards slept.

CHAPTER 19

Wednesday 6th April

Less than five miles away from the old farmhouse where MacKenzie was being held captive, Anna awoke in a strange bed in the village of Blanchland to the sound of birdsong, alongside an odd, rumbling sound which reminded her of a steam engine. Rubbing sleep from her eyes, she padded barefoot down the narrow stairs of the holiday cottage to seek out the source.

She found Phillips half-sitting, half-lying in an armchair he had dragged from the sitting room into the hallway to face the door. After Ryan's call last night, they had re-doubled their efforts to go through the old files from Edwards' past, searching for any mention of a location in the North Pennines region to the west of Durham. When nothing had turned up and they were unable to stay awake any longer, Frank had resolved himself to protect her in Ryan's stead but Anna was glad to see he had obviously fallen into a fitful sleep at some point during the night and his snores now filled the small house. She stood quietly watching him, wishing there was something she could do to help put an end to his heartache, when she noticed that he clutched a firearm against his chest.

Her heart skidded at the sight of the small handgun, which she knew to be the same model as Ryan's, currently in a locked box upstairs. The Glock-17 was the semi-automatic pistol of choice for Authorised Firearms Officers at Northumbria CID and she knew that Phillips, Ryan and MacKenzie had completed their training at the same time before she'd met any of them. It was the kind of knowledge she often forgot about, having rarely seen them holding a gun or having one anywhere within sight. It was only when she queried the little metal box Ryan chose to bring with him from their cottage in Durham that he had reminded her of its contents.

The knowledge left her feeling uneasy.

That same uneasy feeling returned as she watched her friend sleeping, his jowly face relaxed into a puppy-dog expression that was at odds with the dangerous weapon clutched in his inert hand. Her father had owned a hunting rifle and she remembered a time when she and her sister had been young, when he'd taken them out to a nature reserve with the long rifle slung over his shoulder.

"*Where are we going, Dad?*"

"*You girls need to learn how to defend yourselves,*" he'd slurred, through his usual measure of alcohol before midday. "*Can't rely on anybody else and there's evil in this world.*"

He'd ushered them under the fence into the wildlife reserve, a place where rare birds and mammals should have been free to roam without man's interference. Her father had warned them to keep back while he shot a kestrel sitting in a nearby tree.

The image of its falling wings was something she had never forgotten.

Another memorable occasion had seen Ryan bursting into the tower room at Lindisfarne Castle two years ago, firing his Glock to wound a man who would have killed her without his intervention. At the time, she was grateful to be alive and didn't overthink the processes. But now that she knew Ryan better, she realised how much it must have cost him to pull the trigger. He devoted his life to preventing human destruction so the very act of discharging a weapon went deeply against the grain, as it did for the gentle man snoring in the armchair in front of her.

Anna clutched her woollen jumper close to her chest and stepped forward, making little sound. She hesitated, then reached out her hand to remove the handgun, intending to put it on a shelf somewhere out of reach. The moment her fingers brushed the metal, Phillips' eyes flew open and his hand tightened.

"Morning, lass."

Ryan stared at the buttons on the vending machine and eventually selected the one claiming to dispense espresso.

As he watched the steaming liquid hit the bottom of a white polystyrene cup, his thoughts wandered back to the investigation. He and Lowerson had been up all night with a skeleton team of staff trying to trace the whereabouts of the stolen Mercedes. They strongly believed it to be the vehicle Edwards was using and they had made some progress tracing it as far as the A69 heading towards Newcastle. There were three smaller exits from the motorway before the next main checkpoint, where a camera would have caught the Mercedes if it had driven past. Since there was no such recording, they had to assume Edwards exited earlier via one of the smaller back roads. Any one of them would lead to the area around Ponteland, Darras Hall and the western edge of the city around CID Headquarters, so it was another kick in the teeth to know that Edwards had practically been on their doorstep and they still hadn't captured him. Lowerson was in the process of obtaining footage from any local businesses or private residences along those back roads, but it was a slow and difficult task which had reaped few rewards so far. Privately, they realised that any progress they made in finding the Mercedes would come long after Edwards had finished his exploits the previous evening, whatever they might have been.

They were constantly playing catch-up.

Ryan experienced a sense of insult to go alongside the feeling of acute failure that intensified with every passing day. Logically, he knew they were doing everything they could. No expense had been spared in their quest to bring

MacKenzie home and Edwards into custody. But still, this was a very personal investigation and he felt a peculiar sense of ownership regarding Keir Edwards. He didn't usually care about who received credit for a final collar but, in this case, he wanted to be the man to plant a boot in the small of Edwards' back as he kicked his sorry arse back into prison—preferably one with a wire net covering over its exercise yard.

It was becoming increasingly clear that, despite all their hard work, the forensic examinations, the television, newspaper, digital and radio coverage, they remained at the mercy of a man who had gone deep undercover with all the skill of a veteran spy. If Faulkner came through with a lead on the geographical origin of the mud found on the Toyota's tyres, they could start going door-to-door in a manageable radius. Likewise, if they stumbled across something buried in one of the old files, it was possible it might lead them straight to Edwards' front door.

On the other hand, they might search and find nothing, leaving him free to kill again. Time was not on their side. Ryan had hoped and believed that Edwards would have contacted them with his demands, using MacKenzie as leverage for a free ticket out of the country or something equally outlandish. It would have been welcomed by all of them because then there would be a chance she was still alive.

But Edwards had not been in contact and Ryan's confidence in his own assessment began to wane.

He took a sip of the heinous coffee and frowned, reconsidering. Perhaps Edwards *had* made contact, just not in the usual manner. It was common for serial killers to employ a signature with each of their victims—Shipman liked his victims to be fully dressed and sitting up to resemble his dead mother; the Wests preferred to bury their victims vertically rather than horizontally—and Keir Edwards was no different. In his case, the signature had always been the anatomically precise way in which he mutilated his victims using a surgical scalpel, after first dosing them with a sedative. Edwards had employed the same methodology with each of his five previous known victims, including Ryan's own sister. In the case of his most recent victim, Beth Finnegan, he had not been able to access his usual pharmaceutical sedative and had opted for an excessive volume of alcohol, according to the toxicology analysis in Pinter's pathology report. It was a variation but still broadly in keeping with his MO. Likewise, he might not have had a scalpel or surgical saw available but he had performed a decapitation and incisions on her body with a high level of skill, which was in keeping with his style of killing.

However, he had added the word 'INVICTUS', which was a departure from his usual style and signature method. Ryan thought at first it had been a last-minute message to show his dominance but now he wondered whether there was something more to it than met the eye.

He drained his coffee, crumpled the cup and tossed it into the recycling bin.

Much as he hated to admit it, perhaps it was time to delve into the psychology of the man he hunted.

He detested head-doctors at the best of times and resented the wishy-washy diagnoses they dished out to desperate murder detectives looking for a miracle to help them track down killers who would be found quicker with a bit of common sense and hard graft. But, since he was a pragmatist, Ryan admitted that any insight could be useful so long as it was not given disproportionate weight over hard facts and evidence.

He turned and went in search of somebody who could read minds.

***

MacKenzie was startled awake by the sound of Pavarotti singing 'Nessun Dorma'. Rather than being able to enjoy his rich tenor, she was almost deafened by the sound of music playing so loudly the notes became distorted. There was no escape. As before, Edwards had positioned an old cassette radio directly outside her bedroom door so she was forced to listen until he grew tired of torturing her.

She tore scraps of material from what was left of the mattress covering and rolled it up into two balls, which she stuffed in her ears to dim the noise. It was all she could do and at least it gave her the comforting feeling of being underwater.

She examined her ankle and wondered whether Edwards' mood was linked to the night terrors he had experienced during the early hours of the morning. It was a question many psychologists must have asked before: did serial killers suffer terrible nightmares? She would have thought Edwards slept peacefully each night, judging by his general demeanour and feckless attitude towards the sanctity of human life. But, on the other hand, she couldn't forget his ear-splitting shriek and she wondered whether the dead came back to haunt him—with their white, expressionless eyes and trailing fingers—after all.

She truly hoped so.

To wake himself up, Ryan made a quick detour to the shower room in the basement. It was situated next to the locker room and had all the decorative charm of a Stalinist reconstruction but he didn't let that put him off and gladly stepped beneath the hot spray in the hope that it would cleanse his mind as well as his body.

It was there that Lowerson found him, calling out above the pounding water to attract his attention.

"*What*?" Ryan shouted. "Wait a minute."

He grabbed a towel and slicked back his wet hair, feeling a bit more human and a little less bleary-eyed.

"What did you say?"

Lowerson looked worried.

"It's the Mercedes, boss. It's been found abandoned on some farmland, not far from here."

"That was quick. Get Faulkner or one of his team to meet us there," Ryan ordered. "Is the scene secure?"

"The farmer walked all over it before he thought to call the police but the first attending officer has closed off a perimeter."

Ryan towelled off and wandered through to the locker room to rummage around in his locker for a change of clothes. He found a pair of jeans and a thin wool jumper, which would have to do.

"Who's the farmer?"

"Some bloke called Healey."

"That wouldn't be Roger Healey, would it?" Ryan replied, tugging on a pair of socks.

"Uh, yeah, it is," Lowerson replied, wondering what he had missed along the way. Catching the look, Ryan elaborated as he tied the laces on his boots.

"You have to ask yourself why Edwards would be driving to some farmland, rather than heading into town where there's an abundance of dark-haired young women he can maim and murder. Why would he be driving to a patch of farmland, Jack?"

Lowerson realised he still had a lot to learn. "He was meeting someone?"

"You've got it. I can also tell you Roger Healey is more than just a farmer. He's a local businessman who wasn't above the odd pyramid scheme in the nineties, or a boiler room fraud in the noughties. A man like that doesn't mind turning the other cheek for the right price. I don't know if he has it in him to get himself mixed up with anything violent," Ryan mused, trying to remember the man he had met only a handful of times. "I seem to remember he was more of a tweed-jacket-wearing sort."

Then Ryan remembered something else and made an immediate connection.

"He's also president of the plushest golf course in the city. D'you know who else likes to work on his handicap at the weekends? Jimmy Moffa." He smiled grimly. "If we're right and Moffa has been financing Edwards all along, they'd need a safe, private meeting place that was off-road, to be sure that some unlucky pedestrian wouldn't stumble across their little tête-à-tête. Neither of them would want to meet on their own turf, so they'd have looked elsewhere for some neutral ground. Healey is the perfect choice for something like that. He probably woke up this morning, found the Mercedes still on his premises and promptly shat himself, because it's been all over the evening and morning news. He couldn't get rid of the car, so he's hoping to come off looking like a concerned citizen by calling it in and playing dumb."

Lowerson listened with admiration. "How do you put that all together so quickly?"

Ryan huffed out a laugh and led the way from the locker room.

"You develop a nose for sniffing out the bullshit," he said roundly.

Irene turned her little mint-green Mazda into the driveway of Jimmy Moffa's home as she sang along to *Dolly Parton's*

Greatest Hits. It was just shy of seven o'clock and she was running exactly on time, as usual. She noticed that Jimmy's big black Porsche Cayenne was still sitting in front of the house and that one of the garage doors had been left wide open, which gave her pause. The garage was filled with expensive cars and motorcycles and, although it was an upmarket area, there were still plenty of thieves about. It wasn't like Jimmy to tolerate that kind of carelessness and she'd have to mention it when she saw him.

She parked the Mazda in her usual spot and reached for her handbag containing the comfy slippers she liked to wear while she was cleaning and a stash of her favourite snacks. She paused to refresh her coral pink lipstick and to fluff her hair, then made her way across the gravel towards the front door.

She was still humming *Nine to Five* when she caught sight of the heavy blood trail leading from the Porsche towards the front door, which stood wide open. When she turned bemused eyes to look at the car, she saw that the windscreen was painted red with spattered blood, so thickly congealed that she couldn't see through it. With wide, frightened eyes, she crept forward to look through the open doorway and into the marble entrance hall beyond. Drying bloodstains cut across the gleaming tiles in a single, thick track towards the staircase.

Phillips stood at the window in the small galley kitchen of the holiday cottage, looking out at the North Pennines Area of

Outstanding Natural Beauty stretching from the village of Blanchland down into the Derwent Valley towards Weardale. The village itself was nestled beside the river in a wooded section of the valley and was a chocolate-box example of medieval conservation, being mostly built from the ruined stone of a twelfth century Abbey which formerly dominated the landscape. Location scouts for period dramas loved its unspoilt character and old-world charm but all Phillips could see was a pretty collection of houses surrounded by acres of land and forest filled with ruined farmhouses and outbuildings where an escaped convict could hide.

It was like searching for a needle in a haystack.

Anna brought him a cup of sugary tea and looked out at the panorama.

"Beautiful," she remarked, watching sunlight spread over the fields and trees.

Phillips drank some tea and felt the liquid warm him from the inside.

"Denise is somewhere out there." His eyes swept over the landscape. "After what Ryan told us last night, we know they're somewhere south of the Styford Roundabout and west of Carterway Heads. Hell, they could even be in this bloody village."

Anna shivered involuntarily. "We'll search," she said quietly, setting her cup on the window ledge. "We'll do it now because neither of us will rest easy until we've eliminated the possibility."

Phillips nodded and downed his tea like a pro.

"Let's go."

What the Chief Constable didn't know couldn't hurt her. At least, that was what Anna and Phillips told themselves as they questioned the villagers of Blanchland. It was still early yet, not even eight o'clock, but they were past caring about social niceties. There was a killer running amok in the area and the residents deserved to know about it. Admittedly, there was a fine line between fearmongering and genuine policing, but it was one they were willing to cross in their effort to find Denise MacKenzie. As Phillips had said from the start, there was no stone he would leave unturned.

But after all the kind offers of tea and biscuits, all the concerned nods and promises to be vigilant, they found themselves walking a full circle around the village without uncovering any information that was remotely useful.

"What we need is a pub," Anna thought aloud.

Phillips barked out a laugh.

"I couldn't agree with you more, but it's a bit early, don't you think?"

Anna grinned and shook her head. "Don't worry, living with Ryan hasn't reduced me to drinking before 9 am. I only meant that the village pub is the epicentre of all local gossip. Particularly in a place like this." She gestured around the main square, with its tea room and gift shops. "People live here, they come to visit and they pass through it. It's a local hub."

The Lord Drewe was a stately historic drinking hole with an enormous fireplace and a rustic atmosphere but it was presently closed and so they decided to pay a visit later in the day, to give the locals a chance to warm up and loosen their tongues.

As they walked back, Phillips seemed to notice the details of the village for the first time.

"Why are all the doors painted the same colour?"

"It's a conservation village, owned by the Lord Drewe Trust," she explained. "There are strict rules on the upkeep and look of the place, to preserve the historic ambiance."

"Huh," Phillips grunted.

It was very pretty but his mind wandered back to the old street where he had been born and he couldn't help but think it had more character. Horses for courses, he supposed.

"Who the hell was Lord Drewe, anyway?"

Anna stopped mid-step and realised that it was the first history question she hadn't been able to answer for quite some time.

"No idea," she said, honestly. "I'll have to look it up."

They strolled back along the cobbled roads towards the holiday cottage and to the stack of files awaiting them, hoping that one of them would hold the key to Edwards' location. As they passed by the visitors' car park, they failed to see the large, rain-damaged sign providing a potted history of the village and the charity set up in the name of the Lord who used to own all the land thereabouts. At the top of the sign there was an image of the Drewe coat of arms, which was also scattered throughout the village on plaques and walls. Above it was written their family motto in Latin:

INVICTUS MANEO

CHAPTER 20

Ryan never made it to see Farmer Healey or the grey Mercedes abandoned on his land. Leaving that task in Lowerson's capable hands, he made a shorter journey from CID Headquarters towards the exclusive housing estate of Darras Hall, to one of its premier but most disreputable addresses.

A crowd had already assembled outside the imposing black gates of Jimmy Moffa's home, clamouring to see what had befallen a man whose shady dealings had been widely known. They wittered about it 'only being a matter of time' before he got his comeuppance, and about the sad decline of the local area thanks to people of 'his sort'. Others speculated whether his house would be offered for sale for a cheap asking price, always on the look-out for a bargain.

Ryan parked his car further down the street, since the driveway was part of the crime scene, and opted to walk the remaining distance. This stretch of Darras Hall was filled with expensive houses but Moffa's was the only house on the street with a high perimeter wall; too high for anyone to climb without injury. Several cameras were positioned at the entrance and at intervals in between a series of enormous plasterwork lions and what appeared to be gargoyles emulating those gracing the north wall of Notre Dame.

Ryan approached the crowd with an ominous expression.

"Move along please!"

Instead, they surged forward with a series of inane questions.

"You are obstructing a crime scene," he said. "If you don't go about your business, I will call a squad car to come and arrest any of you who continue to cause a nuisance. A police caution goes on record," he added silkily.

With satisfaction, he watched them scatter like rats deserting a sinking ship.

"Yates?"

As he approached the gates to Moffa's big, semi-circular driveway, he recognised the police constable guarding the scene.

"Yes, sir."

Melanie Yates was a capable woman, whom he'd already earmarked as having a lot of potential after some solid police work over the past couple of years and particularly over the course of the last week. He also happened to know that Lowerson had been working himself up to asking her on a date for at least six months.

Ah, youth.

"Report please," he said, and looked over her shoulder towards the house, getting a lay of the land.

"At approximately ten past seven this morning, Control Room received a report of suspected foul play from a Mrs Irene Duggan. She works as the housekeeper at this address, sir. After arriving for work at seven o'clock, she immediately noticed bloodied drag marks leading from the car to the entrance of the property. Mrs Duggan ran immediately to a neighbouring house to call it in."

Ryan nodded, searching the vicinity for a woman matching her description. He spotted Yates' squad car parked further up the street and assumed Irene Duggan was in there.

"Is the housekeeper in your car?"

"Yes, sir. My partner is with her, taking a preliminary statement."

"Good. Have you been inside?" He nudged his chin in the direction of the house, which was a large red-brick affair with white balustrades and columns in a mix of Grecian and Colonial styles.

Yates adopted a shuttered expression and concentrated on relaying the facts, whilst blocking the images branded in her mind's eye.

"Yes, sir. My partner and I were the first officers to attend the scene. We met Mrs Duggan at the neighbouring property"—she pointed to the gigantic house directly across the street—"following which we accessed the property using the secure code provided by her."

Ryan nodded, watching her face lose a bit of colour.

"Take your time, constable," he murmured.

Yates nodded gratefully.

"It's…sir, it's a bloodbath in there. It appears to me that at least one person died in the Porsche sitting on the driveway, losing a lot of blood judging by the interior. That person seems to have been dragged from the car inside the house, although I can't imagine why."

Yates swallowed.

"We needed to ascertain whether anybody was in urgent need of medical attention, so we took the decision to enter the house. I'm sorry, sir, we weren't wearing protective clothing."

"Don't worry about that now," he said. "Keep going."

"Yes, sir. We followed the obvious drag marks through the hallway and upstairs to the first floor. The blood trail leads to one of the main bedrooms, where we found…we found…"

Yates thought for one humiliating moment that she would vomit, but then Ryan placed a hand on her shoulder, to focus her attention elsewhere.

"Alright now?"

"Yes. Sorry."

She still looked a bit peaky, he thought, but she'd hold up.

"How many victims?"

"Two, as far as I could see. We—they were found in a—compromising position," she stuttered, trying to find a professional way to say that Jimmy Moffa and his driver had been staged on the bed in a gross parody of lovemaking, their dismembered bodies covered in blood and gore.

Ryan read between the lines.

"Anything else?"

"We—ah—we didn't enter the room, sir, but we made a sweep of the property to ensure there weren't any other individuals on site. It was clear."

Ryan blew out a long breath.

"Alright, Yates, you got through it. That's the first step on the ladder to becoming a murder detective; you have to be able to look at a scene like that with dispassion."

And preferably without passing out, he added to himself.

"Thank you, sir."

With that, he left Yates to her sentry duty and stepped over the threshold.

Ryan pulled on his protective overalls and crunched across the driveway, careful to walk on the plastic sheeting that had been laid down to protect areas of interest pinpointed by a series of yellow markers. He spotted Tom Faulkner standing among a group of similarly clothed CSIs outside a tent that had been erected to protect the scene around the entrance to the house. Weathercasters had predicted a fine, sunny day with scattered showers, which naturally meant that the people of Newcastle took up their umbrellas and prepared themselves for torrential rain. With a dubious glance towards the sky, Ryan had to agree that things did not look good. Storm clouds were gathering high in the sky, blotting out the sunshine and threatening to wash away DNA evidence. He heard the tread of heavy footsteps and half-expected to see Phillips ambling along behind him but was disappointed to find that it was only Jeff Pinter, come to look at the bodies *in situ*.

"Morning, Ryan!"

The Chief Pathologist loped across the drive in an oversized suit, waving a small holdall in his right hand.

"Morning, Jeff. Thanks for getting over here so quickly." He shook the man's hand and together they walked the remaining distance towards the group of forensic specialists.

"Tom," Ryan said, as he shook the senior CSI's hand and nodded to the rest of his team.

Faulkner frowned. "Where's Frank?"

Ryan rolled his shoulders. "Indisposed," he said curtly. He would not speak of Phillips being suspended. As far as he was concerned, it was a travesty and he didn't want news of it spreading any further than necessary.

"Let's get this over with, shall we?"

A cursory glance at the interior of what had been a brand-new Porsche SUV told Ryan that whoever had died inside that vehicle had not died well. Blood coated much of the driver's area and was spattered in an arc across the steering wheel and dashboard, reaching as far the windscreen.

"Throat slashed, I reckon," Faulkner said.

Ryan nodded, eyes tracing the line of blood leading from the car to the front door.

"The body was moved. Why? It's a messy, heavy job. Why not just leave it in the car?"

"Couldn't say." Faulkner pulled a face as he thought of the possibilities. "Perhaps he was trying to hide it?"

Ryan looked pointedly at the obvious blood trail and Faulkner shrugged.

"Let's take a look inside the House of Horrors."

Ryan led the way inside the double doors of Moffa's house, resplendent with abstract art on the walls and glitzy gold clocks which were probably the real thing but were so garish they appeared fake. The hallway was large and square, tiled with white marble to match the walls and giving the place a clinical, hospital feel. Directly ahead was a staircase leading to a galleried landing on the first floor and an ostentatious Louis XVI chandelier hung in the centre of it all.

Pinter raised his eyebrows at the décor. "It's, ah—"

"Yeah," Ryan snapped. "I'm not interested in how the man lived. I'm interested in how he died."

With extreme care to avoid touching the banister or the crusting trail of blood tarnishing the pale grey carpet on the stairs, they made their way to the first-floor master bedroom.

The first thing Ryan felt when he opened the door to Jimmy Moffa's bedroom was overwhelming relief. The tableau was viciously brutal but he didn't feel a tenth of the emotion he had experienced when they discovered Beth Finnegan's body. He found that he could look at the details of the room with his usual objectivity tempered by compassion. Moffa might have been a criminal who lived off the misery of others but he could not bring himself to feel anything but pity because nobody deserved to die in that way.

Edwards had excelled himself this time, Ryan thought. Not only had he staged the bodies in a coarse rendition of intimacy to remove their dignity, he had also removed most of their organs and propped what looked like liver, kidneys and intestines in a neat row at the end of the bed.

As he moved further into the room and the putrid stench of death became almost unbearable, he realised that the organs had been arranged into another Latin word: MANEO.

"Oh, dear God," Faulkner choked out, breathing through his teeth. "What does it mean?"

"It means, 'I remain,'" Ryan answered. "Putting the two words he's given us together it forms a well-known Latin motto: 'I remain unvanquished.'"

Ryan tore his eyes away from the gory spectacle.

"Pinter?"

The pathologist looked across and only his eyes were visible between the hairnet and face mask he wore, but they were wide with shock. For a man who dealt with death every day, that was quite something.

"Thoughts?"

Pinter just spread his arms in an all-encompassing gesture.

"Where do I start? The smaller body appears to be Moffa, but with all the blood..." He shook his head. "I can't tell you anything quickly. There are too many variables. But at a glance, it looks like the taller of the two is the man who was dragged in from the car. You can see the throat has been severed all the way to the trachea," he held out a retractable pointer, and Ryan made a polite sound of agreement. "As for Moffa, any one of these injuries could have killed him. I'll need some time."

Ryan nodded and turned to leave.

"Let me know when you've got an update. I have to go and inform two gangland bosses that their baby brother has been murdered."

It wasn't every day you made that kind of house call.

CHAPTER 21

Fate finally smiled upon Ryan in the form of leading forensic psychologist Doctor Alexander Gregory. The man was the closest thing Britain had to a criminal profiler since the demise of the government's fledgling effort to establish a criminal profiling think-tank to rival the FBI Behavioural Science Unit. Their efforts had come to a disastrous end following a series of failures and the wrongful imprisonment of innocent men and women. Yet one specialist remained, having had the foresight and wherewithal to realise that his methods were superior to those peddled by his former colleagues and having resigned years before the project's ultimate closure. Gregory worked on a freelance basis now and his skills were in high demand from police forces across the globe. It was therefore a stroke of incredible good fortune that he happened to be visiting Durham University to give a series of guest lectures when Ryan looked him up.

They agreed to meet outside the Palace Green Library at two o'clock, which allowed Ryan time to gather some files together and recover from his unnerving interlude with Jimmy Moffa's grieving brothers. There was one positive he could take from his visit to their lair, and that was the sure and certain knowledge that the Moffa brothers' hatred of him was now outweighed by their hatred of Keir Edwards. Of course, until the DNA results came back, nobody knew for sure that Edwards was the man to blame, but he was certainly the most likely candidate. Without his name ever having been spoken, it was clear from their faces and demeanour that the Moffa brothers knew it too and it was some comfort to know that, if Ryan failed to find the Hacker first, they would undoubtedly be waiting in the wings to deliver their own punishment to the man who had killed their brother.

Ryan was inclined to think that police custody would be the safest place for Keir Edwards now, in more ways than one.

The skies were still heavy, with rainclouds threatening to spill over at any moment, casting a daytime shadow across the wide expanse of lawn known as Palace Green. In years gone by, it had been a bustling marketplace but it was now the domain of bookish types coming in and out of the library, or tourists snapping pictures before the rain forced them indoors. Ryan had no idea what Gregory looked like— he hadn't had the time to scroll through online images—but the man's stellar reputation preceded him. He imagined it would come with a hefty fee but, if necessary, Ryan would pay for it out of his own pocket. Anything to help bring MacKenzie home.

As the rain finally started to fall, first in a drizzle and then in fat droplets, he ducked beneath the cover at the entrance to the old library and watched passers-by run for cover. He looked out for a man he imagined to be somewhere in his fifties or sixties, perhaps with a stoop and a paunch to go with his bifocal lenses. Anyone who had developed the kind of professional résumé that Gregory had would probably be getting on a bit.

"Chief Inspector Ryan?"

He turned at the sound of his name, spoken with the kind of transatlantic drawl many Englishmen developed after spending years abroad. It spoke of international schools in Switzerland, or winters spent skiing in St Moritz.

The man looked nothing like Ryan had imagined. They were of a similar height and Gregory appeared to be somewhere in his late thirties, much like himself. He sported an enviable tan and a pair of assessing green eyes that instantly put Ryan on edge.

"Yes?" he said, tersely.

Gregory held out his hand, smiling inwardly at the automatic defensiveness he found all the time with new clients.

"Alex Gregory." They exchanged a firm shake. "Shall we see if there's a coffee shop nearby?"

The two men walked briskly through the rain and found a quiet, unpretentious little place where they could sit without fear of being overheard and they both ordered strong coffee.

At least that was something they could agree on, Ryan thought, making a conscious effort to push his natural cynicism to one side.

"Thank you for finding the time to see me," he offered, with a grateful smile for the waitress.

"Not at all," Gregory replied. "I've been following your case with interest."

"Then I don't need to tell you about the kind of animal we're dealing with."

Gregory smiled over his cup.

"What I read in the papers is often a far cry from the reality." He raised an eyebrow towards the file Ryan had brought. "Is that for me?"

Ryan placed his hand on the top of the file, strangely unwilling to part with it.

"Look, doctor—"

"Call me Alex."

Ryan wished the man wouldn't be so damn *affable*. It made it infinitely harder for him to stereotype him as an interfering know-it-all if he went around behaving reasonably.

"Alright. Look, we normally work with another psychologist, attached to the department." Ryan thought it was best to come straight out with it. "I haven't cleared this with the Chief Constable but it's within my power to instruct you, so I'm going over her head on this."

Ryan frowned at himself. What on earth had possessed him to confess that? He'd only been in the man's company for five minutes, and already he was spilling his guts.

Gregory read the confusion and irritation on Ryan's face and smiled inwardly.

"Why don't I put your mind at ease and tell you a bit about myself and my methods?"

Ryan said nothing but picked up his coffee and took a sip, which Gregory took as an invitation to proceed.

"I started out with a degree in law," he said. "Then I realised that I was more interested in getting inside the heads of the criminals I was reading about, so I cross-qualified in psychology and did my clinical training." He rattled off a list of well-regarded hospitals in London, then shrugged. "I worked for two years at Broadmoor Hospital before I transferred to the Criminal Profiling Section at the Met—"

"Oh yeah?" Ryan's ears pricked up. He'd cut his teeth at the Metropolitan Police over ten years ago. "When were you there?"

"Back in 2003," Gregory replied. "A couple of years before your time, I think."

Ryan nodded.

"Organisation and funding failed the Criminal Profiling Section, so I wanted to strike out and try my hand at freelance. I found myself most interested in what makes criminals tick and in prevention rather than cure, although I admire those who try."

Ryan raised an eyebrow at that. Gregory was the first psychologist he'd ever spoken to whose approach mirrored his own. Usually, it was all about curing the diseased mind of the criminal, but here was a man who was concerned with protecting others first.

"What happened to you?" Ryan asked, forthrightly.

Gregory smiled and cocked his head at Ryan.

"Are you sure you're in the right business? With perceptive skills like that, you should be doing my job."

Ryan raised his coffee cup in salute.

"You're right, of course," Gregory said, and his eyes dulled slightly at the memory. "But that's for another day, over a glass of single malt."

"Fair enough."

"For now, let me say that my basic approach is a combination of different psychological models. I've worked alongside criminal profiling units around the world, chief inspector—"

"Ryan."

"Ryan," he corrected. "And I've learned lessons from all of them. The basic idea is that Keir Edwards' behaviour reflects his personality." Gregory leaned back in his bistro chair to make himself more comfortable. "The Americans believe there are four 'crime phases' that help us to gain an insight into a serious offender's personality."

"I'm familiar," Ryan interrupted him. "It was part of a weekend 'teambuilding' course I was subjected to, a few years ago."

Gregory surprised him by laughing richly.

"You're a tough nut," he observed, and took another sip of coffee. "Alright, I'll assume you know all about the importance of ascertaining the subject's fantasy; it's the reason they act on some days and not others, it informs their overall plan. Thereafter we look at the methodology of killing and disposal, and then post-offence behaviour."

"Edwards is a textbook case on three of those," Ryan commented. "His method of killing and disposal are well documented. He likes his victims to be found quickly and he doesn't mind a bit of media coverage afterward. He loves the limelight, in fact. But the problem I'm having is understanding his overall plan, his underlying fantasy, you might say. I know that he goes for young brunettes, but I don't know why. I can make assumptions but his personal history is so limited, I can't say for certain. It won't help me find him, per se, but I need to understand why he's deviated from his usual MO."

Gregory nodded his understanding.

"Yes, I see that Edwards gave interviews to various news outlets while he was incarcerated and the information he gave rarely matches, which makes it difficult to sort truth from lies," Gregory said. "I don't ascribe to the organised—disorganised model of criminal behaviour. That is to say, I don't think there is a straightforward split between 'organised' criminals who are believed to know right from wrong, who leave little evidence and who have no sense of remorse, versus 'disorganised' criminals, who have traditionally been painted as young, mentally ill, or under the influence of drugs or alcohol."

"What makes you so different?" Ryan queried, finding himself drawn into the discussion despite his previous doubts.

"I have accumulated a body of empirical, peer-reviewed research that shows serial killers of Edwards' kind are almost always *organised*. Although killers like him might appear insane to the layman, they are rarely 'insane' in the clinical or legal sense of the word. The positioning of the bodies and the method of killing all demonstrate organisation. What sets killers apart from one another is the *way* they interact with their victims."

"What do you mean? The way they kill them?"

"Not only that," Gregory explained. "I'm talking about control, sex, mutilation, execution and so on. I group together different offender behaviours using these specifics. For instance, were any of Edwards' previous victims sexually assaulted prior to death?"

Ryan thought back and shook his head slowly.

"He has a very sexualised mode of expression," he murmured. "But, now I think of it, there was never any evidence of sexual assault, only severe mutilation and sometimes decapitation, as with his most recent female victim."

Pity flickered in Gregory's dark green eyes, and Ryan was perversely glad to see it because it made him human like the rest of them.

"What about his latest victim?"

Ryan finally relinquished his file and pushed it across the table for Gregory to leaf through. He signalled for more coffee while Gregory silently turned the pages with agile fingers, his face completely impassive as he surveyed the photographs taken of Jimmy Moffa earlier that day.

Eventually, Gregory shuffled the papers back into a neat pile.

"It's an interesting departure from his normal victim type, but I presume his purpose was to execute Moffa for different reasons. Relating to money, perhaps? Have you had a post-mortem done?"

"It's in progress."

Gregory nodded.

"I anticipate there will be no sexual assault, despite the highly sexualised manner in which the bodies were staged. It's a little theatre production he's put on especially for you rather than for his own pleasure. It's likely that he's completely impotent, which contributes to his feelings of anger and aggression. The degradation he inflicted on Moffa and his bodyguard was a form of punishment, for their virility, apart from anything else."

Ryan listened intently, watching him with clear grey eyes.

"More interesting is his systematic slaughter of beautiful, brunette women," Gregory continued. "His approach is unusual because it crosses the ordinary boundaries of the 'types' of serial killer I often find operating worldwide."

"I thought for a person to be defined as a serial killer, it was just a case of killing three or more victims, with a cooling off period between each one." Ryan's brow furrowed.

"That's part of it," Gregory agreed. "But from a psychological perspective, we usually find three main types of serial killer: the thrill seekers, the missionaries, and those obsessed with power and control. In the case of Keir Edwards, you have a man who seems to enjoy the thrill of evading capture and taunting the police, as well as the power and control of torturing his victims. This methodology indicates a real enjoyment of the process of killing, rather than a swift, execution-style murder."

As they delved into the subject, neither man noticed that the rain had stopped.

"Why the protracted, drawn-out killing? Why not something quick and simple?"

"It's likely that he derives his pleasure not from normal sexual acts, but from the act of killing itself, so he likes to make it last," Gregory said, conversationally. "He probably has a paraphilia of some kind. His sexual gratification—if any—comes from exposure to internal organs or the mutilation of them. You said he was a consultant doctor in the A&E department before his arrest?"

"Yes," Ryan nodded, thinking of Edwards roaming about the hospital wards with distaste. "He had an exemplary record and he was loved by all who met him."

Gregory gave a knowing smile.

"Yes, that'll be the veneer he developed, to operate in society and continue to have access to what he enjoyed. You see, he probably enjoyed being exposed to serious injuries on an hourly basis. All the car crashes, all the gangland stabbings, the gunshot wounds—"

Ryan pressed a hand to his temple as he tried to step into the mind of a disturbed man.

"It's probably what kept him going between kills," he realised suddenly. "I thought it was the memories of his previous victims because Edwards kept stacks of photographs taken from each scene. They're in an evidence box, back at CID," he murmured. "But it's more than that, isn't it? He didn't just manage to go without killing for months at a time because he had his photographs to keep him company, he managed it because he had fresh images provided on a rotating belt, every day."

Gregory polished off his coffee and thought that he'd found a quick study.

"Exactly. If you want to find out why he kills brunette women, you need to find out what happened to cause his killing spree in the summer of 2014, which was out of character for him. It's likely he'd been quietly picking off victims for years without detection, feeding his addiction and his needs. What happened to make him snap and go on what appeared to be a frenzied spree without his usual cooling off period?"

Ryan paled slightly.

"We know he had an interest in sado-masochism as early as ten years ago," he muttered. "We always assumed he was a sick bastard but there were no other victims to pin on him; just the ones from 2014, including my sister."

"I'm sorry," Gregory said, and meant it.

Ryan wanted to stay focused. "You're saying it's possible that Edwards was a different kind of killer before 2014. One who killed quietly, without the pomp and circumstance, without the need for attention and recognition that seems to define him now. There'll be a life event that affected him, maybe *released* him, from his earlier restraint?"

"That's what I'm saying." Gregory tapped a finger on the sheaf of papers. "But I'm going to go through this and any other information you can give me to see what else I can do for you. I'd suggest you look for the brunette who ruined him for all other women—it's usually the mother."

Ryan shook his head. "We haven't been able to locate Edwards' mother," he said. "We know that Keir Edwards isn't the name he was given at birth; he changed it when he was sixteen and went to boarding school. Before then, he was Charles Adams."

"How intriguing," Gregory remarked, green eyes shining with renewed interest. "Why would he do that?"

"That's something we clearly need to find out," Ryan agreed. "His mother is listed as Jenny Adams and his father is listed as unknown on his birth certificate, which doesn't help. We've tried and failed to locate Jenny Adams and there was never anybody present at any of his hearings or at the trial. There's no log of anyone by that name having visited him in prison."

"She could be dead," Gregory surmised, and Ryan nodded.

"Ah, we haven't talked about your fee..." Ryan began, but Gregory simply smiled.

"This one's on the house."

CHAPTER 22

By the time Ryan returned to CID Headquarters, the rain had completely dried up. He decided to take that as a good omen, until he was intercepted by Lowerson who was waiting anxiously for him in the foyer.

"Don't tell me another Moffa brother has been found dead?"

"No, sir, but the Chief Constable wants a word."

Ryan sighed deeply. "Alright, Jack, thanks for the heads-up."

Ryan stopped at the gents to splash cold water on his face once, twice and then a third time. Coffee had ceased to work and his body was going through the unpleasant stages of severe sleep deprivation but he would not allow himself to shut down. Not yet.

The reflection staring back at him from the mirror was of a pale man, blurry-eyed from stress and fatigue and fit to drop. But he scrubbed a hand over his face and went in search of the Chief Constable, hoping that nothing else had arisen to add to their already back-breaking workload.

He tapped on the appropriate door.

"Come!"

Why did they never say 'in'? Ryan wondered. Every commanding officer he'd ever had spoke like a corporal from the 1940s. He entered the office and came to a shocked standstill as he was faced with a roomful of people and what appeared to be a professional film camera.

He pointed an accusing finger towards it.

"What is *that*?"

Morrison walked around to the front of her desk and sent him a warning glance.

"Ryan, this is Lucy Pembleton from BBC Newcastle and Martin Sampson from *The Journal*. They're here to do an interview with you."

"Was it too much for you to discuss this with me before arranging an ambush?"

Morrison had the grace to blush.

"Would you excuse us for a moment?" Smiling genially, she led Ryan back out into the corridor. As soon as they were out of earshot, he rounded on her.

"This is low, even for you."

"I'm sorry if this has taken you by surprise," she said, in a calming tone. "There wasn't a lot of room for debate. The Commissioner wants to restore public confidence and the best way to do that is to speak directly to the public."

"Send one of your other dancing monkeys in there," Ryan replied. "I'm sure you can find plenty of people to toe the party line. Count me out."

He started to turn away but the tone of her voice stopped him.

"*Please*! I don't like this any more than you do," she said furiously. "Do you think I want to waste time on media calls? Of course I don't, but life is full of moments like this. Sometimes, you just have to jump through the damn hoops."

"I've never jumped through a hoop in my life and I don't intend to start now," he said flatly.

"You're so bloody superior!" she exclaimed, and he raised an eyebrow. "Too good for televised appeals, too busy for the mundane crap that the rest of us have to deal with?"

He shuffled his feet. "That's not what I meant."

"Isn't it?" she raged. "Do you think I like having to dance to the Commissioner's tune? Do you think I like suspending one of my oldest friends? Of course I bloody don't! But life is full of bitter pills we have to swallow."

Ryan folded his arms and waited for her to finish.

"The fact remains that you're the SIO heading Operation Ireland. You've got the gravitas and experience and, much as you might not like it, much as I might not *understand* it," she added, with a short laugh, "the public seem to love you. So, for once, set aside your lofty ideals and bring this home for the department."

Ryan stared at her flushed face for a moment and then gave a brief nod.

"Alright, if you need a show pony, I'll trot out some tricks."

Phillips and Anna surrounded themselves with paperwork at the holiday cottage in Blanchland. Rain pattered against the single sash window in a steady fall and the radio played easy-listening music in the background. By mutual consent, Phillips had siphoned off the more explicit imagery relating to Edwards' past offences so that Anna could concentrate on her portion of the papers in much the same way as a history research project, without any of the trauma.

"There are hardly any personal records in Edwards' paperwork," Anna remarked. "Is that usual?"

Phillips looked up and scratched the top of his balding head.

"I wouldn't say it's usual, no. We did a thorough search," he assured her, "but the best we could drum up was Edwards' birth certificate from the public records office, listing his date of birth and the fact he was born locally in Hexham, his mother's name and her date of birth. There was a change of name by deed poll, back in the early nineties."

Anna shuffled through the papers to find the photocopies.

"Oh yes, I see it. Why would he change his name completely?"

"Who knows?" Phillips shrugged. "Perhaps he wanted something fancier. You have to give it to him, 'Keir' does have a certain ring to it."

"A certain ring of madness," Anna muttered, as she thumbed through the papers. "How about schooling? I can only see a record of his time at boarding school, which coincides with the same year he changed his name."

"There were no nursery or school records before then."

"How is that possible?" Anna queried. "Surely he would have attended a local primary school or something?"

Phillips lifted a shoulder.

"No doubt he's educated, so we assume there was either a blip in the records or he was home-schooled to a decent standard. It's a sorry state of affairs, love, but a lot of kids just fall through the gaps. Social Services aren't overrun with staff and they weren't any better resourced twenty-five years ago."

Anna tugged at her lower lip.

"Something feels off," she murmured. "Shelford School is one of the premier boarding schools in the country. Why the sudden change at sixteen? And who paid for it? Was his mother well off?"

Phillips abandoned his own work for a moment to talk it through.

"We don't know much about Jenny Adams. He's never once spoken of her, or mentioned a father figure of any kind. Essentially, we know nothing about Keir Edwards until after the age of sixteen. For all the years when he was still little Charlie Adams, your guess is as good as mine. We did a full run on Jenny but we don't know where they lived or what she did for a living. There aren't any income tax records or NI contributions since the mid-eighties, when she was living at home with her parents and working as a barmaid. They're now deceased."

Anna wandered across to the kettle in the tiny kitchen, set it to boil, then turned to lean back against the kitchen counter.

"What about the hospital records, from when Jenny Adams gave birth? Surely they'd have made a note of her circumstances—of a father, of a home address?"

"If they did, they don't have it on file anymore. We already checked all those things, when it all blew up the first time around. Like I say, the only thing we could dig up was that birth certificate and then the change of name document because they were both listed as public records. We have his school years at Shelford and all of his life as Keir Edwards the doctor, followed by his life as the Hacker."

"Shelford might be able to give us a clue," Anna said. "They might be able to tell us who paid the bills. Maybe they'll have an address on file?"

Phillips rubbed his eyes.

"Ryan called them, back in the day. They refused to give out personal data, even with a warrant. They took it all the way to court, as I remember, and won on the grounds that it wasn't pertinent to Edwards' prosecution. In fairness to the judge, it probably wasn't important then to know all about his family history so long as we could prove he killed those five women, but it's sure as hell important now."

Anna stirred instant coffee into two flowery porcelain mugs with a thoughtful expression.

"Here's what strikes me as odd," she said, setting a steaming cup in front of Phillips. "Why would Shelford School fight so hard not to give away the information? Surely, they would want to be seen to be cooperating with the police?"

Phillips took a sip, swilled the coffee in his mouth. "You're right. It doesn't make sense."

The light of battle began to shine in her dark brown eyes. "You call Ryan and ask him to get a warrant for the release of records at Shelford. I'm going to ring the school administrator and see if I can't persuade them in the meantime."

"You're a force to be reckoned with and no mistake."

"You're not wrong, Frank."

Ryan felt like the Christmas turkey, all trussed up in the shirt and tie he kept hanging in his locker in case of emergency situations such as the one he found himself facing now. He was seated in front of the window in Chief Constable Morrison's office and somebody had dragged a plant behind him so its half-dead leaves flapped against the back of his neck. A camera assistant fussed over him and tried to fiddle with his hair but one ominous look had put a stop to that.

The room was full of superfluous staff, nagging him to project an air of *quiet authority* without seeming too *arrogant.* Somebody who identified themselves as the new media liaison briefed him about what he could and couldn't say, as if this was his first time discussing an active investigation, or indeed his first time in front of the camera.

Just before the cameras began to roll, Morrison requested that he stop glowering.

Glowering?

The newscaster for BBC Newcastle pouted, massaged her cheeks and made wide 'o' shapes with her mouth before she tossed her hair and made a little rolling signal to the cameraman. It was her first real break reporting on the biggest serial killer case for a decade, talking to a famously private detective who looked like he had just walked off a Hollywood film set. As far as ratings were concerned, it was gold dust.

"Ready?"

She didn't wait for Ryan's response but immediately dived into her pre-rehearsed introduction to the segment that would be shown on every news programme available.

"Two years ago, the people of the North East lived through a summer of terror while former doctor Keir Edwards unleashed a brutal killing spree claiming the lives of five young, innocent women, before he was eventually stopped by one man, Chief Inspector Maxwell Finley-Ryan. In a tragic twist of fate, his own sister was the Hacker's final victim—"

"Stop."

Ryan's voice cracked like a whip.

"I won't have my sister's memory used as a cheap way to boost your ratings," he ground out. His anger was cold and quiet. "And you have an entire taskforce to thank for bringing Edwards to justice, not just me. I won't be party to this."

The newscaster flushed an embarrassed shade of red and bristled in her chair. Morrison could see the situation becoming nuclear very quickly, so she stepped into the breach.

"I don't think it's necessary to rehash old news," she said firmly. "Our agreement was to issue an appeal about the present investigation."

The woman shot Ryan a look that was both wary and resentful, before firming her glossy lips and giving the motion to start rolling the camera again. It was remarkable, Ryan thought, how her face transformed into a caring façade, for all the world as if she gave two hoots about the lives of those who were lost. She began again, in the same serious, haunted tone as before whilst looking directly into the camera.

"Two years ago, in the summer of 2014, the North East was terrorized by a series of brutal killings, all perpetrated by the same man. Formerly a doctor, Keir Edwards became known as the Hacker thanks to the particularly vicious methods he used to torture, maim and kill five women before his killing spree was brought to an end by a task force headed by Detective Chief Inspector Maxwell Ryan, who joins us now."

Ryan could have laughed. It all sounded so neat, so packaged, so far removed from the memories he carried of that last day.

She turned in her seat and faced him.

"Chief inspector, thank you so much for agreeing to talk to us today."

She waited for some sort of polite rejoinder but when none was forthcoming, she gritted her teeth and carried on.

"The Hacker was imprisoned following his trial back in 2014 and the North has been preoccupied with other sensational crimes while he was incarcerated at HMP Frankland, the maximum-security prison where he was supposed to spend the rest of his life. Little did any of us know that he had been hatching a plan to escape. Did *you* have any inkling that the Hacker was capable of such a coup?"

Ryan detested her choice of words, but he answered the question.

"Anything is possible, with enough money and connections," he said. "There have been several high-profile helicopter escapes around the world, so he hasn't broken new ground there. Durham Police have the investigation into his escape fully in hand."

Morrison closed her eyes and was grateful that his nonchalance managed to project the impression that the Prison Service weren't at fault. It was a good start.

From Ryan's perspective, his words were chosen in the full knowledge that Keir Edwards might be listening, whether on the radio or television. If that was the case, Ryan wanted him to know that he wasn't special; he was just another commonplace killer.

"That is reassuring to know." The newscaster flicked a glance towards the camera again, entranced by her own reflection in the lens. "But these are worrying times, I'm sure you'll agree. Detective Inspector Denise MacKenzie is still missing and presumed dead—"

"Nobody presumes she is dead," Ryan interrupted. "We assume that DI MacKenzie is still very much alive. We are searching for her, night and day."

His voice softened just in case, by some miracle, MacKenzie should be listening too. He wanted her to know that she was not alone and she was not forgotten.

"But, with the Hacker's history," the newscaster persisted, "it's surely becoming less and less likely that your colleague will be found alive?"

"Keir Edwards is a functioning psychopath," Ryan said simply. "He acts according to a specific plan, not in frenzy. He is intelligent and methodical, and I know he understands the value of keeping DI MacKenzie alive in order to bargain with us."

Clever, Doctor Gregory thought later, when he saw the interview running on the evening news. Ryan managed to flatter Edwards' ego at the same time as issuing a warning.

"But, how do you explain the deaths of Bethany Finnegan, a mere girl of fifteen, and James Moffa, a well-known restauranteur and local businessman?"

Sticky ground, Ryan thought.

"The death of Bethany Finnegan not only shattered her family and friends, but every member of Northumbria CID and all the police men and women of the neighbouring forces who are working tirelessly to find her killer. My heartfelt condolences go out to her mother, whom I've spoken to personally. I want to reiterate my promise to her and to tell her that Beth was and is important to all of us. It is my strong belief that her death followed a specific plan and that was to mimic the death of one of Edwards' previous victims, Natalie Ryan."

He would not say 'my sister.' He wouldn't be able to continue, if he did.

"Edwards killed Bethany Finnegan to strike out at the officers who originally brought him to justice in 2014, and in particular…me."

The newscaster turned shocked eyes to the camera, then back to Ryan with excitement.

"You believe the Hacker's recent killings represent an elaborate vendetta against you and the task force who incarcerated him the first time around?"

"Yes, that's what I believe."

"How do you explain the death of James Moffa?"

Ryan ran his tongue across his lower lip.

"We are still in the process of investigating his murder and I cannot say for certain at this stage that Keir Edwards is responsible for his death. That being the case, I do not plan to comment further."

The newscaster gave him a petulant look.

"I understand that you would like to make a very personal appeal to the Hacker, if he is listening?"

Ryan turned his flinty grey stare fully at the camera.

"If Edwards happens to be listening to this interview, I want to give him one, very important message. You've won. I'll say it again: *you've won.* I speak on behalf of all the constabularies in this region, in fact across the country, as well as myself, when I say that you have demonstrated your superiority."

Once again, Gregory smiled as he watched him play the right notes.

"You could have fled the country at any time. You could have killed Denise, our friend, whenever you wished. We know that and we respect it."

Ryan leaned forward in his chair, speaking earnestly to the camera and whoever might hear him.

"I understand that your actions over the past week have been a demonstration of your power and we have failed to apprehend you. But now is the time to claim your prize." Ryan's voice became more persuasive, dripping like honey. "Your anger is towards me, personally, as the man who put you in prison. I stopped you…I nearly killed you, as you nearly killed me. That gives us a connection and I understand that I am no better than you."

Ryan thought the words would choke him but he forced them out.

"Let's stop wasting time and cut to the real fight, the real reason you're still hiding out in the North East. If it's me you want, Keir, then I invite you to call me directly on the number for the Incident Room and I will meet you at any place of your choosing, on the condition that you do not harm another person until then. You *remain unvanquished*," Ryan said, "but for how long? Call me to find out."

Ryan sat back and made a weary sweeping gesture with his hands, signalling for the camera crew to stop the tape. The room was buzzing with excitement as the journalists imagined the headlines they could spin but Morrison stepped through the chattering crowd to put a slim hand on Ryan's tense shoulder.

"Thank you," she said.

He rubbed a tired hand across his eyes. "If that doesn't tempt him, I don't know what will."

"What happens now?"

"Now, we wait."

CHAPTER 23

Just before six o'clock, Anna stood beside the radio in the small kitchen of the holiday cottage, the paperwork forgotten. Her hands shook against the countertop as she listened to the news bulletin that had interrupted the constant stream of easy-listening classics she and Phillips had been using to keep them company through their repetitive task.

"Did I—did I just hear Ryan send out a challenge to Keir Edwards?"

She turned wide, horrified eyes towards Phillips and he hurried across the room to take her arms in a gentle grip.

"It's talk, lass," he tried to reassure her. "It's fighting talk, to flush the man out. Ryan knows Edwards has an ego the size of a small planet and he's using it against him. He knows if he lays down a challenge, Edwards won't want to lose face. He's baiting him, that's all."

Anna held a trembling hand to her lips.

"Frank, what if Edwards finds him? What if it isn't all talk and Ryan wants to face him, to risk everything to see it through to the bitter end?"

Phillips pulled her into his barrel chest for a bear hug and ran a hand over her head, much as he might have done his own daughter, if he'd ever had one.

"I don't know if I ever spoke to you about the last time," he said quietly, casting his mind back. "But on the night Natalie Ryan died, I was nearly too late. Ryan had called for back-up but I was driving and in those days, we didn't have hands-free. I had an old brick of a thing and we had clocked off our radios. I dropped him off at Wharf Square in the early hours and we were both exhausted. I carried on driving home, thinking that his sister would be there to look after him. We never thought—"

Phillips drew in a shuddering breath, filled with remorse.

"We never thought Edwards would stalk Natalie. It didn't fit the pattern of his crimes but his intention was payback. He planned to kill Natalie in front of Ryan and he managed that much. He planned to kill Ryan next and, by rights, he should have. To this day, I don't know where Ryan found the strength—he was badly injured and souped up with sedatives."

Anna knew that part of the story and the image of Ryan reduced to crawling, barely able to raise his head, was almost unbearable.

"He found the strength," Phillips continued, in the same quiet tone, while Anna rested her head on his shoulder and allowed herself to be held. "God knows how but he found the strength. By the time I got his message and rushed back, Natalie was dead and he had his hands around Edwards' neck. The man had four broken ribs and his pretty face was smashed up. I've never seen that look on Ryan's face before or since. It was pure hatred, sheer animalistic hatred. In that moment, I believe Ryan could have killed him."

"Ryan always told me you stopped him," Anna whispered.

"No, lass. Wild horses couldn't have stopped him unless he'd wanted to be stopped. The fact is, Ryan just doesn't have it in him to kill, not in cold blood like that. He'd already overpowered Edwards and that was enough. Even through his pain and his grief, lying in a pool of his sister's blood, he still had enough humanity to step back."

Anna let the tears come and held on tightly.

"That was back then, before he'd met you," Phillips added. "He has a lot more to lose now. There's no way he'd sacrifice everything he has with you, the chance of a happy future, just to finish Keir Edwards."

"I hope you're right, Frank."

The radio had been playing all day long.

At some point, MacKenzie heard him walk along the landing corridor to stop and remove the cassette playing Pavarotti but instead of unlocking her door to allow her the usual toilet break, or some measly scraps to eat, he had merely turned up the radio and walked away. She didn't know why today was different or why he had deviated from the usual prison routine but she knew that it didn't bode well.

Edwards never left food or water in her room; whenever he brought her anything she was required to eat and drink it straight away and he removed the crockery afterward. Consequently, she hadn't drunk anything for hours—perhaps nearly twenty hours—and she had a pounding headache as well as a scratchy, dry mouth.

She closed her eyes and did something she hadn't done in years: she meditated.

MacKenzie had laughed at it before, putting it down as one of those 'New Age', jingle-jangle, tie-dye fads. But as she forced her mind to drown out the deafening sound of the radio outside her door and asked it to ignore the clawing hunger in her stomach, she began to see what all the fuss had been about.

In her mind, she walked along the beach at Caherdaniel, the village where she had been born in County Kerry in Ireland. She and Frank walked hand-in-hand along that bracing, windswept stretch of the Atlantic coast, arms swinging like a couple of teenagers. She smelled the sea air, she felt its breath against her face and the warmth of his rough palm clutching hers…

The loud music was interrupted by a news bulletin.

"This is Mike McCauley's Drive Time Show! If you're just tuning in, we'll be playing five of your favourite power

ballads, back-to-back, right after this important news bulletin which was pre-recorded earlier today."

MacKenzie's eyes flew open.

She hadn't heard any news of the outside world in over a week and she waited impatiently for the report before Edwards could come and turn it off.

"Chief inspector, thank you so much for agreeing to talk to us today…these are worrying times…Detective Inspector Denise MacKenzie…missing and presumed dead."

The voice of a female reporter boomed into the hallway and through the door to MacKenzie's cell, where she listened with detached fascination as they spoke of her in the same way she had discussed the dead, so many times before.

When Ryan's voice followed, it was all she could do not to burst into hysterical tears at the welcome sound of it.

"Nobody presumes she is dead," he said, and his words rang out clearly. *"We are searching for her, night and day."*

MacKenzie started to sob uncontrollable tears of relief.

They had not forgotten about her.

Nobody presumes she is dead. We are searching for her, night and day.

She held her head in her hands and listened to the remaining interview, hearing for the first time the names of the victims whose blood had covered Edwards' clothing the previous two nights. She said a quiet prayer for the girl Bethany, who had died simply because she looked a certain way and Edwards needed somebody to kill. She even prayed for Jimmy Moffa's soul despite all he had done because, as Ryan had said that very morning, nobody deserves to die like that.

Then she heard Edwards' footsteps charging upstairs. She braced herself against the bed and tried to hold Ryan's voice inside her head, to take it with her when she needed it the most. It was the closest thing she had to Frank, and she knew they would be working in partnership.

Unexpectedly, she heard Edwards stop beside the radio but he did not switch it off.

He turned the volume back down to a manageable level as the interview drew to its conclusion and he heard the final, most important piece of Ryan's message.

"*I want to tell him one, very important message. You've won… your actions over the past week have been a demonstration of your power…now is the time to claim your prize. I stopped you…I nearly killed you, as you nearly killed me. That gives us a connection and I understand that I am no better than you.*"

MacKenzie listened with bated breath, realising that Ryan was bargaining with Edwards to keep her alive.

"*If it's me you want, Keir, then I invite you to call me directly on the number for the Incident Room and I will meet you at any place of your choosing, on the condition that you do not harm another person until then. You remain unvanquished but for how long? Call me, to find out.*"

There was a momentary pause before the radio presenter began again, recapping for listeners who had just tuned in. He was cut short as the radio was finally turned off and silence fell in the old farmhouse. MacKenzie pushed her worn-out body up from the bed and took up her usual position, in case Edwards decided to pay her a visit after all. Although Ryan had pitched his message exactly right, playing on Edwards' personality traits to perfection, it was impossible to know how he would react.

As he had said once before, he could kill her any time he chose.

Once again, she heard him move off down the hall but this time he turned into one of the other bedrooms to drag an old chest of drawers out onto the landing, straining to wedge it against the locked door to block her inside. Then came the sound of his footsteps, quick and light on the stairs before she heard the front door open and close again.

MacKenzie rushed to the tiny window and watched him stride around the edge of the house, towards the other side where she had found the worn pathway leading back towards the road. He must have hidden his car somewhere down there, she realised, and he was heading out.

She sent up a final prayer, and this time it was for Ryan.

"Sir!"

Ryan spun around from the display board in the Incident Room, where he'd been adding a series of notes following his consultation with Dr Gregory earlier in the day.

He saw one of the telephone operators waving a feverish hand to attract his attention and hurried across the room.

"What is it?"

The operator covered the small mic attachment on his headset and simply said, "It's *him*."

Ryan felt an odd little tremor, as if somebody were walking across his grave, but he motioned for the operator to hand over the headset and he slid into the chair instead. Nearby, people dropped what they were doing and gathered around to listen to the conversation.

Before speaking, Ryan checked to make sure the call was being recorded and traced, then took a deep breath.

"This is Ryan."

"I received your invitation."

It had been over a year since Ryan had last seen or heard from Keir Edwards. Even then, it had been within the safe confines of a prison interview suite, while the other man was handcuffed and guarded by two armed officers. It had been unpleasant to see him face-to-face again after the trial but somehow listening to his voice at the other end of the telephone line was even more so. The medium lent a strange sort of intimacy to the situation, one that he could happily have done without.

"So I see," Ryan replied. "I presume you're calling to arrange a meeting?"

Edwards chuckled hoarsely. "Not so fast. Why ruin all my fun? I've always considered you a worthy opponent, Ryan, so don't disappoint me now. I'm ringing because I've decided to give you a clue."

Ryan continued to listen, all the while watching Lowerson for any news of the caller's whereabouts.

"Landline," the other mouthed, and immediately began running a search for its registered address.

"You're getting sentimental," Ryan said aloud. "It isn't like you to want to play games."

"I think it's only fair to give you a sporting chance," Edwards snarled, gripping the telephone so tightly his knuckles turned white. "And there's a very big incentive for you to perform well in this little game."

Ryan's stomach plummeted. "Oh? Do I get a certificate?" He tried to keep his voice strong but it wavered because he knew what was coming next.

"I will kill Denise MacKenzie at eight o'clock this evening if you do not arrive, unarmed and alone, to replace her. That gives you nearly four hours, Ryan. Plenty of time for a man of your capabilities, I should have thought."

Ryan's eyes flew across to Lowerson, who scribbled a note on his pad to say, 'PETROL STATION, CARTERWAY HEADS'.

"Tell me the clue."

"It's very simple," Edwards said, with a laugh. "Just ask the wife of my first victim where to find me."

"Your first victim was a young woman and she was unmarried."

"It's a conundrum, then, isn't it?"

Ryan heard his soft, malicious laughter down the line and he asked the most salient question.

"How do I know MacKenzie is still alive?"

"You'll have to take my word for it," Edwards replied silkily.

"No offence, but your track record doesn't exactly inspire trust in our relationship."

"Ouch," Edwards rasped. "That really hurt."

"If she's hurt, in any way—"

"Save your threats for somebody who cares," Edwards interjected. "The clock is ticking."

With that, the line went dead.

CHAPTER 24

Ryan made an immediate request for an armed response team to be sent to the petrol station at Carterway Heads but by the time they drove from the nearest police station to that remote spot, the Hacker was long gone. At the petrol station, they found a young service assistant hunkered down behind the counter with blood streaming from a deep cut to his eye, courtesy of an 'angry-looking' man who had walked into the empty shop and demanded to use their landline telephone.

Evidently, the assistant hadn't noticed that the man bore a remarkable resemblance to a dangerous serial killer on the loose, whose image graced a poster on the wall right beside the till. It was a stark reminder of how unreliable eyewitness statements were, Ryan thought, because people rarely remembered the physical details of one person to the next, not even when there was a photograph to remind them.

Thanks to a statement from Jimmy Moffa's housekeeper, Irene, they had already determined that a vintage 1929

Harley Davidson Two-Cam motorcycle had been stolen from the extensive selection of luxury vehicles in Moffa's garage. CCTV showed the stolen motorcycle making its way through the quiet streets of Darras Hall with a single male driver matching Edwards' description, along his favoured route via the A69 to the Styford Roundabout and from there along the A68 towards Carterway Heads. As before, the petrol station camera confirmed that the motorcycle had made a right turn into the dales but they had no way of knowing which direction he had taken from there.

Being unfamiliar with two-wheeled vehicles, Ryan had deferred to Lowerson's superior knowledge of flash engines and was reliably informed that a Harley Two-Cam in good condition could easily sell for six figures at auction, owing to its rarity. It was not the choice of a shrinking violet, or indeed an obvious choice for a fugitive wishing to maintain a low profile, but it was certainly the perfect choice for someone like Keir Edwards.

Looking at its classic lines on a computer screen, Ryan thought that the motorcycle was better suited to the Californian hills than the fells of the North Pennines but, on the plus side, it was a very rare vehicle with a loud engine. There was every chance that Edwards would have been seen on his journey to and from the petrol station, but they simply didn't have the time to complete door-to-door enquiries. Edwards had issued a four-hour warning and that gave them very little time to spare, so Ryan asked local Durham police to canvas the area for a motorcycle matching the description while he and his team focused on deciphering Edwards' cryptic clue.

But before all that, Ryan had an important call to make.

Anna was speaking to the School Administrator at Shelford, in Somerset, when Phillips' mobile phone began to shrill. Noting the caller, he snatched it up immediately.

"Well, lad? Any word?"

Ryan didn't answer directly.

"You saw the interview I gave? Morrison sprang it on me out of the blue."

"We heard it on the radio. It was good," Phillips said. "But Anna's worried about you offering yourself up like that."

Ryan leaned his back against the whitewashed wall, next to a faded poster about mobile phone theft and another touting a forthcoming police comedy improv night. He didn't think it would be well attended.

"Edwards is escalating," Ryan answered. "If he were thinking straight, he would never have killed Jimmy Moffa. Now there's an army of violent criminals hell-bent on avenging his death and it makes no sense. Edwards must have known we would find out about Moffa's involvement but there was no need to finish the man, not in such an obvious way."

"He did it because he needed to kill," Phillips guessed.

"Yes." Ryan switched the phone to his other hand and closed his eyes, just for a moment. "There's something else,

Frank. He killed Moffa's new bodyguard. It was the same one from the Diner."

"Tony?"

"Yeah."

Phillips inhaled sharply, thinking of how he had gone to school with Tony's father before he'd been killed in an accident on an oil rig. His only hope would have been for Tony to make something of himself and keep his widow company. Instead, the young man had become a stooge for a gangland boss and been killed on his first day on the job.

He cleared his throat.

"I warned him, when I saw him there. I told him to go home."

"I know you did," Ryan murmured. "There isn't anything more you could have done. Tony was a free agent and he knew the risks associated with a man like Moffa."

"Aye, but it's sad, all the same."

Ryan opened his eyes again and looked at the opposite side of the corridor, feeling numb.

"There's something else, Frank. It's worse than Tony."

"Denise. She's—?"

"No, she's not dead, as far as we know," Ryan said quickly. "But I had a call from Edwards, less than ten minutes ago. He's issued a deadline of eight o' clock tonight. If I fail to show up wherever he's hiding out, alone and unarmed, he'll kill Denise."

Phillips felt himself sway and he gripped the back of a chair for support. There was a short silence while Ryan listened to his friend breathe in and out, commanding his body to remain calm.

"What—what's being done? How can we find him?"

"Edwards gave me a clue to finding him but it seems like nonsense. He said I should ask the wife of his first victim."

Phillips shook his head and tried to slow his irregular breathing so that he could concentrate on what Ryan was telling him. He moved across to the kitchen table and the stack of files there, rummaging with one hand until he found the one he was looking for.

"His first known victim was a woman called Isobel Harris." Phillips read out the name printed neatly on the front of the plain cardboard file, then flipped it open to see her face smiling back at him. She had been twenty-two and worked on the perfume counter at Fenwick's, one of the oldest department stores in Newcastle. "He followed her home one night after work, after he'd bought some aftershave from her counter earlier the same day. Seems he took a fancy to her."

Ryan remembered listening to Edwards' cold dissection of her attributes, as if she had been an object for him to do with as he chose. But Isobel Harris had been a young, heterosexual woman who hadn't been married with a wife.

"He's telling us she wasn't his first victim."

Phillips sat down heavily at the kitchen table.

"We had a list of other potential victims we hadn't been able to pin on him but a lot of those were crossed off when we investigated Paddy Donovan last year."

Ryan pushed away from the wall to start pacing again, thinking back to another killer at another time.

"Yes, Donovan was credited with most of those. Even if he hadn't been, we come back to the same issue. Whether the victims were attributed to Donovan or Edwards, they were all dark-haired, young women who identified as heterosexual. We're looking for the *wife* of Edwards' first victim, so logic tells me the victim was probably male."

They fell silent for a moment, then Ryan sighed.

"Faulkner is working his socks off to get those soil samples back to me so we can try to narrow the field but it won't be enough to track down a specific address, only a more specific area. Have you found anything that might be useful? Is there anything at all we've missed?"

Ryan wished he didn't sound so desperate.

"Edwards has been careful, right from the start," Phillips replied. "There's no mention anywhere of his life before the age of sixteen, of a family home address, or even somewhere he liked to go on holiday when he was a nipper. No mention of a traumatic experience on the fells around here or of a farm where he first learned how to kill chickens." Phillips broke off as Anna walked back into the room, looking vaguely triumphant. "Just a sec, we might have found something after all."

Ryan waited while Phillips handed the receiver to Anna and felt a powerful wave of emotion wash over him when her soft voice came down the line.

"Ryan?"

"Anna," he murmured. "Have you got something for me?"

"Maybe," she said. "I've just had a long and interesting discussion with the administrator at Shelford School. The *new* administrator, I should say."

"Were they more forthcoming than the battle axe I spoke with two years ago?"

"Now, don't get mad," Anna said.

Where have I heard that before? he wondered, while he waited to hear what new mischief she had been up to.

"I decided to take a different approach, since I can't very well claim to be a police officer. When I rang, I said I was calling from the Information Commission and that we'd received a complaint the school had been giving out personal data about an infamous former student of theirs, Keir Edwards."

Ryan waited for her to continue.

"Well, as you can imagine, the administrator was mortified. I told him, to make matters worse, we'd received the complaint from a private individual whose address had been given out and they'd been receiving hate mail since the manhunt started last week. There was obviously a new family living in Keir Edwards' former listed address, so I was calling to check that their old records were correct and to give them an informal warning. I suggested some refresher training for his staff at the school to ensure there weren't any further slip-ups, in future."

Ryan grinned at the empty corridor.

"You're a tough cookie. Needless to say, he cooperated. What was the address?"

His heart began to beat just a bit faster in anticipation of a fresh lead.

"I can hardly believe it," Anna said, "but the address they have on file for Keir Edwards is *Castle Drewe*."

Ryan was shocked into silence for a full ten seconds. Even with his limited knowledge of local history, he had heard of the Drewe family. They were landed gentry and, until recently, their estate stretched across hundreds of acres through the North Pennines.

"If he's a member of the aristocracy, I'll eat my hat," he said roundly. "But Castle Drewe is right in the middle of our search area. Who lives there now?"

"I already looked it up," Anna put in, delighted to be able to help. "Lady Drewe is still in residence."

"Then I'll need to have a chat with her," Ryan said decisively.

"Ryan, there's something else I found when I was looking into Shelford School. The Drewe family are listed as benefactors and have been ever since the early nineties."

Ryan nodded, finally beginning to feel the pieces slot into place.

"Which coincides with the time Edwards joined the school."

"Yes." Anna sensed Phillips pacing around the kitchen beside her. "There's one final thing. The entire village of Blanchland is owned by the Lord Drewe Trust. We noticed it yesterday and even the pub is named after him. I did a bit of research into the family history and when the last

Lord Drewe died, he left no heirs. Rather than the estate reverting to his wife, he left everything in trust for conservation purposes."

"Misogynist old git," Ryan remarked. "What year did he die—and how?"

"He was involved in an accident in 1992." Anna had already guessed the direction of Ryan's thoughts. "He fell from the cliffs at High Force waterfall after a late-night hike and his body was recovered on the rocks the following morning. If Lord Drewe was in any way connected to Edwards, the boy would have been sixteen when he died."

"The same year Edwards changed his name and went off to school, hundreds of miles away," Ryan put in. "Another coincidence."

"I'm betting his school fees were paid for by Lady Drewe, which is why her address is listed on his record."

"It would also explain why Shelford fought tooth and nail not to let that information see the light of day when we were investigating two years ago. I could never understand why they kicked up such a fuss but now I see they were protecting a wealthy benefactor. What is Lady Drewe's situation?"

"All I have is what I've been able to pull up from the internet," Anna said. "According to the Lord Drewe Trust's website, Lady Drewe is permitted to live in the castle for the remainder of her life but when she dies, it reverts to the trust."

"The question is why she paid for Edwards' schooling," Ryan murmured. "He has to be connected to her husband—

who must have been Edwards' father. What happens to her if an heir is found?"

"He could be entitled to the castle and have a legitimate claim that the estate should have reverted to him, not to the trust. But Ryan, there's no mention of an heir, or at least no legitimate one."

"Does the Drewe family have a motto?" Ryan asked.

"Invictus maneo."

"Looks like we've found his first victim," Ryan said, and relief vibrated through his entire body. Here, finally, was the clue they had been waiting for. "Tell Phillips to hang tight. I'll let him know when we've got a rendezvous point. It'll take some careful planning so that Edwards believes I'm going in alone."

"Please, please be careful," she begged him.

"I will," he promised.

CHAPTER 25

Twenty miles south of Blanchland, the medieval palace-fortress of Castle Drewe was surrounded by two hundred acres of deer park spanning County Durham to the east, the North Pennines to the west, and the Wear and Derwent valleys to the north. Its foundations dated back over a thousand years and its walls and towers were so much a part of the verdant landscape that it seemed to Ryan that it had stepped straight out of a Turner painting.

Ryan had telephoned the castle and asked to speak to its mistress, Lady Sophia de Jacquette-Drewe. Having suffered the ignominy of a double-barrelled surname for his entire life, Ryan could hardly cast the first stone, but it had to be said that if there were a prize for the most ridiculously elaborate surname, hers was a real contender. Unfortunately, the Lady herself was disinclined to talk to the police without her solicitor being present and certainly not over the telephone. Ryan had made a supreme effort to appear sensitive and even deferential but the prospect of a violent killer preparing to take another life was not enough to move her and his patience wore thin. Time marched sickeningly onwards and the skies were already turning a darker, cardinal blue as the sun fell lower in the sky, so he elected to override her protestations and drive out to the castle to make a personal appeal to her better nature.

In times like these, Ryan felt he could draw upon his own family background in a manner he seldom chose to otherwise. It was embarrassing for him to admit that the Finley-Ryans were listed in *Debrett's* and *Who's Who*. His own mother had formerly been a London debutante before meeting and marrying his father, a former British ambassador to France and a minor peer. He had attended the 'best' schools and had called a stately manor house in Devonshire his childhood home. He even knew how to play polo, if he had to. Ryan didn't know who had been more uncomfortable when he had first confessed all of this to Anna but he suspected it was him. With the kind of innate class that was nothing to do with title or breeding, Anna had taken less than five minutes to settle into comfortable conversation with his parents, to laugh with them and see them for the real people they were. They might not be perfect, he thought—with hindsight, he would not send any child of his away to boarding school—but they were good people. But then, he had always gone his own way, setting himself apart from what he considered to be 'The Establishment'. Perhaps it was why he preferred to be known simply as 'Ryan', because 'Maxwell' was a reminder of a privileged childhood from which he now felt very far removed.

However, as he steered his car along the beautiful tree-lined driveway through the acres of woodland leading to the main entrance of Castle Drewe, he was thankful that his upbringing enabled him to cut through the usual hogwash that might intimidate somebody less familiar with the kind of exalted circles Lady Drewe preferred to move in. Then again, he was fairly certain that Frank Phillips could have achieved the same result by sheer force of personality if he were there.

Ryan completely ignored the liveried butler who emerged from the gatehouse to point an imperious finger towards the service entrance. Instead, he swerved his car under the archway of the gatehouse and into the main courtyard of the castle, coming to a stop outside its dramatic entrance portico.

"Um, shouldn't we have gone around the back?" Lowerson worried, glancing nervously towards the red-faced butler now hurrying across the courtyard.

"Bollocks to that," Ryan muttered. "Stick with me, kid, and try to act snooty."

Lowerson affected an uppity tilt to his chin.

"How about this?"

"Not bad," Ryan said, before slamming out of the car.

"Stop! Stop right there, young man!"

Ryan turned to glare at the puffed face of a butler in his late forties, wearing a severely disapproving expression on his shiny, rounded face. It was mildly amusing to be referred to as a 'young man' when there was only a handful of years between them, but it was just another example of the kind of ridiculous etiquette he hated.

Ryan stared down his nose from a superior height of five or six inches.

"Detective Chief Inspector Finley-Ryan and Detective Constable Lowerson to see Lady Drewe," he said, with an imperious flick of his own wrist as he whipped out his warrant card. "We are pressed for time, so we would like to see her immediately."

Ryan turned to walk inside the castle.

"My Lady has already declined an audience with you." The butler hurried to bar the entrance. "If you persist in this harassing manner, I'll be forced to call the police."

"By all means," Ryan said. "I was about to do the same thing, myself. Lowerson?"

The younger man stood to attention, dragging his jaw from the floor at the sight and sound of Ryan conversing in his most cultivated accent, with an aristocratic demeanour he had only seen in small doses before now.

"Yes, sir?"

"Put a call through to the Commissioner." Ryan turned back to the butler with a self-effacing smile. "Norman will likely be at home at this hour but, thankfully, he's a close, personal friend."

"What should I tell him?" Lowerson made as if to key in a number.

"Tell him to authorise a full tactical response team. I want the works: sniffer dogs, helicopter search, CSI team. It'll mean a lot of upheaval at this time of night and, of course, we'll need to notify the press—"

"Now, just wait a minute!" The butler looked between them. "You have no authority to order a search of the castle."

"I will have the proper authority within a matter of minutes," Ryan said, in bored tones, holding out his hand to Lowerson while he made a pretend phone call. "Is he on the line?"

"There's really no need for you to disturb the Commissioner," the butler interjected, with a pleading look towards Lowerson, who waited until Ryan bobbed his head like a Roman Emperor before sliding the phone back into his coat pocket.

"Take us to Lady Drewe," Ryan snapped.

The Rt Honourable Sophia de Jacquette had been a plain-faced, mousy-haired girl of the best breeding and manners when she had made her debut into London society aged eighteen. It had taken three waltzes and one fumbling goodnight kiss for her to fall head over heels in love with Charles Drewe, who had been several years older and under pressure from his mother to find a suitable wife. Having only known the stolen pleasure of Barbara Cartland's back catalogue, Sophia was expecting a lot from her would-be husband and was disappointed almost from the first night. For Charles had been completely uninterested in her and had performed his marital duties in a perfunctory fashion, always with the lights out. Over the years, her husband's increasing distance and coldness towards her had killed any feeling she might have once had towards him. She maintained their home and social calendar for the sake of appearances but in all other respects they led very separate lives.

When Ryan and Lowerson were shown into one of the smaller drawing rooms in Castle Drewe, they were met with a woman of around sixty who was almost unrecognisable from her former self, complete with extensive plastic surgery and six-inch designer heels.

Ever the professional, Ryan kept his thoughts to himself and his face carefully neutral. Lowerson, on the other hand, still had a lot to learn in the way of tact and stared with goggle-eyes at the woman's super-sized lips and bulging cleavage.

"Lady Drewe." Ryan removed his warrant card and showed it to her. She flicked a glance at it, then a much longer glance over him.

"Chief Inspector Ryan." She smiled slowly. "I must say you're vastly more impressive in person than on the television screen."

Ryan wasn't going to indulge her mindless flirtation, not when the grandfather clock standing against the wall had just chimed six o'clock.

"You know why we're here," he said.

"I am not discussing my private affairs without my solicitor present." She gave him a haughty look and began to signal for her butler.

"That is your right," Ryan shot back. "But if you fail to cooperate and it later comes to light that you are withholding evidence pertinent to our investigation, we will not hesitate to charge you with an offence. If your obstruction of our investigation leads to our suspect killing another innocent individual this evening, we will treat you as an accessory to murder. I can't begin to imagine what the papers would have to say about that."

Her face paled beneath her tan.

"I do not respond to threats. I never have."

"Who's threatening you?" Ryan said, blithely. "I'm simply stating facts. Now, are you going to make the intelligent choice or not?"

She looked at him, then around at the sumptuous drawing room that had been her home for forty years. With a sigh, she waved away the butler, who slunk from the room with a small bow.

"You've found out about Keir, I suppose," she said candidly, and offered them both a seat on the delicate little French lounger opposite her.

Lowerson took his cue from Ryan and remained standing.

"Tell us everything you know." He didn't beat around the bush.

"You're not much for small talk, are you?" she said coyly, but then her face fell again and she reached for her silver cigarette case on the coffee table between them. Ingrained manners had him leaning forward to light it with a mother of pearl cigarette lighter he swept up from the table. "Thank you," she murmured.

They gave her a moment to inhale.

"Keir Edwards is the bastard son of my late husband's mistress." She delivered the words dispassionately and took another long drag. "She had the nerve to name him after Charles."

"I never knew about him," she continued, with a faint air of surprise. "Not until he turned up with his wanton mother on my doorstep after Charles' death, demanding that I support him through school and university otherwise he would go to the press and play the wronged party. He said he would be claiming his rightful inheritance as soon as he found the money to pay for lawyers but of course what the poor boy didn't realise was that Charles had left everything to the trust and to his country. Not to his wife," she said, with some bitterness, "and certainly not to his illegitimate son."

"You believed that he was Charles' son?"

Sophia smiled a private smile and rose on her precarious heels to retrieve a photograph from one of the small bureau desks. She handed it to them and sank back down on the delicate sofa, taking another deep drag on her menthol cigarette.

Ryan showed the photograph to Lowerson and he could see why she had smiled. Keir Edwards was the spitting image of his father, Charles Drewe.

"You see now why I didn't need to question it, chief inspector? There used to be an enormous portrait of Charles on the wall—just there, above the fireplace."

She gestured to a gilt-framed painting of the castle, dated sometime during the 1800s.

"That portrait was one of the first things I had removed," she said, with another smile. "He really was the most hideously conceited man."

Another hereditary characteristic, Ryan thought.

"So you paid for his schooling to avoid a scandal?"

"Seems silly to you, doesn't it?" She stubbed out her cigarette with three vicious taps into a fine ceramic bowl. "Back then, I'd spent twenty years trying to maintain the impression of a happy marriage. We were patrons of the theatre, the races, the literary societies, the Farmers Guild…I could go on. I panicked, chief inspector. I didn't want to lose everything I had worked so hard to build."

"What happened to your husband, Sophia?"

Ryan thought that it had probably been quite some time since anybody had called her by her given name and not the pompous title she wore like a noose around her scraggy neck.

"Charles used to tell me he was going walking or climbing or some such nonsense. We are all adept at self-deception and I'm no different. A part of me knew that he was seeing another woman and I looked the other way. He gave me no choice," she said, and realised some of the hurt was still there, buried deep. "The night he died was a night like any other.

He said he was going for a walk along the stretch between the two waterfalls—Low Force and High Force. It was one of his favourite routes, or so he told me."

She reached for another cigarette to calm her nerves. It felt cathartic, she realised, to offload the secrets she had held onto so tightly from the past. It was amazing how little they seemed to matter anymore.

"It's a stretch of about a mile and a half, if you follow the banks of the River Tees, but it's rough terrain in parts. Charles was always complacent, bragging about how well he knew his own land, but at night it can be treacherous. They found him at the bottom of High Force waterfall, his brains splattered all over the rocks."

She said it quietly, Ryan thought, but there was a thread of pity woven through her rounded tones and he realised this woman had lived through her own share of pain.

"Do you know where Keir lived with his mother?" Lowerson piped up. It was the kind of information they could look up but it would take time they simply didn't have. They needed an address, and fast.

Sophia shook her head.

"I didn't *want* to know. I wanted as little contact as possible. But if I were to hazard a guess, I'd say it was somewhere within walking distance of those waterfalls. He went there every week and that's where he was found."

Ryan nodded and looked across at Lowerson, who was trying to bring up a map of the area on his smartphone. Then he remembered that there had been no record of Keir's mother, Jenny Adams, on the official radar. That meant it was likely someone had financed her home and living costs.

"Did your husband own all the property in that area?"

"Most of it." She nodded. "There are several farms, cottages and outbuildings."

"Can you tell us anything—anything at all—about Jenny Adams?"

Sophia closed her eyes for a moment, remembering the first time she'd seen the woman who had stolen her husband, perhaps long before she'd ever married him. It was painful but only as a distant ache.

"Jenny was lovely looking," she admitted. "Young, considering she was mother to a sixteen-year-old boy. Long dark hair, big brown eyes like a helpless fawn, that sort of thing. I asked her how she'd met my husband and she told me they'd first met when she was seventeen and working behind the bar at The Lord Drewe, in Blanchland. It was one of the inns Charles owned and he used to pop in regularly, when he was doing the rounds of the estate. I don't know what happened to her, after Keir left for school. He was still Charles back then but he wanted to be known as something different. As you may imagine, I was happy to accommodate his request."

Ryan searched her face and could see the signs of strain. He was also satisfied that she had told them the truth, as far as it went.

"Thank you," he said meaningfully.

She blew out a ring of smoke and looked him dead in the eye. "Did he kill Charles?"

Ryan considered giving her a meaningless reply but he decided to repay her openness in kind. "Yes, I think he did."

Her hand started to tremble and she stubbed out her second cigarette before linking her fingers together in a tight clutch on her lap.

"Inspector, there's—there's something else you should know. It isn't easy for me to tell you this. I haven't spoken of it, not to another soul."

Ryan broke his own rule and sank down into a chair beside her, to create a sense of confidence between them.

"Go on."

She needed another minute before she could speak of Charles and the real man he had been.

"You're Eve's boy, aren't you? I thought I recognised the name."

Ryan nodded.

"Tell her—tell her she should be very proud of you." She sucked in a long breath to stem an unexpected flow of tears. "I don't mean to waste your time, chief inspector. I'm about to speak of things I've never uttered aloud, not even to my priest."

"We understand. Take your time," he soothed, but his eyes strayed once again to the grandfather clock.

Six-thirty.

"Charles was—he was very proper, very courteous on the outside. He never raised a hand to me in all our years of marriage. But I saw him do things—things to the horses, or the dogs. Violent beatings, or a quick slash of a horse's tendon. He'd starve the dogs so that they were ravenous, nearly out of their minds. One time, he went too far and attacked one of the stable boys. He paid him to keep his mouth shut about it, but you never forget a thing like that. Something wasn't right..." She looked up at him and fear shone from her eyes, even though the man was dead and buried. "He wasn't interested in me as anything other than a trophy and not a very good one at that. But some nights, when he was very drunk, he'd tell me what he imagined doing to me. Vile, repulsive things that gave me nightmares. I started locking my door at night. There was a darkness to him and I sensed it every single day."

Ryan felt compelled to take her hand and give it a quick, reassuring squeeze.

"He's gone now."

"But his son is still here," she whispered.

Ryan and Lowerson left the grounds of Castle Drewe with a screech of tyres.

"Jack, get me a list of every dwelling within a five-mile radius of those two waterfalls. Low Force is only a ten-minute drive from here and High Force is another five minutes further west. Edwards has to be using his mother's old house somewhere in that area."

Lowerson made a humming sound of frustration as he typed furiously into his smartphone but failed to get a signal.

"I'll have to radio through to the office for that. An e-mail came through from Faulkner while we were at the castle. He attached a full report but I can't download it," he grumbled. "I can still see what he said in his covering e-mail, though. Apparently, the soil on the tyres of both the Toyota and the Mercedes had an abnormally high lead content. He's spoken with a geologist friend of his and they've also isolated elements of limestone, sandstone and dolerite."

Ryan pulled the car over to the side of the road and turned on the internal light. He reached under the seat to fish out an old A-Z of Great Britain, something he hadn't needed to use since the advent of GPS technology.

He flipped the pages until he could see their current location.

"We're here," he muttered, tracing the road from Castle Drewe towards Low Force waterfall. "You can see several old lead mines and a museum marked nearby as points of interest, which would explain the lead content of the soil. They used to mine lead veins in the Victorian era and if there's a property anywhere near the old mines, maybe along a dirt track where the cars would've picked up some soil, that'll be the place."

"How d'you know all that?"

"Until two days ago, I lived a few miles yonder with a beautiful historian who likes exploring the local terrain every chance she gets. I've been on more guided tours than you've had hot dinners," Ryan replied, with the air of one who owned a National Heritage annual pass.

Lowerson gave him a pitying look. "You've been suffering in silence."

"Yeah, but she's promised me a hot tub at our next place," Ryan reminded him, and picked up his radio to issue a series of urgent demands as the digital clock ticked onwards.

CHAPTER 26

Anna and Phillips approached the problem of finding the Hacker's current location from a different angle. The sky was turning dusky when they crossed the street from the holiday cottage to The Lord Drewe but they weren't intending to join in with the Wednesday night revelry. If Jenny Adams had once worked there as a young woman, there was a chance that somebody might remember her or where she had moved to. Memories were long in these parts and communities were close-knit.

The main bar area comprised of a medieval vaulted room with a long, polished bar lit up by dozens of fat candles and a large, crackling fire. Locals huddled together and mingled with travellers passing through or staying in one of the inn's bedrooms. All heads turned when Anna and Phillips entered, bringing a gust of cold night air with them.

By unspoken agreement, they decided to try the bartender first.

Alan Ingles was a thick-set man in his early sixties with a craggy complexion; whether from sampling too much of his own craft ale or from spending most of his free time enjoying the moorland walks, they couldn't be sure. He gave them a ready smile, finished polishing the wine glass he had in his hand, and crossed his arms on the top of the bar.

"Evening, folks! What can I get you?"

Neither of them felt remotely in the mood for alcohol but for appearance's sake Anna ordered a small glass of the house white and Phillips automatically ordered the same, uncaring of the fact that he hadn't drunk white wine since the eighties.

"This one's a nice choice," Alan suggested, running through the options on the extensive wine list because business was slow and he was a sociable man.

"Ah, I'll just take your recommendation," Anna said a bit impatiently, then chewed her lip to remind herself she was supposed to be snooping for information and nobody would be inclined to tell her anything if she came across like a grumpy tourist.

Her eyes strayed to the fancy, Victoriana-style clock on the wall.

Six-forty-five.

Meanwhile, Alan studied the newcomers with a sharp eye. He was an observant man and could see straight away they were the people renting the middle cottage across the road. He also happened to recognise them from his wife's description of the man and woman who had knocked on their door this morning asking about that runaway convict.

He didn't think they looked like police, although they both had the same watchful eyes about them. Maybe they were family of the victims, he mused, or of that missing woman. That would make more sense and he had a lot of sympathy for that.

Not much he could tell them but he had a lot of sympathy all the same.

"You were gaddin' about this morning, weren't you?" he said conversationally. "What's your interest, if you don't mind me asking?"

He began to measure out two small glasses of wine.

"The missing woman is very important to us," Anna said, seeking out and holding his eyes to drive the point home. "Her name is Denise MacKenzie. She's a very good friend of mine and she's the woman Frank plans to marry."

Phillips started to smile at the thought of marrying Denise, because it wasn't something they'd really talked about. She was so free-spirited and he didn't need the formal paperwork to know that they loved each other. But things had shifted in his mind over the last seven days and the thought of being without her, of never seeing her standing beside him promising to be together always, was unthinkable. So, yes, he damn well wanted to marry her. Just as soon as he'd kicked Keir Edwards' teeth down his throat.

"Aye, that's a shame," Alan clucked, leaning his arms against the counter again. "I was sorry to hear about it on the news. But what brings you over to this neck of the woods?"

"The man who's taken her, Keir Edwards, wasn't always known by that name. He was called Charles Adams."

"You don't say?"

"Yes. His mother was Jenny Adams and she used to work as a barmaid here, years ago, in the early seventies. Do you remember her at all? Do you know if she's still living in the area?"

The bartender frowned, as if thinking back.

"Please," Phillips put in. "It's important."

Alan sighed heartily and shook his head.

"I'm sorry I can't help you," he said in aggrieved tones. "I wish I could, and I hope you find your lady soon enough. That'll be nine-fifty for the drinks."

With heavy hearts, Anna and Phillips paid their bill and asked the same questions of the groups of huddled locals who occupied the tables in the bar. Alan watched them from the corner of his eye and breathed a long sigh of relief after they'd left.

He'd worked at The Lord Drewe for twenty-five years and had been in love with Lady Sophia Drewe for every one of them, ever since she'd come in one day with her sour-faced husband and asked him for an Aperol spritz. It had been lust at first sight for them, he remembered, and he'd enjoyed the lazy evenings they'd spent together when her husband was out and his wife was at her book club. It was the romance of a lifetime and he didn't care whether she dyed her hair or injected Botox into her lips. She would always be his Sophia and anybody threatening to upset her, upset him.

Those two would just have to go looking for gossip elsewhere.

It was fortunate for them that not everybody shared Alan's staunch loyalty to the Drewe family. When Anna and Phillips headed out once again into the chilly night a voice called them back.

"Wait! Hold on a minute!"

A local woman hobbled towards them on arthritic hips.

"I didn't think of it before, when you asked," she rasped, drawing air into her lungs like a dying person. "Did you say Jenny *Adams*?"

"Yes, that's her," Anna said eagerly. "Do you know her?"

"I know a Jenny *Adamson*," she offered. "I met her while I was doing one of those holistic retreats at Minsteracres Retreat Centre last year. She works as one of the helpers and lives there all year round. A bit like a nun, except she's never taken vows as far as I know. Anyway, I'm sure I remember her saying she once worked as a barmaid in Blanchland, when I mentioned that's where I'm from. It just strikes me as very similar, and she's about the right age. I don't want to send you off on a wild goose chase…" she trailed off.

"No, no," Anna said quickly, while Phillips simply turned to retrieve the car. "You've been very helpful. I can't thank you enough."

"Don't mention it!"

The woman's mouth hung open with a comical 'o' of surprise as Anna and Phillips dived into his car and reversed with more haste than precision, almost taking out one of the decorative bollards lining the street.

Minsteracres Retreat Centre was a fifteen-minute drive from Blanchland, back in the direction of the A68 leading north to the Styford Roundabout and skirting around the Derwent Reservoir. Originally a mansion house built in the middle of thick woodland, it had served variously as a Roman Catholic mission, a monastery, a novitiate centre and more recently as a retreat for religious and lay people. Its community adhered to Passionist beliefs, taking inspiration from St Paul on the Cross and dedicating their lives to a simple existence of prayer, solitude and penance.

"What if she isn't there or it's the wrong woman?" Phillips asked, as he steered the car through winding roads towards the small brown-signposted turnoff that would take them to Minsteracres.

"It's all we've got," Anna said bluntly, watching the passing fields as they sped along the road. "We have to hope it's her."

Phillips braked and turned the car into an ungated road lined with colossal sequoia trees that must have been hundreds of years old. They grew tall and straight at perfect intervals, soaring into the night sky at over a hundred and fifty feet high. In the daytime, bluebells and daffodils carpeted the forest floor leading up to the eighteenth-century building at the end of the driveway but they were hidden in darkness. As they emerged from the avenue of trees, the road wound around to the main house, past a 'peace garden' and other areas used for quiet reflection and healing.

It took a while for anybody to answer their knocking at the main doors, even after Phillips took to hammering against the wood.

Eventually, they opened and a priest gave them a placid, inquiring stare.

"Can I help you?"

"We need to come in."

"Our doors are always open," he said, imagining them to be people in need of peace and solitude.

"We need to speak with Jenny Adams, or Jenny Adamson."

The priest looked more closely at the pair of them and noted the air of fizzing tension surrounding their arrival.

"May I ask your names and what it's concerning?"

"Tell her it's the police and we've come to ask about her son. The one who's been marauding around the countryside killing people."

The priest made a funny little sound in his throat.

"Right. Ah. Right. Wait here."

He scurried off and they were afraid for a moment that she wasn't coming but a minute or two later a petite woman of around sixty walked into the hallway. Her face was practically unlined and she wore a serene expression that seemed to suggest she had lived a good, wholesome life.

But it was the eyes, Phillips thought. She had the same eyes as her son.

"I'm told you're from the police?" Her voice was soft, breathy almost.

"Yes," Phillips confirmed, grateful that he had retained his warrant card to be able to show her. She didn't need to know that he was on suspension. "The information you give us now could mean the difference between saving a woman's life and—and not," he finished inadequately, unable even to form the words out loud.

"Please think carefully," Anna urged. "We don't care about your past or about why you left it behind. If you want, we'll never tell a soul we found you here. But please, tell us where you used to live, down near the waterfall."

Jenny Adamson—formerly Adams, until she'd made the slight change to her name—had spent nearly two years inside the protective confines of Minsteracres. Every day, she had prayed for Christ to redeem her and wash away her sins, but every night the past came back to her and the cycle began again. She would always remember and she would always know that she was to blame. No amount of art or dance therapy, of healing hands or walks among the trees would remove the ever-present knowledge that she had borne a killer and, she feared, made him that way in the first place.

She turned without a word and led them into a small sitting room that reminded them of an old people's home, with beige-coloured high-backed chairs and a lingering scent of custard pudding. She turned the light on and the room was instantly lit by a bank of energy-saving bulbs that hardly lifted it from the general gloom.

"I don't know how you found me," she said, and let herself sink into one of the stiff chairs.

"It doesn't matter now," Anna urged her. "Please tell us where he might be, Jenny. If we don't find him in the next hour, he's going to murder somebody else."

The woman pressed shaking fingers to her eyes.

"If he finds me here, he'll kill me. Do you understand? He'll kill me."

"Why would he want to do that?"

"I…I was young when I had him and it wasn't planned. I didn't want a baby. I only wanted Charles," she whispered.

"But you had him, all the same."

"Yes, but I didn't give him much of a life. All my love and attention was for Charles. That was the way it was."

"He killed his father, in the end," Phillips said flatly. He wasn't interested in this woman's stumbling confession. She'd had more than enough time to make her peace with the things she had done.

"I think—yes, I know he did." She dashed away a tear but it wasn't for the degeneration of her child, it was for the man she still loved, despite all the years that had passed. "Charlie—Keir—went out one night, he said he was going for a walk. I didn't care because I was expecting Charles and I preferred to have him out of the way."

Anna's heart hardened towards the quivering, grey-haired woman sitting delicately on the stained old chair. It was hard to imagine a woman being so unfeeling towards her own child, even though that child had long since grown into a man, and that man was a killer.

"Charles never made it to the house that night and his body was found the next morning, smashed against the rocks at the bottom of High Force. I knew it, though, even before word started to spread. I knew it because Charlie came home and his shirt was covered in blood."

Tears began to stream down her face and she let them fall.

"I t-told him I wanted him out. He took Charles from me, I know he did."

"Tell us the address," Anna growled, and the older woman looked up in shock at the undertone. "Tell us where he is, before he kills again."

Jenny hiccupped and wiped at the snot dripping from her nose. Nobody offered to find her a tissue.

"You've known all along where he might be," Phillips managed. "All this time when we've been chasing our tails, searching high and low, you *knew* and you never told a soul."

"You don't understand," she wailed. "He doesn't know I'm here. The summer before he started killing all those girls, I moved here and changed my name. I didn't want to live in fear anymore, terrified that he'd eventually do what he'd threatened to do so many times before. He hated me but he loved me, I think. I don't know." She shook her head. "I asked the sisters to help me because I didn't want to be in the world any longer. I left him a note, telling him it was the end, I didn't want to be his mother anymore. I think he believed—*still* believes—that I'm dead or somewhere very far away. If he knew I was still alive and living so close, he'd kill me."

"He's killed three other people instead because of your silence."

The woman made a cross against her chest. She clasped her hands together and then recited an address in a dull little voice.

"I'll pray to God for forgiveness," she finished.

Anna took Phillips' arm and tugged him away, fearful of what he might say or do.

"Come on, Frank. Come away now. We have everything we need."

CHAPTER 27

Unable to contact either Ryan or Lowerson by telephone, Phillips radioed through the address Jenny Adams had given them. Ryan took comfort from the crackling sound of his voice coming through the speaker and, for a moment, it was as if they had gone back to a simpler time when nobody had smartphones or tablets. He acknowledged safe receipt of the information and radioed his colleagues in Northumbria and Durham Constabularies who had been on standby for an alert over the past three hours. The address given as Edwards' childhood home was a small farmhouse located a mile or so south of High Force waterfall, perched on high ground between two forested areas and accessible via a single track. It was among those barren fields, volcanic outcrops and thickets of forest that a young Keir Edwards had lived his lonely childhood as Charlie Adams, wandering the hills and ravines, swimming in the lakes and listening to the unfortunate comings and goings of a domineering, absentee father and a submissive, selfish mother whom he would eventually feel compelled to kill, time and again.

With an hour to go before the eight o'clock deadline, Ryan set about the business of ensnaring him. It was imperative that Edwards should not be alerted to a police presence. Small teams of plain-clothed police officers set about evacuating the houses close to Edwards' farmhouse, although given its sheltered location there were very few of those and none within a half-mile radius. It was not outside the realms of possibility for Edwards to take hostages from any of those houses, or indeed from the jolly-looking pub opposite the tourist entrance to High Force waterfall which lay to the north on the other side of a forested area. For that reason, residents were swiftly removed from the designated high-risk zone and road-blocks were set up at every major road exit. It was all done quietly and without fuss, under the velvety fold of darkness. People mostly came willingly and without complaint—for those who didn't, the casual mention of an escaped serial killer was enough to make them hustle into the backseat of an unmarked car to be driven to safety.

By the time the digital clock on Ryan's dashboard showed seven-thirty, inner and outer cordons had been successfully arranged. Armed response teams seconded from neighbouring command areas were in position to the north, south, east and west of the Hacker's location. Ordinary police manned the outer cordon to ensure no passing civilians entered the danger zone. It was a risky proposition to override Edwards' explicit instruction that no other police should be present but Ryan had already received Phillips' blessing that he was taking the right course of action as far as he was concerned.

The only problem was, Ryan would be going in without any means of communication—Edwards would be sure to spot any bulky radios or wires and, if he did, it was more likely he'd execute MacKenzie on the spot. Ryan was therefore relying on their deal, offering himself in exchange for his friend Denise, who must have lived through untold nightmares over the past week. It would be a straight switch to get MacKenzie out as swiftly as possible, following which the armed response teams were free to enter immediately afterward.

Unlike the man he hunted, Ryan did not consider himself superhuman or above taking obvious safety measures. With Anna's face printed clearly in his mind, he wore a bulky stab vest, as did every one of the police staff who made up the response team scattered across the quiet countryside. He also wore steel-capped walking boots, having already learned that his usual thin brown suede boots were wholly inadequate for hill walking. Headgear rested on his lap, which he fully intended to wear when approaching the farmhouse. From his current position on the main road to the north of High Force, it would take him perhaps fifteen or twenty minutes to walk along the single track, arriving at approximately seven-forty-five. The response units had been told to surround the farmhouse if MacKenzie had not exited by five-past-eight, which roughly coincided with the time the sun was due to set. Chief Constable Morrison approved his strategy and so all that remained was for Ryan to approach the farmhouse on foot and prepare to face his personal demon one last time.

Ryan had ordered that Phillips and Anna should head back to the holiday cottage and stay well out of range of the action. Phillips would have stayed to protect her, entrusting the safety of MacKenzie to his best friend and superior officer, but it would have gone against his every instinct screaming for him to be there when Denise was brought to safety.

Anna agreed wholeheartedly and suggested they join Lowerson in position on the north side of High Force waterfall. The River Tees separated the north and south sides and, since the farmhouse was on the south, they would be far enough away not to present a distraction or interfere with the police operation.

Phillips was supposed to be on suspension but CID bureaucracy meant diddly-squat to him at that precise moment, when the only thing occupying his mind was ensuring Denise was safe and unharmed. If it came to it, he'd risk another disciplinary. So thinking, Phillips stopped to retrieve his firearm, checking the safety clasp and tucking it into his holster before making for the front door.

Anna paused at the bottom of the stairs.

"What's the matter, lass?"

She glanced upstairs in the direction of the safe box she'd hidden beneath one of the beds.

"Just a minute."

She took the stairs two at a time and scrambled to retrieve it from beneath the bed. Her fingers shook a bit as she unlocked the box and lifted Ryan's firearm out of its leather case but her movements were sure and quick as she checked the mechanism.

Her father had done little enough for his family but he had taught her how to fire a gun.

The weight of it felt alien and dangerous in her hand and she thought about returning it to the safety box but instead she shoved it into the deep pocket of her waxed Barbour jacket and ran lightly back down the stairs.

"Ready," she said.

Phillips gave her an odd, searching look but he gestured for her to go ahead. She was a capable woman who'd been brought up on the land. She was no trigger-happy fool and, besides, he hadn't seen her take anything.

Had he?

Keir Edwards lay atop a high ridge of craggy whinstone rock overlooking the River Tees near Low Force, his belly flattened to the rock as he surveyed a group of seven or eight firearms officers huddling around an armoured vehicle, scratching their arses. He watched them for another minute or two through his binoculars and felt anger run like lava through his body.

Did Ryan think he was stupid?

Did he imagine that he wouldn't have prepared for *every* eventuality, *every* possible misstep?

His plan had always been to wait to kill Denise MacKenzie in front of Ryan for maximum impact. He would savour the pain on the other man's face as if it were a fine wine, something that had taken years to mature.

Then he would kill Ryan too.

It was unfortunate that time constraints would not allow him to truly relish the experience but his hands were nimble and he was sure he could achieve something quite spectacular in only five minutes. After that, he would leave via his planned route. There was nobody who knew these hills as he did, nobody who had traced every crop of heather, every juniper bush and rock formation. He could have walked blindfolded through the dark and would still be able to outrun a team of CID plodders.

Edwards had a rucksack packed full of Ryan's fine clothes and a passport with Ryan's name and face on it, carefully doctored so that the eyes appeared a darker shade to match his own. He was sure he would enjoy spending some time playing a dead man.

Slowly, he wriggled backward on his belly until he could be sure that nobody would see him, then jumped to his feet and ran back towards the farmhouse with a loping, sure-footed stride. There was a mile to cover but at this speed, he would be back within five minutes. His quarry had been in captivity for over a week and it was time to put her out of her misery, at least after the first few cuts.

Jack Lowerson coordinated Response Team B which was stationed in the visitors' car park immediately north of High Force waterfall, about a mile away from the action. His task was to prevent anyone rabbiting away from the scene and to move his officers into a support position once Team A confirmed that MacKenzie had been safely picked up. They were positioned with Ryan at the foot of the narrow lane just off the main road, which turned into a winding, disused track leading directly to the farmhouse.

Ryan was already en route to the farmhouse, walking along the track dressed in protective clothing but without a radio or communications device so as not to enrage the man who held MacKenzie's life in his hands. Lowerson heard crackling updates from one of the armed officers of Team A, who estimated Ryan's progress as an average distance covered per minute.

"*ETA is two minutes,*" the voice said, and Lowerson continued to stare at the asphalt car park as he imagined what might be going through Ryan's head as he made that long walk through the fields.

After arguing their way through the first roadblock, Phillips and Anna found Lowerson like that, staring fixedly at the ground with one index finger to his ear, presumably holding the small radio earpiece in place.

"Jack," Phillips said, and waited for a response. "Jack!"

Lowerson looked up in surprise and gave them a funny half-wave, concerned by the prospect of a civilian on site when Ryan had given express orders that there should be none—and especially not his fiancée. Still, he walked to the boot of his car and retrieved another two radio headsets and stab vests, which they shrugged on without complaint.

The three of them settled back against the side of Lowerson's car and listened to the disembodied voice of a firearms officer from Durham Constabulary counting down to Ryan's arrival at the farmhouse.

"ETA is one minute."

Ryan maintained a steady pace as he followed the long, single-track road leading south from the main road, curving up and over the landscape with its jutting rocks and uneven fields separated by crumbling walls or windblown hedges. It would have been a lovely sight, to stand and watch Nature's majesty as the sun reduced to a tiny sliver of light and the sky was painted a deep inky blue. But he continued onward, walking further into the fold of the valley until the road changed from tarmac and became long, overgrown grass.

He heard nothing except the sound of his own light breathing, the hum of crickets and the call of birds circling high in the sky above. It was a humbling experience to feel so alone in the world and with every passing step he realised that, without Anna and Phillips, he would never have found the location of this farmhouse. Not in time, at least, and not amid the countless other similar dwellings scattered across the fields and tucked away in the shadowy corners of the valley. The terrain was so unpredictable; sometimes the track would plateau, other times it dipped and fell before rising again to look out across the valley. To his left, he could hear the faint sound of High Force waterfall through a thicket of dense trees and it sounded like a running tap, rather than the rushing deluge he remembered visiting once before.

He rounded a bend and a simple two-storey stone building came into view, little more than a dark silhouette against the navy-blue sky. A light shone in the downstairs window, bidding him welcome.

He glanced at the watch on his wrist.

Just in time.

CHAPTER 28

Five minutes earlier

MacKenzie could feel a change in the air and a change in *him*. It had taken her a while to realise precisely *what* had changed but, when she did, the truth came crashing down on her like a tonne of bricks. The reason why Edwards had chosen not to see her all day was because he didn't want to waste time on a woman he planned to kill within a matter of hours. The prospect of him coldly planning his attack was bowel-loosening and she'd vomited into the pathetic bucket in the corner of the room, already filled with her own faeces in the absence of a toilet.

MacKenzie was past caring about the indignity because her entire being was focused on survival. As the hours dragged on and the intermittent bursts of 'fight or flight' adrenaline coursed through her veins, she burned it off in a series of abdominal crunches rather than allow herself to sit jittering on the bed, waiting for death to come. Her ribs were still painful but each day she had forced herself to endure higher levels of discomfort, to desensitise her body against the final push that was to come—and it was working.

Her bare feet had been taped up with long strips of denim taken from the bottom of her jeans. It was the toughest material she could find in the sparse room and it would go some way towards protecting the soles of her feet in the absence of shoes. When she grew too cold, she jogged on the spot. There was not much energy to spare but what little she had left she decided to use to fuel the endorphins in her injured body.

She watched the approaching sunset with tears in her eyes, wondering whether it would be her last. She spoke aloud in the empty room and imagined Frank was there to listen.

"I'm sorry it took me so long to tell you how much you mean to me," she began. "The time we've spent together has been the happiest two years of my life. You're my love, Frank, and you're my best friend in this world."

She paused to take a shaky breath, fighting back tears.

"I don't know if I'm going to come through this or if we'll see each other again. You and I were never ones for believing in an afterlife but, standing here now, looking out at that sunset, I have to wonder if we were wrong. Maybe I'm a hypocrite. I don't know. A part of me hopes it's all true because it means there's a chance I'll see you again, even if things go wrong tonight."

She paused her monologue when her keen ears picked up the sound of a key turning in the front door downstairs and she knew she didn't have much time left.

"If I die tonight, Frank, I want you to know that none of it was your fault. You did your best, you searched for me and fought for me, just like you always have. But in the end, this isn't your fight."

She heard Edwards' footsteps coming quickly up the stairs.

"It's mine," she vowed.

Edwards hooked the strap of his binoculars on the butt of the hunting rifle propped beside the front door. He would move it before Ryan arrived but first he needed to retrieve his fatted calf and move her into position. He selected the long carving knife from the kitchen—the same one MacKenzie had stolen. He'd been sharpening it for most of the day until it was a gleaming blade worthy of a shogun.

His heart pounded in anticipation of the kill and he imagined the sweet warmth of her blood flowing onto his hands. He'd seen no sign of Ryan approaching the house, so he had a few minutes to spare before his guest of honour arrived. He was sure he could put on a fitting display to greet him when he walked through the door.

Whistling beneath his breath, he ran lightly up the stairs and clucked his tongue when he remembered he needed to move the chest of drawers blocking the door.

Silly me.

"Ruth! Daddy's home!"

He smiled to himself and rolled his neck as he pushed the chest of drawers to one side and unlocked her bedroom door.

Edwards didn't see it coming. He didn't think she had any fight left in her but he was wrong.

As the door swung open on its hinges, he had no time to react before the heel of MacKenzie's injured foot shot out to kick him full in the face, while she pivoted on her stronger foot to maintain balance.

He stumbled backward, blood spurting from a broken nose but he still gripped the knife and started swinging it, swearing wildly.

She followed up with another hard kick to his crotch but he was expecting it this time and caught her leg in full extension. Panic flitted across her face as she tried to tug it back, tottering on her pivot foot and he began to laugh maniacally. Then his arm swept downward and slashed her calf, slicing through muscle.

She screamed in pain but when he let her go, she didn't crumple to the floor. She clutched the edge of the bedroom door and rammed it against his approaching figure, twice in quick succession until he jerked backward. She took her opportunity and hurled herself desperately towards him, kicking both feet against his midriff so that he staggered back against the banister rail overhanging the stairs.

His spine bent backward against it and time froze for a second as his fingers clutched for support but then she heard the splintering crunch of the old wood buckling beneath his muscular frame. As the banister gave way, he fell backward, tumbling heavily with a series of hard *thuds* down the stairs.

MacKenzie hurried to the top of the stairs and saw him lying at the bottom, his body twisted awkwardly. Blood gushed from his nose and the knife had fallen from his right hand. There was no way to avoid walking around him.

Her heartbeat thundered in her ears, so loud that she couldn't hear any other sound for a moment as she limped closer and closer to his bulky body blocking the bottom of the stairs.

She watched him for a second and saw that he was still breathing.

It could be another one of his games.

With a cry, she made a leap over his torso and landed painfully on her wounded leg, which was starting to bleed badly.

No time to think about that now. She had to get out.

As she grasped the front door handle and pulled it open, one of his hands shot out to grab her ankle in a vice-like grip while the other reached for the blade.

MacKenzie didn't hesitate.

She used her other foot to kick against his wrist but he wasn't budging. Frantically, she looked around for a weapon and grasped the rifle propped beside the door. There was no time to see if it was loaded, so she used the butt against his head. His neck snapped backward and he brought up his other hand to shield himself from another blow.

His fingers slackened against her ankle and she didn't think, she just ran.

Still clutching the rifle, MacKenzie staggered outside into the twilight and was disorientated for a moment. She could feel the blood from her leg soaking the material of her jeans and she knew she needed to tie a tourniquet to stem the flow.

First, she needed to put some distance between them.

She hobbled around the side of the farmhouse and made directly for the track she had found the other day. She had almost reached the gate at the end of the field when she heard his voice calling out into the night.

"RUTH!"

She didn't look back this time but increased her pace until she reached the old entrance with its rotten wooden gate hanging against the hedgerow, dragging the rifle with her.

"*RUTH!*"

She gritted her teeth against the throbbing pain in her leg, reaching down to clasp a handful of her jeans so that she could physically propel her damaged leg forward. She hurried through the gateway and saw a single-track road curving around into the valley, covered with thick grass from disuse.

But on a straight track, there was nowhere to hide.

To her right, there was a short wall whose stone had crumbled years ago and had never been replaced or repaired. Beyond it lay the thatch of forest she had spied before, offering concealment in the dense undergrowth beneath the trees.

She heard his footsteps pounding the earth towards her, crossing the distance from the farmhouse and MacKenzie threw herself over the gap in the wall, her blood staining the limestone. She ran as quickly as she could across the uneven ground, tripping against the tufts of earth.

Behind her, a stone dislodged and she glanced behind in reflex to see him vaulting over the low wall. For a moment, their eyes met across the fields and it was as if a lion had spotted his prey and was preparing to pounce.

Her hands gripped the rifle and cocked it, ready to discharge. The light was dimming but she raised it and took aim at the centre of his torso, tracking his tall body as he ran steadily towards her.

Her finger squeezed the trigger and the rifle jarred her right shoulder with its hard recoil but she maintained her shaking position.

He was still coming.

Dear God, he was still coming.

How had she missed? The calibration was off, it had to be. There was no way she could have missed that shot.

No time to worry about it now. He was covering ground, and fast.

MacKenzie sobbed out harsh, panting breaths as the sweat poured down her face and into her eyes, blurring her vision so she could barely see the opening into the trees.

Don't look behind.

She reached the outskirts of the small forest and dragged herself beneath its dark canopy, adjusting her eyes to the sudden darkness for a moment as she made a split-second decision. Which direction?

Which direction!

The sun was almost setting in the west, so she continued northeast and followed the faint sound of a river somewhere nearby. If she found the river, it would eventually guide her to civilisation. She veered right, her feet stumbling against the sharp edges of fallen pine-cones and drying leaves as she made her way blindly through the forest.

She heard his heavy footfall somewhere behind her, perhaps twenty metres away, as he burst into the forest. She froze and shrank back against the bark of a tall pine tree, listening intently as she gripped the rifle.

He was so good, she thought, *his movements were almost silent.*

But she had trained herself to listen for the past week, tuning herself into his unique frequency so that she would be prepared for this moment.

Crack.

She heard his foot snapping a small branch underfoot and estimated that he was about ten metres away.

Rustle.

The sound was further away that time, and she realised he had started to walk in the opposite direction. She held her breath, scanning through the trees for any obvious way out, when she spotted something dark and metallic in the undergrowth fifty metres further east.

Was that the wheel of a car?

So this was where he'd been hiding his vehicles.

There were no further sounds and she knew she could not stay there, waiting for him to find her. She had to strike out or die.

It was inevitable that she would make some noise alerting him to her location. Her only hope was that she could hot-wire the car or take another shot with the rifle. She dried her sweating brow with the sleeve of her jumper and focused her eyes and her mind on a fixed point. She visualised herself running for the car and using the butt of the rifle to break into the driver's window. She could defend herself once she was inside.

Now.

Now!

She pushed away from the bark and bolted through the trees.

CHAPTER 29

Ryan approached the farmhouse at five minutes to eight. Its location was completely isolated, with only fields and trees to be seen in any direction. Even the track he had taken to reach it was overgrown with tall grass almost reaching his knees, although a way back there he'd seen the signs of a vehicle having turned off into one of the open fields leading to the forested area he'd passed on the way. Dusk lent everything a supernatural quality, as if the house had been dropped onto the earth by a higher power, to remain surrounded by flora and fauna for all time.

But there was life to be found. He knew that much.

A light burned in the ground floor window of the farmhouse and he looked at the open gateway ahead of him with caution.

Something wasn't right here.

Rather than proceeding directly past the rotting gate, he circled around to the left until he found a gap in the hedgerow around the back of the farmhouse. He stepped inside the perimeter and scanned the area, half expecting Edwards to take a shot at him, or to lunge out at him as he had done once before.

Nothing moved on the air and Ryan experienced an increasing sense of disquiet as he approached. Some instinct told him there was no life here, no other warm bodies sharing the crisp night air that he breathed.

Reaching the farmhouse, he paused to take a quick peek inside the lit window and saw a dated living room with moth-eaten furniture and the signs of food and drink debris. A small fire was petering out in the grate. There was no door on this side of the house, so he skirted around to the other side, sticking close to the outer wall and moving with slow, quiet steps. As he rounded the corner, he saw a shaft of light emanating from the front door, which was thrown open to the wind. He was about to approach it when he heard the unmistakeable sound of a single gunshot, somewhere back in the direction he had just come.

"Denise!"

Ryan sprinted back around the side of the house towards the gate and looked ahead at the track he had just followed, finding it empty. Then, his eye caught something he had missed the first time: a slash of blood lying dark and wet against a low stone wall in the hedgerow, leading across the fields towards the forest.

He stopped only to tug off the headgear he was wearing, finding it cumbersome. He flung it to the ground and leaped over the wall to run full pelt across the fields, his long legs tearing up the ground.

Denise stumbled through the thicket and could barely feel her leg now as the blood loss numbed it of sensation. She dragged herself through the darkness, ignoring the thin, whip-sharp branches that slapped against her face and clawed at her like fingers. Her jumper snagged on wiry shoots, tugging her backward, and she tore herself free in her single-minded journey to reach the vehicle she'd seen hidden among the trees.

"Ruth," he sang out, from somewhere nearby and to her left.

Her heart hammered against her chest so hard she thought it would break from her body. With something that sounded like a battle cry, she pushed her way through the remaining trees until she ran into something hard and metallic.

But it was not a car; it was a big, black motorcycle.

MacKenzie heard his footsteps approaching and cocked the rifle again, aiming first left, then right.

Where was he?

He had stopped dead still and was waiting.

She tried to quieten her own breathing but it was impossible. Her lungs laboured to keep the oxygen pumping through her body and she was already feeling light-headed from the blood loss in her leg. She didn't think he'd severed an artery—if he had, she wouldn't have made it this far.

Still no sound.

Night owls screeched in the distance and she heard the scuffling of a small forest animal but no other human.

She had to move.

MacKenzie spun around and felt for keys in the ignition but found none. She didn't know how to hot-wire a motorcycle and her escape plans evaporated.

Through the trees, she heard the sound of keys jingling, followed by laughter.

"Looking for something, sweetheart?"

He laughed again and the darkness seemed to close in around her. She didn't know how many rounds she had left in the six-shot rifle but she took a chance and fired one in the direction of his taunting voice to buy herself some precious time. She cocked the lever to expel the used shell and stepped back to fire again into the front wheel of the motorcycle. It would be harder for him to follow with a flat tyre.

Then she ran.

Ryan reached the edge of the forest just as another two gunshots sounded out into the quiet night, disturbing a flock of resting birds that fluttered from their branches in protest. He paused to consider the direction it had come from, his eyes adjusting to the changing light as he tried to make out any signs of life through the murky trees ahead.

There was no time to waste.

He dived into the forest, which was small but thick with mature trees whose roots carpeted the undergrowth in a network of trip-hazards. The failing light outside cast barely a ray into the gloom and Ryan began to rely on his other senses.

There was no breeze beneath the forest canopy and the air felt damp and stuffy. His hands brushed against the damp fungus creeping its way up the bark as he wound his way through the trees like a blind obstacle course. He stopped frequently to listen for the sound of footfall and thought he heard running feet up ahead. Quickly, he scoured the floor with outstretched palms until he found a thick branch, heavy enough to serve as a weapon.

Then came the alien sound of a powerful engine bursting into life.

MacKenzie heard the motorcycle too, its fearsome engine crashing like thunder through the silent trees and she tripped and fell against the forest floor. Her knee cracked painfully and her hands reached out to break her fall, landing inside something cold and wet.

It was a dead animal, bloated and festering.

She let out a small cry of horror and snatched her hand away, pushing to her feet to continue running. She didn't know where she was going; she had no idea of distance or direction beneath the shadowed trees.

She only knew she had to get away.

She had lost all feeling in her lower leg now but there was no time to stop. Her body was shivering, freezing cold but still sweating so much that her hair matted against the side of her head.

Behind her, the motorcycle crashed through the low branches and as she glanced back, she saw the glare of its headlight shining an eerie white light through the brush. She saw the outline of its driver revving the engine as he guided it through the packed trees, the flat tyre presenting no hindrance at all.

He was gaining on her all the time and she felt her legs slowing down. The ankle that had been sprained now felt like it was broken and the rifle dragged behind her, scuffing against the floor as she no longer had the strength to hold it up.

Suddenly the floor fell away as a sharp rift appeared in the valley, out of nowhere. MacKenzie pulled herself back just in time, falling to the floor and grasping at the roots of a tree to gain purchase. The motorcycle engine was a roar in her ears and she turned to look fully into the glare of the single headlight.

She swore she saw the whites of his eyes.

Edwards spotted her and started to brake but MacKenzie grasped the slippery surface of a log and wrenched it with all her might, throwing the weight of her shoulder behind it so that it crashed into his path. She threw herself backward again and watched as the front wheel of the bike connected with the log, braking too late to avoid the impact. The wheel buckled and the bike flipped over onto its side, crashing through the leaves and sending its driver skidding down the steep incline towards the river below.

Ryan moved quickly through the trees, following the roar of the engine as it disappeared further into the forest. He picked up its trail and followed it, arms shoving at the wispy branches that snaked like tentacles across his face. He could hear it, gears grinding and engine blasting up ahead and he commanded himself to move faster.

Faster!

His thighs burned and he drew short, gasping breaths of the stagnant air into his lungs, labouring to cover the ground without losing his footing. He was almost there. He could see the artificial glimmer of a red taillight up ahead.

Then came a growl of tyres and the heavy clunk of metal hitting the forest floor, followed by a skid and the crashing of leaves and branches as the bike and its rider were dragged down into the gorge.

Ryan skidded to a halt a few seconds later, following the track of the motorcycle until it disappeared. He peered down the steep incline and saw it smashed against a tree at the bottom, metal twisted and headlight still flickering on and off.

Then he spotted the man shaking himself off, limping away from the motorcycle but otherwise unharmed.

Ryan watched him stalk through the trees, looking for his prey. Ryan cast his eyes around and in a burst of almost paternal love, found her lying a short distance away, curled up in the foetal position.

MacKenzie.

He swiftly crouched down to check the pulse at her neck and found it uneven but strong. He might have wept at the sight of her bruised, torn face and feet; at the ankle that had now swollen to the size of a cricket ball. But it was the blood seeping from her leg that gave him most cause for concern. He didn't hesitate and removed his jacket to keep her warm, then felt around for a thin, sapling branch, rubbery and pliable which he used to wind around her calf to stem the blood.

Ryan heard rustling leaves nearby and he did the only thing he could, which was to create a diversion. Reluctantly, he left MacKenzie and stepped forward to look down into the steep incline.

"Edwards!" he called out.

He stood at the top of the incline as the other man crouched at the bottom, poised like an animal about to take flight. Edwards' head whipped around and up, following the sound of his voice.

Then he let out a snarl and began to charge back up the hill.

Ryan had the better of him to start with. Being on higher ground allowed him to choose his moment and, as the shadowy figure drew near, he charged down to meet him. They met like two rutting stags, light and dark clashing together, melding and rolling down the ravine. Arms thrashing, legs kicking out as they slid down and down through the trees, hurtling towards the whinstone rock overlooking the river at the bottom.

CHAPTER 30

"It's been too long," Phillips muttered.

Anna looked up and met his worried eyes. They were still huddled in their position on the north side of the river in the visitors' car park near High Force waterfall. There had been no report of MacKenzie emerging safely from the farmhouse about a mile further south and it was now almost eight o'clock. Another five minutes and Ryan had given orders for the armed response team to go in.

Lowerson spoke in urgent tones into his radio, querying positions, asking for updates, but finding there were none. Beneath the yellowish-green light of the solitary street lamp, his young face appeared faded and worn down by worry.

"Ryan said to give it until five-past-eight," he said, for the tenth time.

The three of them looked among themselves and Phillips fixed his young protégé with a meaningful stare. Understanding it, Lowerson nodded and spoke again into his radio.

"They've heard gunshots," he said. "Response Team A is going in now."

It felt like a lifetime while they waited for the response team to make their way to the farmhouse. Through their radios, they heard raised voices and gas canisters being released as armed officers made the premises safe. When they did, the news was not good.

"Target clear," came the ultimate response. *"But there are signs of assault beside the door. The chief inspector's headgear has been found discarded on the grass outside."*

Lowerson listened as the response team searched the immediate area in expanding circles, while Anna sank into a crouched position, breathing hard. Phillips stooped to put a protective arm around her shoulder, but then rose again and removed the headset he wore, slinging it onto the back seat of the squad car.

"Frank? Frank, where are you going?"

"I'm going after Denise," he told them. "If they're not at the farmhouse, it's because they've gone off on foot. The only place that isn't cordoned off is the river, down there."

He jabbed a finger towards the wooded entrance leading down to High Force waterfall and the river flowing into it.

"That's where they'll be."

When he lumbered off towards the tourist entrance leading down into the falls, nobody tried to stop him.

Nobody could.

MacKenzie was lying face down in the mossy undergrowth when she came around. She must have fallen unconscious at some point after Edwards' crash, her body giving in to stress and exhaustion after her desperate flight through the forest. The rifle still lay beside her, blending into the dark brown compost and she reached for it like a comfort blanket.

Pain ricocheted through her body and suddenly everything came back to her. The flash of his knife, the sight of him chasing her atop the angry, monstrous roar of the motorcycle. Her teeth began to chatter and she reached down to rip a blood-soaked strip of denim from the bottom of her frayed jeans, already cut short to use as strapping for her feet. Her right eye was blurry and stung painfully, and she knew a branch had caught it somewhere through the trees.

She forced her fingers to work but then realised somebody had already tied a long, rubbery shoot just above her knee to stem the blood loss. Then she noticed a thick black parka jacket had been draped across her back to keep her warm. She recognised the scent and feel of it.

Ryan!

MacKenzie started to cry silent tears of relief, unable to believe they had found her when it seemed like all hope had been lost. She struggled to her feet and, using the rifle as a walking stick, moved to the edge of the incline to peer down into the darkness. She saw the flashing headlight of the motorcycle but in the thin light surrounding it she could make out no sign of Edwards or Ryan.

Fear made her tremble again and, for a moment, she didn't know if she could carry on. It was hopeless. Then she heard a voice, one she thought she might never hear again.

"*DENISE!*"

It seemed to come from very far away, across on the other side of the trees, and for a moment she thought she'd imagined it, like a mirage.

Then it came again.

"Frank," she croaked happily, and began picking her way down the hill towards the river.

Ryan and Edwards tumbled down the steep incline in a flurry of leaves and twigs, battering against the sides of trees until the land evened out towards the edge of the forest. A hard ridge of whinstone rose up ahead of them, flanking the river on either side, and they were thrown apart as each man tried to stop himself falling over the high edge of it and down into the rocky waters below. Winded and bruised, Ryan recovered himself as quickly as he could and stood on shaking legs, absurdly grateful for the stab vest that had cushioned some of his fall.

Edwards was on his feet again and Ryan looked at him properly in the fading light. His face was covered with blood from the injuries MacKenzie had inflicted and the wounds were caked with dust and soil. His clothing was torn—

His clothing was torn, Ryan corrected, noticing that Edwards seemed to be dressed entirely in clothes stolen from the cottage in Durham before it had been burned to the ground.

As he studied Edwards, he felt as if he were coming face-to-face with a rabid dog; an animal that had returned to its natural habitat and knew every inch of it better than he did. Edwards was unrecognisable from the pampered man he had known and the only thing that shone clearly through the mud and grime was the white flash of his teeth.

"I believe I said, 'no police,'" Edwards growled, in a voice so low Ryan struggled to hear it.

"I must have misheard you," he countered. "I thought you said, 'bring all the police.'"

Edwards started to laugh and it was an ugly sound. "I'm going to miss the banter we have together, when you're gone," he hissed.

"Really? Because the moment you're back behind bars, I'm not going to miss anything about you."

Edwards took a step closer, then another.

"That's far enough," Ryan snapped. "Come quietly, now. There's no way out of here; the entire place is surrounded by armed police."

They must have made it to the farmhouse by now, Ryan thought quickly. They would be combing the area in circles that would lead them here, eventually.

The question was whether it would be soon enough.

And was Denise alright?

"Where's Denise?" Ryan asked, feigning ignorance. "I couldn't see your usual efforts up at the farmhouse, so I presume she got away from you."

Edwards felt his anger grow to fever pitch. "I dumped her body in the forest."

"I think not," Ryan said. "If that were the case, you'd be parading around telling me how brilliant you are. Instead, you're standing there looking like a poor man's Rambo."

Ryan took a step forward himself, risking a quick glance over the edge of the whinstone cliff to his right. It was a high drop to the waters below and the stone was wet and slippery.

"I'll find her easily enough," Edwards said. "It won't be hard hunting down that lame bitch."

"You'll never get that far."

"Want to know how far I got? Or shall I wait to share that with Phillips? I'm sure he'd *love* to hear about it."

Ryan just laughed. "You know something, Keir? You're full of shit. You couldn't get it up even if you wanted to. Those days are long gone, aren't they? The only time you feel like a *man* is when you're killing women who look like your *mummy*. You're pathetic."

Edwards began to shake violently. "Shut up. Never speak of my mother."

"Why not? We were just chatting to her earlier. She's been living right under your nose these past few years, Keir, and you never knew it."

"You're lying. You're *lying*!"

Ryan threw his arms out wide, deliberately goading him.

"Look at me. Take a good, long look. I don't need to lie. I don't need to change my name or kill people just to feel normal. It's a sickness, whatever has made you the way you are, and it's something I can't and don't even want to understand. Maybe you had a bad mother—who knows? But people get over things like that. They grow up and they move on. You never did. You wanted her all to yourself, didn't you? But she gave it all to *him*. And even after you'd killed him, got rid of him for good, she *still* wanted him and not you."

Edwards made a deep sound in his throat unlike anything Ryan had ever heard before.

"She's dead. She told me she was going away, that she couldn't stand living anymore."

"No, she's not dead." Ryan shook his head and felt a queer sense of pity creep into his bones, something he never thought he would feel for this man. "She's alive. But you've tried killing her so many times before, haven't you? Did you feel robbed—is that what sent you spiralling two years ago? She'd robbed you of the dream of killing her yourself."

Edwards closed his eyes. Fleeting images of dark-haired women popped into his mind and every one of them looked like his mother.

He opened them again and began to clap slowly, the noise reverberating around the rock face.

"Bravo, chief inspector. That was an excellent effort. Eight out of ten for delivery but I'd have gone with the daddy angle, myself. Charles Drewe really was a bastard, you know. Completely insane, when you think about it." Edwards cocked a hip, as if settling down for a cosy chat. "The things he used to do to her…well, is it any wonder that the apple didn't fall far from the tree?"

Edwards gave a self-deprecating laugh, then surveyed Ryan with his own measure of pity.

"Poor Ryan," he said. "Always looking for an *underdog*. Always hoping for the *best* in people. Always trying to understand the reasons why."

Ryan inclined his head. "It was worth a try."

Edwards snorted. "Didn't it ever occur to you that I *like* who I am—who I've come to be? I've never felt more free, more *liberated*. For years, I had to pretend to be just like everybody else. I moved among the herd, smelling their stench, but all the time I was waiting. Waiting to flourish; to be my finest, basest self. The self that we all want to be, if we ask the voice buried deep inside."

He dropped his voice to a murmur, coaxing Ryan to agree with him.

"If you listen to it, that voice will whisper the same thing to you. We're like two sides of the same coin, you and me, but only one of us has been brave enough to *grasp* life. I don't go through the motions anymore and I don't answer to the laws that man has made for me. *I am my own law*."

Ryan listened to his ravings and he heard the search team moving closer through the trees.

"Don't tell me you've never looked at a body and *wondered*," Edwards continued.

He had also heard the approaching officers and started to step backward along the whinstone, his feet parallel to the jagged edge and an eighty-foot drop below.

"You must wonder what it feels like." He watched Ryan with his hypnotic black eyes. "The indescribable power when their blood runs through your fingers. The look in their eyes when they realise you're the last thing they'll ever see before they die. The pleasure is exquisite," he moaned.

Ryan felt bile rise up in his throat but he kept a sharp eye on Edwards' movements.

"I remember the look of blind fear in *your* eyes, when I had my hands around your throat. Is that the kind of thing you're talking about?"

Edwards smiled at the tactic, then looked downward as Phillips' cries echoed up from the pathway below.

"Let's see if you can recreate the magic, shall we?"

Before Ryan could stop him, he turned and ran along the whinstone wall, his footsteps barely an inch away from the slippery edge and Ryan could see he was going to try making a break for it along the eastern path of the river, over the top of the waterfall.

He threw caution to the wind and sprinted after him.

CHAPTER 31

Phillips burst through the small tourist gate leading down to High Force waterfall, intending to cut across the river to the other side. It would save time, rather than running all the way to the bridge and circling around to the south side. But either way, he knew anyone in their right mind would head for the river; it was a natural pathway to civilisation.

His feet skidded on the narrow, tarmacked path leading down to the falls. It was damp from the wet air rising from the bubbling water and trees had grown in a natural arch above the pathway, some of them fallen and crushed after high winds. He almost lost his footing and threw out a hand to grab the wooden handrail separating him from a steep fall to the river on his left.

Eventually, Phillips came to the bottom of the pathway and heard the waterfall even before he saw it. Thundering gallons of water from the River Tees cascaded over the jagged outcrop of rock known as Whin Sill, eroding the softer limestone and sandstone beneath the hard dolomite that had risen as molten lava some three hundred million years ago. He stood overlooking it, squinting in the very last light of day and scanning the riverbank and the rocky clifftop on the other side.

"*Denise!*"

The sound erupted from him like a primal scream that could not be contained. When there was no reply, he tried again.

"DENISE!"

Again, there came no reply and he was about to start picking his way across the rocks when two tall, male figures appeared silhouetted atop the cliff on the other side of the gorge.

Phillips tugged his firearm from its holster and aimed it high.

He lowered it again when he realised that, in the near-darkness, he couldn't distinguish one man from the other.

Anna stood beside Lowerson's squad car with her hands in her pockets, staring out at the trees and fields surrounding the visitors' car park at High Force. There was an inn directly opposite the tourist entrance where walkers could stay overnight and enjoy the warm hearth and convivial atmosphere after a long day hiking the fells. It had been evacuated but the landlord had left it open for the police to use as a temporary base of operations. Lowerson bustled off in that direction to help formulate a new action plan as it became increasingly clear that the Hacker was at large again, and on foot. They were yet to find Ryan or MacKenzie, although blood trails had been reported through a wooded area to the south side of the river, alongside a fresh motorcycle trail leading north.

Anna's right hand closed around the heavy firearm in her pocket, burning a hole through the material.

Police in full safety gear talked among themselves and some of them sent her a friendly smile every now and then, recognising her as their chief inspector's fiancée. They were probably trying to be kind, to reassure her that she was not alone and that everything would turn out for the best.

But Ryan was out there, against a man without principle and without conscience. There was no reasoning with somebody like that and no mercy either.

She brushed her fingers against the firearm and thought again of how Ryan had once overcome his natural aversion to violence to save her life.

He might be out there right now, desperately needing her.

Anna picked up her heels and ran towards the tourist gate, ignoring the shouts from the officers who tried to call her back.

———

Ryan chased after the Hacker, relying on the thick tread of his hiking boots to provide traction against the slippery surface of the stone. Night had fallen and the world was nothing more than shades of grey, the waterfall a curtain of silver in the light of the moon. They were approaching the highest point of the falls, where the river gushed over the lip of the whinstone, and Edwards stopped just beside it. Ryan realised he was about to try to cross to the north side, where it was possible for him to slip along the riverbank.

Sheer madness.

Ryan skidded in his haste to stop him, arriving just in time to grasp a handful of Edwards' jacket and haul him away from the edge.

"Give it up, man! There's no place to cross. Give yourself up!"

Edwards' only response was to lash out violently, landing a hard punch to Ryan's face that left his ears ringing. It bought Edwards some time to break away and plunge into the freezing cold water, to make his way across the rocky path hidden underneath. His feet remembered the journey and knew exactly where to step but all Ryan saw was the possibility of a man falling to his death.

He had not come this far, nor given up the chance of killing him two years ago, to watch Edwards commit an act of suicide. Ryan knew he could not live with the knowledge that he might be able to prevent it.

"Stop!"

Edwards carried on wading, almost reaching halfway across the waterfall.

Ryan swore violently but lowered his feet into the water, feeling the icy shock of it penetrate his bones. He was a strong swimmer but the waterfall hadn't been named 'High Force' for nothing; the impact of the water nearly swept him off his feet. He hunkered down against it, feeling the rocks beneath for toe-holds to help him cross.

Up ahead, Edwards seemed to have frozen.

"Wait there!" Ryan called. "I'll help you out!"

He gritted his teeth and continued across, blinking the water spray from his eyes. When he reached Edwards, the other man turned around to face him with a bold, fearless expression. His face had taken on the quality of a waxwork dummy after the water loosened the dried crusts of blood so that it ran in tiny streams down his pale face.

Edwards grinned and felt the power of the water rushing around him, making him feel like a god.

"My father taught me to cross this waterfall," he boasted. "The Drewes have owned the land around here for centuries and every man learned the path beneath the water."

He laughed and raised his hands to the wind.

"Did you think I was going to kill myself? Is that what you thought?"

He threw his head back and laughed again.

"You're priceless," he told Ryan, before his eyes darkened. "But it's time to say 'goodbye' now."

With that, his hand shot out to grasp Ryan's neck like a cobra's fangs, his fingers digging into the sinews until Ryan heard the blood roaring in his ears.

MacKenzie reached the edge of the forest and limped out onto the cliff overlooking the river gorge. She scanned the area for signs of Phillips or Ryan, and saw the back of two running figures further up, in the direction of the waterfall. She recognised them instantly as Ryan and Edwards and they were covering the ground at speed. She knew there was no hope of catching them up but she looked down at the rifle and wondered if there was another way to help.

Carefully, so as not to slip and damage her leg any further, she hobbled across to a collection of small rocks and lowered her body onto one of them, using one of the smaller rocks as a prop for the rifle. She stayed like that, tracking the progress of the two running men until she had a clear shot. The moon was almost full so it acted like a spotlight and she hoped that, if the time came, her aim would not be off.

Phillips spotted MacKenzie the moment she emerged and was about to call out to her, his joy at finding her still alive almost too much to contain.

But he had seen the same crisis unfurling and, now that he knew Denise was alive, he could turn his attention elsewhere.

His heart rose to his throat as he watched Edwards, then Ryan, wading out across the top of the waterfall.

What had possessed him?

But he knew why Ryan had followed. He believed Edwards was going to jump, to deprive the families of the dead of any rightful punishment in one fell swoop.

But there was a confidence in the way Edwards walked across the water and Phillips knew he must have done it before. He had not gone out there to die—he had gone out there to kill.

Phillips raised his firearm again and waited for the right moment to pull the trigger.

Anna flew down the pathway leading to the waterfall but didn't see Phillips standing a little way off, beside the rocks. The moon shone down on the two figures above the waterfall, seeming to dance against the sky as they battled each other and the water. Her heart seemed to stop and then restart, violently slamming against the wall of her chest as she saw the man she loved standing precariously on top of the falls, locked in a fight that would surely end badly for one of them.

Working on instinct alone, she scanned the rocks for a way to get up there to help him but the rocks were pitch black and slick with water. To her right, there was a small gate marked 'DANGER—DO NOT ENTER' and a narrow flight of stairs that would take her to the top of the waterfall from the north side. She flung it open and raced up the steps, her palm slipping against the handrail as she forced her legs to move faster.

She reached the top and raced along the narrow path running beside the cliff face until she could find a position where both men were clearly in sight.

A large boulder sat just inside the river—it would take a dangerous jump to get to it, but from there she would have the perfect view.

And a perfect shot.

Not giving herself time to panic, she rocked back on her heels and then leaped across the rushing water, fingers splayed to grasp the stony edges before she could tumble across the other side. Her feet splashed into the water but she scrambled up onto the surface of the boulder and pulled the firearm from her pocket.

She had to focus for a moment to distinguish between the two men grappling violently in the moonlight but she would have recognised Ryan anywhere. Her hands might have shaken from the cold but there was no fear as she raised the gun and aimed it directly at Edwards' head.

Ryan broke free from Edwards' grip and landed a hard blow to his face, bringing the heel of his hand upward to connect with his already broken nose. Blood poured from the wound and Edwards screamed, clutching his face with a look of surprised anger. In the moments it took him to react, Ryan had him by the throat.

He felt the terrible urge to finish the job this time, to rid the world of Edwards once and for all. Ryan saw nobody else, just Edwards, and his fingers tightened against the thick cord of his neck in an effort to shut off the blood supply. He didn't know where he found the strength. It wasn't muscle alone, it was force of will. Ryan could feel the sinews in Edwards' neck straining, could feel the skin of his face and hands tearing as the other man tried to claw himself free, but the muscles of his arms were locked in position and he knew that, in another minute or so, it would be over.

Over.

The roaring in Ryan's ears started to slow and his fingers relaxed, bit by bit.

He had never killed a man.

He was not a killer.

His grip released and Edwards fell away, gasping and spluttering for air, hands clutching at his throat. Ryan watched as the river current took him by surprise, sweeping him off his feet towards the water's edge. He began to turn away, pushing through the water to return to the safety of the riverbank while the anger drained from his body, no longer caring whether Edwards was swept away.

He turned again at the last moment, but it was too late.

Edwards reared up and threw himself across the waves, the heavy weight of him toppling Ryan into the water so that his head submerged and he began to choke. He twisted and turned, thrashing against the hard body pinning him beneath the water. His lungs screamed, begging for air, and freezing water ran up his nose and into his mouth. His ears rang and the splashing waves dimmed to a gentle hum.

Beneath the water, he heard a single shot fire. It sounded like a tape being played in slow motion; a record skidding and slowing to play out the final long note of a melody.

The pressure on his back lifted and his head burst from the water, mouth wide and searching to draw deep, nourishing breaths of air into his bursting lungs. His body heaved, expelling the river water from his stomach as he fought to make his way through the current.

Ryan collapsed against the riverbank, legs shaking and body shivering from the icy cold, then turned to look back across the water. There was no sign of another living person and the river continued to flow, surging over the dolomite ridge as it had done for millions of years.

EPILOGUE

Phillips found MacKenzie collapsed against a huddle of rocks atop the cliff face and radioed for immediate medical assistance. Somewhere in the corner of her mind, she heard Frank's voice as she was moved onto a stretcher. Her skin remembered the feel of his calloused hand rubbing her chilled fingers, clutching them as he walked along beside her towards the ambulance. She felt herself being hoisted upward and frowned at the blaze of interior lights against the thin wall of her eyelids.

"Come on, lass. Open your eyes."

Phillips sat beside her as the ambulance began to trundle back across the bumpy track toward the main road, moving slowly so as not to dislodge its patient. The harsh light showed up every cut and bruise marring her lovely face and he swallowed back tears of rage, raising her hand to his lips to place a gentle kiss against her dirty skin.

"Please…" His voice shook. "I've missed you so much. Please open your eyes."

MacKenzie gripped his fingers a bit harder and he let the tears come, falling against the back of her hand.

Her eyelids flickered open and he could see that her left eye was completely bloodshot, the eyelid torn by the sharp branch of a tree. He wanted to look away, to pretend he hadn't seen it, but instead he raised a gentle hand to smooth the hair away from her face.

"My love," he said.

"Frank," she said hoarsely. "Oh, God, Frank."

"You're safe now," he managed.

"You came for me," she sobbed. "He said you wouldn't but I knew. I knew you would."

Phillips dashed the tears away from his eyes and kissed her gently on the lips.

"I've thought of nothing but you." He rested his forehead against hers.

"You saved me."

He looked up and shook his head. "I wanted to," he admitted. "I would have gone to the ends of the earth, but you saved yourself. You did it, Denise."

Her lips trembled into a smile.

"I always said you were a handful," he added, with a lopsided grin.

MacKenzie managed a weak laugh and breathed in the scent of him. It was like coming home. Then a shadow crossed her face.

"Where—where is he?"

Phillips sat up to look deeply into her eyes, understanding that she needed this closure.

"Edwards is gone, lass. Smashed against the rocks at the bottom of the waterfall, not ten feet from where they found his father twenty-five years ago. He'll never hurt anybody ever again."

MacKenzie closed her eyes and thought of a small, lonely boy living out on the moors. But then she remembered the emptiness behind his eyes, the brutality, and when her eyes fluttered open again, they burned a bright, emerald green.

"He's at peace," she whispered.

AUTHOR'S NOTE

Although it has been noted elsewhere that this is a work of fiction, wherever possible I like to remain true to the landscape of my beloved North East. For any readers who feel compelled to visit after reading *High Force*, you should find it largely similar to the country waterfall I have described. However, it is worth mentioning that distances between landmarks and villages have been lengthened or shortened to fit the pace of the story. Likewise, certain geological landmarks have been shuffled around here and there to create a more impactful chase scene at the climax of the story. For all that, the Pennine Way walking route which takes you past High Force waterfall remains a stunning scenic outing and is well worth the trip.

Many readers have asked me whether Anna's little stone cottage in Durham is real—I am sorry to tell you that it is entirely fictitious but the city itself is beautiful and I have tried to capture its essence in these pages.

One final point to note is a matter of genealogy. The village of Blanchland is, in fact, a conservation area operated under Lord Crewe's Charity. It was established under the terms of the will of Nathaniel, Lord Crewe, Bishop of Durham, to distribute the income from his estates following his death in 1721. When I visited Blanchland prior to writing *High Force*, I was struck very much by its charm and beauty, and the history of the area inspired me to think of the fictional *Drewe* family which, needless to say, bears no resemblance to any members of the Crewe family or their descendants.

LJ ROSS
19th January 2017

ACKNOWLEDGMENTS

I can hardly believe that *High Force* is the fifth DCI Ryan mystery book—it feels like it was only yesterday when I was tentatively publishing *Holy Island* and hoping that one or two people might like it! To say that I am grateful to the hundreds of thousands of readers who have invested their pennies in my books would be an enormous understatement. Your faith and support has meant so much to me over these last two years—thank you all so very much.

Likewise, my thanks go out to all the wonderful book bloggers and enthusiasts who have read my stories and taken the time out of their busy lives to write such beautiful reviews, I am grateful to all of you!

Particular thanks to Jim Kitson, my Dad, for his location scouting. As always, his nose for what would be an atmospheric site for a murder mystery is spot on! Thanks also to Gordon Spedding for his very useful advice around the local boxing scene in the North East—it is fascinating to learn about its proud traditions and I'm sorry that DS Frank

Phillips isn't in better condition but I'm afraid he likes his ham-and-pease-pudding stotties too much! Sincere thanks to Charlie Charlton for his excellent photograph of High Force waterfall, which provided the base for the book's cover.

Lastly, but never least, to my wonderful husband and family. James, you are my rock and without your unstinting support I doubt any of these books would have been written. Mum, Dad, Rachael and Ethan—your love and laughter is infectious and I love you all very much.

ABOUT THE AUTHOR

LJ Ross is an international bestselling author, best known for creating atmospheric mystery and thriller novels, including the DCI Ryan series of Northumbrian murder mysteries which have sold over five million copies worldwide.

Her debut, *Holy Island*, was released in January 2015 and reached number one in the UK and Australian charts. Since then, she has released a further eighteen novels, all of which have been top three global bestsellers and fifteen of which have been UK #1 bestsellers. Louise has garnered an army of loyal readers through her storytelling and, thanks to them, several of her books reached the coveted #1 spot whilst only available to pre-order ahead of release.

Louise was born in Northumberland, England. She studied undergraduate and postgraduate Law at King's College, University of London and then abroad in Paris and Florence. She spent much of her working life in London, where she was a lawyer for a number of years until taking the decision to change career and pursue her dream to write. Now, she writes full time and lives with her husband and son in Northumberland. She enjoys reading all manner of books, travelling and spending time with family and friends.

If you enjoyed reading *High Force*, please consider leaving a review online.

DCI Ryan will return in

CRAGSIDE

A DCI RYAN MYSTERY (Book #6)

Are you afraid of the dark..?

After his climactic battle with notorious serial killer The
Hacker, DCI Ryan is spending the summer with his fiancée
within the grounds of Cragside, a spectacular Bavarian-style
mansion surrounded by acres of woodland. When they are
invited to attend the staff summer party – a Victorian murder
mystery evening – it's all a joke until the lights go out and
an elderly man is found dead. It looks like an unfortunate
accident but, as the dead man's life begins to unfold, Ryan and
his team of detectives realise that all is not as it appears.

When a second body is found, terror grips the close-
knit community and Ryan must uncover the killer who
walks among them, before they strike again...

Murder and mystery are peppered with romance
and humour in this fast-paced crime whodunit set
amidst the spectacular Northumbrian landscape.

**CRAGSIDE will be available in all
good bookshops in July 2020!**

LOVE READING?

JOIN THE CLUB...

Join the LJ Ross Book Club to connect with a thriving community of fellow book lovers! To receive a free monthly newsletter with exclusive author interviews and giveaways, sign up at www.ljrossauthor.com or follow the LJ Ross Book Club on social media: